THE LOW ROAD

MARTIN MCCAW

ISBN: 978-0-945917-00-4

Printed in the United States of America

Front Cover Photo: courtesy of mostnatures.com
Back Cover Photo: Maddie Fenton

"Making other books jealous since 2007"

Big Table Publishing Company
Boston, MA
www.bigtablepublishing.com

For Libby

PART ONE

MONDAY, JUNE 16, 1986

The white-clad woman who listened in the doorway is gone. I hear the click of Luke's guitar case snapping shut. My brothers' last song, requested by Mama, lingers in my head, "Take my hand, precious Lord, lead me home."

My back hurts. No wonder. I've spent three days sitting on a hospital chair that belongs in Henry the Eighth's torture chamber. Not that anybody cares. No one's waiting for me in my apartment, and I've got no job.

Mama's teeth grin at me from a glass of water on her bed stand. Her hair is white and her mouth is puckered in an "O" shape, like a sucker's. I've been taking deep breaths–like this, Mama–but the air smells used up, like the poker room's air.

I watch the heart monitor, willing it to zigzag again. The line stays straight. Her heart has stopped beating.

Someone touches my arm.

Outside, the night air is fresh and warm. Timothy waves from the passenger window as Luke's car leaves the parking lot, heading across the state to Seattle. Tiny flies swarm around me, big as bats when I look up into the floodlights. I find my old Ford and drive north to drop off the plastic bag that contains Mama's purse and clothes. After twenty miles I slow down, watching for the kitchen light to guide me into the lane. I pass the mailbox and have to back up. No lights tonight. Halfway down the lane I hit our prize pothole with a bang that rattles my teeth.

I park behind Mama's car and scan the northern sky until I locate the big dipper. It looks as close as it did fifty years ago, but I know it's moving away from me faster than the speed of light, like Mama.

Her left rear tire is still flat. I let the air out after a neighbor tipped me she was driving again. I'd confiscated her two sets of keys, but she must have found a spare. Two weeks ago when I pulled into the lane, she was pushing down the handle of a wobbly tire pump. Was it a coincidence she'd decided to pump up the tire at the exact moment she knew I'd arrive?

"It's not filling up very fast," she said.

"It's flat."

I helped her up. She was bent at the waist, clutching her back. "Now you've given yourself a back spasm," I said. "Go in and lie down."

"After I rest a bit I'll finish pumping it up."

Half an hour later I watched from the kitchen doorway as she shuffled into the living room. "Here comes the queen," she said. She paused by the recliner, teetering on her cane, lips pursed as she pondered something. I wanted to go up and hug her, but I knew I'd choke up. Besides, the shock might trigger a tachycardia spell. I'd hug her next visit.

Yeah, next visit.

I kick the flat tire, which doesn't inflate it any more than Mama's tire pump did. Inside, the plastic bag clinks when I toss it onto her bed. What's in her purse, silver dollars? I turn to leave the bedroom, but something whacks my shin. The bureau's bottom drawer juts out a few inches. As I lean down to shut it, I see something that makes me pull the drawer out farther.

A cardboard box lies on top of Mama's stockings and bras. What caught my eye is a crayon drawing of Uncle Wiggily the rabbit, so primitive I must have been a toddler when I drew it. I

2

carry the box to the kitchen table. Beneath the drawing are folded sheets of stationery in Mama's elegant handwriting. The top page begins "My Sweetie" and is undated. These must be letters Mama wrote to Daddy during their courtship. I lay them on the table.

Still in the box are a couple of envelopes and three small sepia snapshots, bordered in white. The top photo shows two young men, one lean and one stocky, standing behind an empty wooden chair. I recognize the ivy that covers one corner of the house behind them, the family homestead that burned down when I was a teenager. It takes longer to identify the two men. I last saw the lean man years ago, and I can't recall the stocky man ever having hair. Both brothers wear striped bib overalls. Daddy's thumbs are hooked in the overall's straps, and a shock of dark hair sprouts above his high forehead. Their faces look calm and confident. They knew how to farm; they could handle whatever came along. But that was before they met their wives.

In the snapshot beneath, the shock-haired man is hoisting a baby over his head. The photo caught them near the top of the hoist, the man's head tilted back, face to face with the baby. I'm sure they're laughing, though their features are blurred. They seem to be in a canyon between two steep hills. A line of stubby fence posts runs along the left hillside. Tumbleweeds clog the fence. The place looks familiar.

The bottom snapshot shows three teenage girls, arms across each other's backs. They're leaning to their right, kicking their left legs toward the camera. They look like can-can dancers except for the bloomers that cover their knees. The girl on the right is smiling, the middle girl looks embarrassed, and the girl on the left is laughing.

I stare at the picture a long time, trying to recall if I ever saw Mama laugh like that, not a care in the world. I also wonder how long it's been since she could bend sideways.

One of the envelopes is empty. It's frayed at the edges, addressed in Daddy's handwriting to Miss Lola Lindsay of Rogue

3

River, Oregon. The return address says "Edward Roundtree, Box 54, Whetstone, Washington." A two-cent stamp has been canceled, partially obliterating some President's face. Although the postmark's ink is faded, I can make out "November 5 7AM 1929." A week before Mama and Daddy got married.

The other envelope is also addressed to Lola Lindsay in Rogue River, but the sender is Mrs. R. T. Wilson of Whetstone. It's dated April 16, 1928. The name doesn't ring a bell. I slide a letter out of the envelope.

Dear Lola,

I hope you and your family are well. How is your dear father? We were so sorry to hear of his heart attack. A pastor's life can be so stressful. We are finally settled here. Richard's sermons have been received very well. Whetstone's congregation is smaller than Rogue River's, consisting mostly of farm families.

I do hope you can visit us when your teaching duties are over in June. Dust storms and pollen would be bad for your hay fever later this summer, but June should be nice, the last month things are green around here.

There is a young bachelor who farms with his family two miles east of Whetstone. I would guess he's in his mid-thirties. His name is Edward Roundtree. He seems a bit shy around women. He never opens his mouth when we sing a hymn. His brother Jacob has a beautiful bass voice and is very active in the church. He leads the congregation in prayer whenever Richard asks him. Unfortunately, Jacob is married.

I have to admit I have an ulterior motive in writing you. We badly need a piano player. I do my best, but sometimes the hymn I hear doesn't sound like the one I'm playing. I can see you now, sitting at the piano in our old church.

So can I. By standing tiptoe and craning my neck I can see over a woman's shoulder to the raised platform up front where Mama plays the piano. Auburn hair falls loose over her ear and down the back of her neck. Her rich soprano voice soars above us, leading the congregation, "Rock of ages, cleft for me, let me hide myself in thee." I stand by Daddy, holding one side of the hymnbook, wondering what "cleft" means. My side of the book feels weightless because we're on page 473, near the back. Daddy holds the book low so I can read the words. He's not singing at all, and neither are my brothers on my right. Luke can't read the big words and Timothy can't read any. The woman in front of me is Bertha Warren, the grocer's wife, and her perfume fills my nostrils, stinging my eyes.

I tip back in my chair, away from the kitchen table, until the chair teeters and I begin to fall backward. But I'm an expert at tipping back in this chair, and my head gently nudges the kitchen wall. I feel suspended in midair, my feet unconnected to the floor. I smile for the first time in a long while, realizing that I still don't know what "cleft" means.

Memories come pell-mell. I lift a tiny, bell-shaped glass of grape juice from the communion tray that Daddy holds above my lap. "This is my blood," the minister says. "Drink in remembrance of me."

Mama shakes an angel food cake out of its pan onto the kitchen counter while Luke and I, waving our spoons, argue over who gets to scrape the pan first.

I hang onto the windshield frame of my cab-less grain truck, coughing from the dust, as I bounce downhill across furrowed rows of wheat stalks toward a cloud of chaff that obscures a combine. The hill is so steep I'm certain I'll land on top of the combine if my brakes fail.

Someone knocks.

I struggle to get up, forgetting my chair is tipped back. The back of my head bumps the wall and I crash to the floor.

When I reach the front door I freeze. Through the door's small window I see white hair, the top of a head. I can't think of any reason Mama would knock unless she has grocery sacks in both arms.

As I stand gaping, the doorknob turns and Aunt Bea comes in, shaking a floppy gray hat.

"June bug got trapped inside," she says.

Uncle Jacob's hat. I squint into bright sunshine at a boysenberry bush twice my height. A thorny branch guards the ripest berry, such a deep purple it's almost black. I reach under the branch, but a thorn pricks me. A bright red drop oozes from the tip of my index finger. Uncle Jacob leans into the bush, stretching for a berry. He loses his balance and disappears into the thicket, leaving his hat drooping from a branch. He climbs out, laughing, and hands me a huge boysenberry. I chew it slowly. The sour-sweet juice puckers my lips.

"You going to take this or not?"

"Huh?" I focus on Aunt Bea. She's holding out a casserole dish covered with wax paper. It's half full of what appears to be scalloped potatoes. I take the dish. "How did you know I'd be here?"

"Luke phoned me from the hospital. You look peaked, Mark. Been getting any sleep?" She lays a cold hand on my wrist. "She's with her sweetie, you know."

"Yeah, my father." I put the dish on the dining room table so she can't see my eyes.

"Not your father," she says from the porch.

"What?" I wheel around. She's striding across the lawn. I see only two cars, Mama's and mine. Did she walk here? I follow her, but I'm so worried I'll step into a pothole that she beats me to the end of the lane. Gravel caves under my shoe. I stumble away from the culvert's edge and turn right onto the highway. Although the lights of Whetstone are two miles away, they blind me. I fall into step alongside Aunt Bea, trusting her to keep us out of the ditch.

"You mean she was in love with somebody else?"

"Yes."

"When?"

"During the Depression."

Half a century ago. "Before she got married?"

"After."

"There couldn't have been anyone after!"

"Don't you yell at me!"

I struggle to keep my voice down. "Who was the man?"

Silence.

The only sound is the scrape of our boots on the asphalt. A breeze chills my face.

"What happened to him?"

"Murdered."

The shovel glides back and forth, smoothing the snow.

I'm standing in the middle of the road, the taste of bile on my tongue. Aunt Bea has vanished into the lights of Whetstone. Maybe my hearing aids distorted what she said. Or maybe she's getting dingy, living alone all these years.

I start back. The sky has clouded over. One star blinks, low in the east. One wish. Let them be alive somewhere, together.

"I want to live my life over again," I tell the star.

The blinking light moves north, heading for Spokane's airport.

Far away a coyote howls–Yip yip yaooo… I am here, where are you? A coyote answers, then another and another, each starting a beat later, like a barbershop quartet. I can't tell where the howls are coming from, the river on my right or the wheat hills on my left. When I reach our mailbox, the howling stops.

As I climb the front steps I remember Mama's salutation, "My Sweetie," on the top page of the folded sheets of stationery. I'd assumed she wrote those letters to Daddy, but after Aunt Bea's visit I've got to make sure.

I sit at the kitchen table, take a deep breath and unfold the sheet.

My Sweetie,

Mark is taking his nap, so I have a few minutes to spare. I had to write you, though of course I can't send the letter. I think about you every minute. This morning I burned the bacon. I was standing right over the frying pan and didn't notice the smoke until Edward came in from the bathroom and asked if something was burning. I ache to hold you again, to feel your hair against my cheek, your breath in my ear.

The page quivers in my fingers. The ink blurs. So that was why she didn't mail the letters. She couldn't let the mailman see the envelopes. But why didn't she destroy them? She must have known one of us would find them after she died.

I carry the folded pages to the back yard and dump them into Mama's burn barrel. Then I ransack every drawer in the kitchen, hunting for a box of matches. No luck.

The first page of the letter I started to read still lies on the table. I turn a stovetop knob to "high" and touch the sheet against the burner. One edge blackens and smokes but won't catch fire. What lingers is the smell of burnt bacon.

I take the page outside, holding it away from my body as if a skunk had sprayed it, and drop it into the burn barrel. I want to go back to my Walla Walla apartment and forget what happened tonight, but I can't leave those letters in the barrel for Luke or Timothy to find. Tonight I'll lie in my old bed, catch up on the sleep I've missed the last three nights. Tomorrow I'll get groceries at Whetstone's little store, including matches to burn those phony letters in the barrel. Maybe I'll remember something that refutes Aunt Bea's lies. That's my curse, reliving the past. Sometimes I lie awake all night because I can't turn off the memories.

I flop onto my chair at the kitchen table, the one I always sat

8

on at mealtimes. I'm unaware of tipping backward until my head taps the wall. My hair makes a funny sound scraping the wall, like a steer rubbing its back against a fence post. As I float in limbo, my feet hanging above the floor, I become aware that other stories fill this house, this farm, including the mystery I've been trying to solve for forty-four years. Tonight more pieces of the puzzle fell into place, and I don't like the picture that's emerging.

The music started just in time. I'd got bored making Luke guess which hand held my collection-plate nickel. He hadn't guessed right yet because I'd been sitting on the nickel.

All these people, fifteen at least, and Mama was leading them all. Without her piano they couldn't find the right notes. On Daddy's left, Aunt Bea strained to imitate Mama, shrieking on the high notes. Uncle Jacob, alongside the aisle, sang way lower than the women, going deeper yet when they went up.

When the song was over, Mama left the piano and sat in the front pew below a stained glass window. Reverend Taylor stood up, a tall man with specks of gray around his temples. He smiled at the congregation with his lips but frowned with his eyes. Looming over us behind the pulpit, he looked fierce enough to keep us from sinning without God backing him up.

"A man was out in a boat with his young son and the son's friend," he said. "His son had accepted Jesus but the other boy hadn't. A terrible storm came up and both boys fell overboard. The man could only throw the boat's lifeline to one of them. The other boy would drown. What should he do?"

He looked around the congregation. This was only his second Sunday preaching, so he hadn't yet learned that Presbyterians aren't allowed to speak during a sermon.

"The man knew his son would go to heaven because he'd accepted Jesus. The other boy wouldn't. So he threw the lifeline to

9

his son's friend and yelled, 'I love you, Son!'"

Three things happened at once. The minister choked up, Mama shook her head, and Uncle Jacob said, "No!"

Reverend Taylor scanned the back pews, blinking through watery eyes. His frown didn't look as scary as his smile. Mama hurried through the door behind the pulpit and reappeared with a glass of water. He reached for it without looking at her. After a couple of false starts, interrupted by coughs that he smothered with his fist, he explained that to be saved we had to be washed in the blood of the lamb. Taking a bath in blood didn't sound like much fun, so I quit listening and counted flies. I couldn't get past three because the flies kept changing their minds about whose head they wanted to land on.

I perked up when the minister talked about starving peasants in the Ukraine. I imagined myself standing on the bed of a loaded truck, peering down at a mass of outstretched arms. I tossed out hams and angel food cakes, mixing in a few references to Jesus, not in a pushy way, and by the time I drove on to the next village, the peasants were patting full tummies and chanting my name. I got so absorbed in my daydream that when the congregation began singing "Blessed Redeemer," I thought for a moment they were singing about me.

While Mama played the postlude, the congregation milled around in the aisle, the women asking each other about sick relatives and the men chewing out President Roosevelt for keeping wheat prices low.

"He's going to drag us into that war," Mr. Morgan said. He didn't realize that I'd joined the Royal Air Force and shot down twenty-five Messerschmitts in our back yard.

As we filed out, women said hello to Daddy but ignored Uncle Jacob.

Outside on the sidewalk I told Mama, "Daddy was so proud listening to you that he forgot to sing."

She laughed and tousled my hair. "He can't carry a tune."

But Daddy whistled. That's how we always knew he was happy. He began to whistle as he backed our car into the street. In the back seat we boys held our usual contest, trying to be first to smell the rotting pea vines Daddy got last summer from the cannery. The smell had gotten worse lately as the weather warmed up. The hogs seemed in no hurry to finish off the pea vines, for which I was grateful. Once they were gone, we'd be able to smell the hog pen again.

"I smell the pea vines!" Timothy yelled.

"You can't smell them yet," I said. "We're only two blocks from the church."

"Roll up your windows," Mama said, giving Daddy a dirty look.

Back at the ranch, Mama pinched her nostrils for Daddy's benefit as she got out of the car. A column of blue smoke rose from the burn barrel behind the house. On the porch she took a deep breath, savoring the smell of singed chicken feathers as if it were perfume.

Daddy went outside to feed the hogs, and Mama cut up the chicken she'd plucked before breakfast. "Would one of you boys please set the table?" she said.

"It's Mark's turn," Luke said, heading for the front door.

"I set it last night for supper," I said.

Mama whacked the cutting board with her butcher knife to dislodge a drumstick. In the living room, Timothy lined up his stuffed animals on the carpet by the radio.

"Timothy's too little," Mama said, practicing her mindreading skills.

Timothy was not too little. He'd been declared exempt from table setting because he copied Daddy's technique of randomly dumping silverware alongside each plate.

I counted out nine plates. With her finger Mama slid a gob of lard off a wooden spoon into her frying pan. She rolled chicken pieces in flour and dropped them into the pan. The lard crackled. She hurried to a counter and began to slice strawberries.

11

In the dining room, I aligned each piece of silver so the bottoms were even with the edge of the plate. I could smell the chicken browning. Through the kitchen window I saw shirker Luke throw a stick to our collie. Did the other martyrs, the early Christians, get fried chicken every Sunday in their dungeons? Maybe just the wings and neck.

The front door opened. "Mmm," Uncle Jacob said as he followed Aunt Bea into the living room, "Fried chicken. My mouth's watering already."

He went into the kitchen and hugged Mama. Aunt Bea watched them, her face screwed up as if she had an itch between her shoulder blades that she couldn't reach.

Mama beckoned to Uncle Jacob. He followed her down the hall into my parents' bedroom. I tiptoed after them and peeked into the room. They stood at the side of the bed, facing the bureau. Its bottom drawer was open. They were looking down at something she held.

"Such great detail," Uncle Jacob said.

"Just three years old."

"Are you ever going to tell Mark?"

Mama shook her head. "He's too fragile."

"He saw us," Uncle Jacob said.

"He was too young to understand."

"You said he still wakes up screaming."

"It was my fault." Mama put the piece of paper back in the drawer. "I'll never forgive myself." She closed the drawer.

"It wasn't your fault," Uncle Jacob said. "Try to remember the good times. We'll always have those memories."

"That's not enough."

Uncle Jacob shook his head. "No, it's not."

My nostrils tickled. I got halfway to the bathroom before the sneeze exploded. Uncle Jacob appeared in the bedroom doorway. "Where's Luke?" he said.

"He took off because it was his turn to set the table."

"Then I get his chicken."

The front door closed. "You do not," Luke said. "The minister's here."

"Go fetch your father," Mama told me.

A sow had got out. I guarded the pen's open gate, waving my arms to keep other pigs from escaping, while Daddy tried to chase the sow back in. Every time the sow approached the gate I had to stand motionless. Then other pigs tried to sneak out and I had to shoo them back in, spooking the sow. After a while she got bored with our game and rejoined her peers.

Daddy shoveled dirt into the hole the sow had rooted under the hog wire fence, which had big squares at the top that tapered downward to small squares at the bottom. Our pigs had dedicated their lives to outwitting hog wire. Over the years Daddy had fastened every piece of wood he could find to the bottom of the fence, one-by-six boards, poles, tree branches, even railroad ties. Nothing worked for long. Any inmate who wanted to escape from prison ought to keep a hog in his cell.

By the time I finished washing my hands, everyone else was seated at the table. The only vacant chair was on Mama's right against the wall, the worst position of all. Platters of food were passed to the left, and I'd planned to sit on Mama's left so I'd get first crack at the chicken breasts.

While Reverend Taylor said the blessing, I prayed a breast half would still be available when the chicken reached me. Timothy grabbed his usual drumstick and Aunt Bea took a wing. Reverend Taylor speared a breast half, then picked through other pieces with the serving fork till he found the second half. The third piece of white meat was still on the platter, smaller than the breast halves but acceptable in a crisis. Mrs. Taylor chose a wing. Daddy forked a chunk of thigh, and so did Uncle Jacob. Luke took the platter and studied its contents.

"Boy, that drumstick looks good," I said.

"I'll let you have it, then." Luke slid off the slab of white meat and handed me the platter, smirking.

I took the drumstick. Mama poked the serving fork among the leftovers. Although the back had the most meat, she chose the neck, raising the martyr's bar a notch higher.

"Interesting sermon," Uncle Jacob said. "Bothered me some when you said the other boy wouldn't go to heaven."

Reverend Taylor's head snapped back as if Uncle Jacob had slapped him.

"Would anyone like mayonnaise for their asparagus?" Mama said.

"I don't question Jesus' words," Reverend Taylor said.

Uncle Jacob raised his shaggy eyebrows, and the mole on his cheek wiggled. "What words?"

"John three, verse three. 'Verily, verily, I say unto thee, unless a man be born again, he cannot see the kingdom of heaven.'"

"Doesn't mention women or children." Uncle Jacob winked at Mama. "Guess you and Bea get a free pass, Lola."

Mrs. Taylor said, "When the Bible says man, it also means—"

"Biblical interpretation is my responsibility, my dear," her husband said.

"I'm sorry, Justin. "I only meant—"

The minister held up his palm like a policeman stopping traffic. His wife looked at her plate. "All of us are born into original sin," he said. "To be reborn we must accept Jesus as our lord and savior. That's why your mother teaches Sunday school, so you children can learn to love Jesus." He smiled at us, scaring Timothy into spilling a spoonful of gravy on his lap.

Timothy wailed. Mama dipped her napkin into her water glass and dabbed his pants. The commotion provided me enough cover to spit out gristle.

"For the sake of argument," Uncle Jacob said, "let's suppose Jesus gets to decide who goes to heaven."

"That's a fact, Mr. Roundtree, not a supposition," Reverend Taylor said.

"The word that I think describes Jesus best is compassionate," Uncle Jacob said. "Do you know the Greek word for compassion?"

Reverend Taylor glowered at him.

Uncle Jacob said a long word that sounded like "spaghetti" interspersed with sneezes.

Daddy chuckled. "No wonder the Greeks' society didn't last. People couldn't understand each other."

"It means a churning of the bowels," Uncle Jacob said. "Jesus got sick to his stomach when he saw someone in pain. Does that sound like a man who'd ban people from heaven because they didn't think he was God?"

"John three eighteen settles the matter," Reverend Taylor boomed in his pulpit voice. "'He that believeth on him is not condemned, but he that believeth not is condemned already.'"

Uncle Jacob said, "The Gospel of John was written a century after Jesus died. Maybe the writer made up that verse to get converts."

"Jacob!" Mama looked at him as if he'd said a swear word.

Aunt Bea sighed.

Mama nodded toward us boys. "Little pitchers have big ears."

Timothy chomped his drumstick, the only one at the table allowed to eat chicken with his fingers. Luke twirled his glass, seeing how high he could make water swirl without slopping over the rim. I spooned a hole in my mashed potatoes to make room for more gravy. Timothy didn't have a clue what anyone was talking about, but Luke and I knew the only way we'd learn anything was to pretend we weren't paying attention to adults' talk.

The minister said, "Mr. Roundtree, it saddens me to hear such blasphemy in a Christian home."

"I need to understand scriptures better," Aunt Bea said. "Could you call on me at your convenience, Reverend Taylor?"

He pulled a black notebook from the inside pocket of his suit coat. "One-thirty tomorrow afternoon." He made a notation with his fountain pen.

"Zelda, this Friday is Decoration Day," Mama said. "Bea and I will be taking flowers to the cemetery. Would you like to come with us?"

"I'd love to," Mrs. Taylor said, looking at her husband.

"Thank you for your kind offer," Reverend Taylor said, "but the only decoration day we observe is Good Friday."

I scraped the last sliver of meat from the drumstick. Luke chewed a hunk of white meat, smacking his lips for my benefit. Aunt Bea and Mama carried dirty dishes to the kitchen. They brought back plates of strawberry shortcake loaded with whipped cream.

"Looks delicious," Uncle Jacob told Mama. "I'll bet your special biscuits are hiding under that whipped cream."

"They got too brown on top." Mama smiled at him. "You're trying to butter me up so I'll give you an extra helping."

I lost track of the conversation because I had to make sure each forkful included three strawberry slices, whipped cream, and part of the top half of the biscuit. The bottom half would be tastier, soggy from strawberry juice, so I saved that for last.

After the Taylors left, Charley Simmons, a neighbor, stopped by to see how our wheat was doing.

"I've got things to do," Aunt Bea told Uncle Jacob. "You can walk home."

Not much of a walk. They lived half a mile away.

Uncle Jacob followed her outside. Through a window I saw them talking on the porch. I went out the back door and ran along the side of the house until I got close enough to hear.

"Stand up to him for once," Aunt Bea said.

"I'll talk to him."

"Whatever's left after he pays off the bank, we get half."

"Bea, they've got three kids to feed."

I flattened my back against the wall as Aunt Bea stalked to their Model T Ford. Uncle Jacob cranked it, spinning the handle until the engine sputtered. He watched his wife put-put down the lane, backfiring instead of waving goodbye.

I tagged along behind the three men as they climbed the big hill behind the barn. It hadn't rained since Easter, and the yellowing wheat stalks rubbed against my legs, hoping to filch a drop of sweat. By the time we reached the hilltop, a wet half-moon had formed on the back of Charley's shirt.

Daddy broke off a head of wheat and pinched its kernels. "Another dry week and we might be hurting a little."

"Another week and we can forget about harvesting." Charley clapped Daddy on the back. "Look at the bright side, Eddie. We won't have to bother getting our combines in shape."

While Uncle Jacob walked down the lane, I kicked a clod and watched the dust float away. "What are we going to do, Daddy?"

"Don't pay attention to Charley. He loses his crop every year and then harvests forty bushels an acre."

I went inside, but Daddy stayed on the porch awhile, looking at a wisp of gray cloud in the west.

It was five o'clock before I had a chance to sneak into the bedroom unobserved. I opened Mama's bureau drawer and found a crayon drawing of Uncle Wiggily. The bunny's top hat was a black lump, and so was his long-tailed coat. His arms and legs looked like sticks. No wonder. Mama had told Uncle Jacob I was only three years old when I drew it. I would draw her a new picture, show Uncle Wiggily bopping the Woozy Wolf with his rheumatism crutch.

We were crowded around the radio, listening to Jeanette MacDonald sing "Ah, Sweet Mystery of Life" on the Ford Sunday Evening Hour when Daddy said, "What's that sound?"

He turned on the porch light and opened the door. Raindrops shimmered against the darkening sky. He started whistling, the same few bars over and over, slightly off-key like a meadowlark's song.

Monday morning Daddy stuck a ruler into the tomato can he kept by the back porch to measure rainfall. "Sixteenth of an inch," he said. "Hardly enough to settle the dust."

After breakfast I rode in his pickup to the other place, the original family homestead. Most of our farm lay north of the highway, but this sixty-acre parcel ran south, from the highway to the river. He passed the house where Uncle Jacob and Aunt Bea lived, the machine shop, the huge pile of scrap iron, the butchering shed.

There was a commotion in the corral. Uncle Jacob was wrestling with a heifer. The calf strained backwards against a rope, one end around its neck, the other around a corral post. He tried to loosen the rope, but the heifer pulled so hard its eyes bugged out and its tongue hung out the side of its mouth.

As Daddy climbed over the railing, Uncle Jacob ran to the post and tried to untie the other end of the rope, but the heifer was straining too hard. Daddy wrapped both arms around the calf's neck and pulled. It looked like a tug of war between him and the heifer. He heaved, and they both toppled to the ground. The calf struggled to get up. Daddy hooked his left arm around the calf's head, dug his fingers between the rope and the neck, and yanked the rope. The heifer jumped up and bolted to the far end of the corral. Daddy sprawled in the mud, holding the empty lasso. He began to laugh, the sound starting deep in his belly, huff-huff-huff. I'd only heard him laugh like that once before, at a Charlie Chaplin movie. He sat in the middle of the corral, laughing as if he couldn't stop, his knees stuck out sideways. The back of his bib overalls was smeared with manure. The calf eyed him warily, wondering what was so funny.

Both men climbed out of the corral. Uncle Jacob said, "Heard on the radio wheat's down three cents this morning."

"It'll go back up," Daddy said.

"Once the price starts dropping, farmers will panic."

"You wanted to sell right after harvest." Daddy clapped his

hands together, missing a blowfly that buzzed around his nose. "Holding the crop made us eighteen cents a bushel."

"Okay, let's cash in that profit. If we have a decent harvest we can pay off the bank."

Last fall I'd overheard Daddy explain to Mama why he hadn't sold our wheat. Other years the brothers sold the harvest wheat in August to pay off the bank, then immediately borrowed enough to finance the next year's farming operation. Last summer wheat prices were so low they had hung onto the grain. They now owed the bank twice the usual amount.

"Let me think about it," Daddy said.

"Don't think about it. Sell the wheat."

I expected Daddy to get mad, but he was still feeling jaunty about the way he'd rescued the calf. "I'll go to Waitsburg this afternoon," he said.

"Go now," Uncle Jacob said, "before the morning market closes."

Mama was unpinning shirts from the clothesline when we got out of the pickup. "Don't you dare walk on my clean floor," she told Daddy. "I just mopped." She snatched a pair of overalls off the clothesline. "Have some trouble with a steer?"

"Pretty good guess," Daddy said.

It wasn't a guess. Mama was the Sherlock Holmes of manure analysis.

After Daddy changed overalls we drove the six miles to Waitsburg. Instead of going to the Touchet Valley Grain Growers' building, he parked by the bank and went straight to the manager's office.

"Jacob wants to sell our wheat," Daddy said. "What do you think?"

Mr. Osborn leaned back in his chair, hands clasped behind his white hair. "The price only dropped three cents this morning. That indicates profit taking, not the beginning of a decline."

"That's what I told Jacob. No reason it won't go up."

19

"Nothing's certain, of course," Mr. Osborn said.

Daddy whistled on the ride back. From the highway we saw Uncle Jacob riding a mule bareback near the corral. Daddy stopped his pickup a little ways off. "Don't slam the door," he said. "We don't want to spook the mule."

"What's he training it to do?"

"He wants to control its hip movement. When a mule turns too sharply, its hindquarters aren't directly behind its shoulders, so it can't push off with much strength. Takes a lot of horsepower to pull a combine up our hills."

Uncle Jacob had been holding the reins slack, but now he tightened the left rein, looking back over his shoulder at the mule's hip. Then he let the rein go slack.

"The mule kept walking straight," I said.

"Not quite. Soon as Jacob saw the hip move sideways an inch, he released the rein. That lets the mule know it did what Jacob wanted. He'll gradually work up to two inches, then three. We want the mule to learn to move its hips just enough to make the turn."

To the west, near the little house where I lived till I was four, Burke Foster scowled at Uncle Jacob from behind the barbed-wire fence that separated our properties. The Fosters lived across the highway from us, and sometimes at night I could hear Burke yelling.

Aunt Ethyl had told me Burke used to drive the wagon that carried children to school. Back then, she said, the Darrell family lived half a mile west of the Fosters. Puffy Darrell was younger than the Roundtree brothers, and he'd been held back several grades. Uncle Jacob kept the bullies away from him during lunch hour. One morning the wagon stopped at the Darrell's mailbox as usual, but just before Puffy reached the wagon, Burke snapped the reins and the horses trotted off. A little ways farther Burke stopped again. Puffy ran after the wagon, but when he started to climb aboard, Burke flicked the reins and the horses took off again. Puffy fell backward onto the road.

"I'll never forget what happened next," Aunt Ethyl had said.

"Jacob grabbed Burke around the waist and wrestled him off the driver's seat. Edward took the reins and stopped the horses long enough for Puffy to climb aboard." She laughed. "Burke was swearing like a muleskinner. Jacob kept him pinned to the wagon bed till they reached the schoolhouse. Burke's face stayed red the whole way."

Uncle Jacob saw us and slid off the mule. "Did you sell the wheat?"

"I asked Mr. Osborne what he thought," Daddy said.

"Did you sell the wheat?"

"He thinks the price will go up."

Uncle Jacob pulled out his pocket watch. "Morning market's closed. Soon as the afternoon market opens at two-thirty, you go back to Waitsburg and sell it. If you don't, I will."

Daddy didn't talk on the ride home. When Mama saw how quiet he was at dinner, she opened a jar of apricots, his favorite fruit, even though she'd made lemon meringue pie for dessert. For once Daddy didn't try to talk me into eating apricots.

As I chewed my last forkful of pie, an equal amount of meringue and lemon filling—I'd engineered the portions perfectly—I noticed the wall clock said 1:23. Reverend Taylor was scheduled to visit Aunt Bea at 1:30.

The minister's car was parked in the driveway. Out by the corral, Uncle Jacob was riding a mule. I crawled through weeds to the back of the house, relying on my jungle experience with Frank Buck, who captured wild animals in Ceylon for zoos. Ever since I'd read his book, I'd been sneaking up on leopards and pythons in the woods by the river.

Crouched beneath an open window, I heard Aunt Bea's voice. "It used to be worse. Years ago he was down at her house every afternoon. Babysitting, he said. As if Lola needed help. She only had the one child back then."

"Why wasn't he out working?"

"Good question." Aunt Bea's voice got fainter, as if she'd left

21

the room, and I had to raise my head higher to hear. "He started getting up at four so he could finish work early. Of course that meant I had to get up at four to cook his breakfast." She said something I couldn't understand. Then her voice got louder. "That was when he had his nervous breakdown."

A chair scraped inside the room. "Thank you," Reverend Taylor said. "Just a little cream, please."

"He lost fifty pounds," Aunt Bea said. "I'd cook him the most delicious meals. He'd take a couple of bites and get up without a word and go outside. He'd walk in the hills for hours, sometimes all night. Winters, I'd worry about him freezing to death. I'd go to bed and lie there worrying about him. I'd wake up, feel across the bed, and he still wouldn't be there. I didn't get any more sleep than he did."

"Such a dutiful wife."

Uncle Jacob came into view, riding a mule past the machine shop. I ducked beneath the weeds until he disappeared again.

I straightened up in time to hear Reverend Taylor say, "Why does he bother going to church?"

"Before he had that breakdown, you'd have thought he was the most devout Christian. Then one Sunday he said he wasn't going to church. No explanation. He didn't go for five years. Never did attend Sunday school again."

"It will be our job, yours and mine, to lead your husband back to Christ. We'll be partners."

"Partners," Aunt Bea said.

Uncle Jacob and the mule came into sight again. This time he looked in my direction before I could drop below the weeds. I left the house and crossed the road. Why did Uncle Jacob have a nervous breakdown? I couldn't recall him ever babysitting me. From the railroad tracks I looked back at the little house, abandoned now, and the ache came back. I'd felt it as long as I could remember, wanting something I couldn't identify, as if there were a hole deep inside me that I could never fill.

I got home in time to ride with Daddy to Waitsburg. I knew he felt more comfortable riding a horse than driving a car, but this trip his hands curled around the steering wheel like fists.

The grain growers' office was crowded with grumbling farmers. Daddy stared at a chalk-covered blackboard on the wall. I heard air hiss from his lungs, like a tire going flat. When a man seated behind a desk beckoned to him, he told me to stay put. The room was too noisy for me to hear what they said. The man at the desk took off his glasses and wiped them with a handkerchief. His forehead looked wet. He wrote something on a printed sheet and handed it to Daddy. Daddy looked at the paper, his right shoulder hitching up and down, something he did when he felt uneasy. The man pushed a pen to Daddy. Instead of picking it up, he watched a grizzled farmer who was talking in an agitated voice to a woman clerk. She kept shaking her head. For a long time Daddy studied the numbers on the blackboard. Finally, he picked up the pen.

Neither of us talked on the way home. I heard a clanging when we got close to the machine shop, bang, bang, bang. Uncle Jacob didn't hear us come in. Using tongs, he lifted a horseshoe off the anvil and inspected it. He thrust it deep into a pile of coals in the forge and cranked the bellows, shooting air into the coals from below. The coals glowed cherry red, hot enough to qualify as fuel for hell. He put the reddened horseshoe back on the anvil sideways, tapped the top prong a few times with a hammer, and plunged it into a tub of water, where it sizzled with a long sigh.

Daddy walked up to the forge.

Uncle Jacob looked at his face and said, "How far did it fall?"

"Thirty-five cents. I sold it all."

Uncle Jacob wiped sweat off his forehead with the back of his gloved hand. He poked the tongs absently into the coals, spreading them around. "We need an inch of rain real quick," he said.

TUESDAY, JUNE 17, 1986

I toddle across moonlit room, bump into chair, fall down, other room, long hair on pillow. Back through doorway, where's other bed? Run through pantry, smell pickles, reach up to doorknob. Slippery, can't turn. Scream, pound on door, feet pad behind me, arms lift me, hug me.

Someone is screaming. I taste salt. Sweat stings my eyes. I close my mouth, and the screaming stops. My throat feels raw. My head's been lying on my left arm, and the arm has no feeling, as if a tourniquet's been tied around my elbow. I flex my fingers until the arm tingles.

It's still dark outside. My back stiffens when I get up from the table. Burning those incriminating letters seems even more urgent now, but the store won't open till eight. I search the cupboards again and find a box of wooden matches behind the baking soda.

I shiver when I step out the back door. Why didn't I bring a coat? In the hall closet I find the ragged jacket Daddy wore every season except summer, the one Mama threatened to burn if he ever wore it to Walla Walla. The buttons are varied shapes and colors, whatever Mama could find in her button jar. Was that why she wouldn't let him wear the jacket to town, because it would tarnish her reputation as a seamstress?

I take the match box and a paper bag out to the burn barrel, scrape a match against the box's sandpaper strip, and hold it under the grocery bag. When the bag flares, I drop it into the barrel on top of the letters I dumped there last night. Flames shoot above the barrel's rim.

I hear a sound that chills me—a human voice. Two syllables, like a name. I think the sound came from the north, but I can't be sure. I can see the outline of the barn in the predawn grayness. Maybe the sound was an owl hooting. I walk past the bunkhouse toward the nearest hill. The lower hundred feet is scabland, too steep to farm. I can make out thickets of Russian thistle at the bottom of the hill. Higher, the hill is a dark mass.

My chest lurches. At the crest of the hill, where the scabland ends and the wheat begins, stands a motionless figure, silhouetted against the charcoal sky. I strain to see more clearly, and the figure dissolves.

Uncle Jacob, still walking the hills.

The hobo fell off the train the first week in June. He may have jumped; none of us thought to ask him. I was counting boxcars from the front yard when I saw him tumble down the embankment. He got up and hoisted a bundle onto his back. I knew he'd be coming here. Tramps kept leaving piles of rocks at the end of our lane, a signal that the people who lived here would provide a meal. Daddy always kicked the stones into the ditch, but a new pile would appear the next time a tramp asked Mama for food.

He trudged up the lane, a small man with a face like beef jerky. I followed him to the hog pen, where Daddy was emptying a sack of grain into a feeder.

"Got any work?" the man asked Daddy.

"Rye needs pulling, but I can't pay you."

"I'll work for a meal."

We watched him pull clumps of rye along a narrow swath on a hill of yellowing wheat. "He knows what he's doing," Daddy said. "Most men wear themselves out going up and down a hill."

"I thought you didn't like tramps."

"He's a hobo, not a tramp."

"What's the difference?"

"Tramps won't work. They just want a free meal."

"But if a hobo works, doesn't that make him a hired man?"

"A hired hand stays till the work gives out. A hobo's restless, wants to keep moving."

Timothy came out on the porch and said, "Where's Mama?"

"Luke might know," I said.

I found him hunting eggs by the chicken house. "She went that way." An egg in each hand, he pointed toward the row of locust trees that separated our hills from the flatland. "She had a bucket."

"Let's go find her."

Luke and I took the cows' pathway under the locust trees. It must have been a hundred in the shade, but there wasn't much shade. Locusts overprotect their young, afraid to sprout leaves till long after the threat of frost is gone.

The asparagus patch had been planted forty years earlier by our grandfather. Now it grew wild, competing with spring wheat for moisture. We found no asparagus stalks taller than two inches.

"That means she's been here today," I said.

"So where is she?" Luke said.

The problem called for the deductive powers of Sherlock Holmes. I searched the ground for a locust twig that resembled a pipe.

"She might have gone to the graveyard," I said.

On a hill just east of our property was an old cemetery, protected by a few gnarled locusts. It was still used for burials by farm families who didn't mind toting a casket uphill.

Three years ago I'd watched from the asparagus patch as Mama clambered up the hill, holding Timothy in one arm and gladiolas in her free hand.

We climbed the hill, trying not to mash wheat stalks. The barbed-wire fence at the edge of the graveyard was so low that Luke put his foot on the top wire and hopped over it. "Aren't you coming?" he said, needling me. He knew I didn't like the graveyard.

"Look for fresh-cut flowers," I said.

"Here's one." He pointed to a pink iris near a leaning fence post. "She must have dropped it when she climbed over the barbed wire."

I took Holmes' pipe from between my lips and spat out a fragment of bark. "The first thing a detective must learn, Watson, is never jump to conclusions. She would have brought the flowers here before she picked asparagus. No sense lugging a full bucket up here."

"Maybe she went to the river," Luke said.

"Our first task is to eliminate the impossible. Mama hates the river." I didn't know why. She never went near the river, although Aunt Bea told me Mama used to love picking blackberries along the bank.

"She didn't go home and she didn't go to the river," I said. "Where else could she have gone?"

"Up that canyon?" Luke said, living up to Watson's reputation for making illogical deductions.

"Impossible. She would have no reason to go up there."

"Mama doesn't always need a reason."

"True, Watson, true." I decided to humor Luke so I could say I told you so.

Two hundred yards up the gully, where it forked at the base of a hill, we reached a meadow of bunch grass and wildflowers. I spotted the bucket before I saw Mama. She lay in the grass, her straw hat covering her face. My stomach tightened. Sunstroke?

"Mama!" Luke cried. He ran to her and lifted the hat.

She smiled up at him.

"What are you doing up here?" I said.

"It's so peaceful. The hills are so quiet. Can you smell the flowers?"

I shook my head.

"I can't because of my hay fever," she said. "Those are brown-

27

eyed Susans, the ones that look like small sunflowers. The blue flowers on the long stems, they're camas. I used to carry Anna up here."

"A tramp came," Luke said.

"A hobo," I said. "He's pulling rye."

Mama jumped up and smoothed her hair with both hands, dislodging dried grass. "I'd better get the bunkhouse ready."

We heard a long bleat. At the canyon's mouth we saw an engine pulling a string of boxcars. Mama waved.

"No one can see you from this distance," I said.

The engineer waved back.

"He always waved at us," Mama said. "Anna would wave till the caboose was out of sight. I promised her we'd go on a train ride someday."

She looked past the railroad tracks at the little house where I'd lived till I was four, where Anna lived all her short life. The outhouse had been tipped over by Halloween pranksters. Beyond the house, hidden by cottonwoods, flowed the river Mama once loved.

She turned and strode along the row of locusts, so fast Luke had to trot.

The bunkhouse stood between the well and the hog pen. Inside were four cots, two on each side, and a wood stove at the back. Although hired men hadn't slept here since spring seeding, the smell of sweaty bedrolls and tobacco lingered. Luke and I liked to sneak into the bunkhouse when the men were working, sniff the tobacco pouches and empty whiskey bottles. If there was liquid left in the bottom of a bottle, we'd swirl it, imagining what it would taste like. Of course we never took a sip. Drinking was sinful.

We never found many personal items because hired men, like hobos, had to carry all their belongings inside their bedrolls. We might study a frayed snapshot, wondering if the woman who smiled back at us was the man's wife, if their kids were still small. Sometimes there would be money order receipts, a few crumpled letters in their envelopes, most of them postmarked years or months earlier, addressed to general delivery in different towns. The states they were mailed from were far to the east, Oklahoma, Texas, South Dakota.

Before meals Luke and I would watch the hired men wash their hands at the faucet by the back porch. Once I'd asked Mama where they went to the bathroom. She hadn't answered.

After she swept dust and dead flies out the bunkhouse's open door, she fixed supper. Because she'd wasted the afternoon, our main dish was macaroni and cheese.

She apologized to the hobo for serving macaroni instead of meat. He made sure she wouldn't feel guilty by asking for seconds and thirds.

"Do you have family somewhere?" she said.

He looked at his plate, as if the answer lay hidden under his mound of macaroni. "I don't know."

"Why don't–"

Mama bumped my knee under the table. "Would you like some more asparagus?" she handed the bowl to the hobo. "I picked it this afternoon."

While she washed the supper dishes, Daddy showed the hobo where the bunkhouse was. Then our family gathered in the living room to listen to Sir Harry Lauder on the phonograph. He sang, "There's a wee hoose 'mang the heather, there's a wee hoose o'er the sea… "

"What's that?" Mama said. "There's no ukulele accompaniment."

She lifted the phonograph's needle. Sir Harry stopped singing, but from out front we heard a scratchy voice, "There's a lassie in yon wee hoose waiting patiently for me."

"I declare," Mama said. She opened the front door.

The hobo sat on the porch steps, strumming a ukulele. His bedroll was spread over some ragweed by the porch.

We brought kitchen chairs to the porch and listened to the

hobo as the sun set and the sky turned purple. In a voice itchy as tarweed he sang about droughts and dust-bowl refugees, about a mining camp where families lived in tents, where strike-busters set fire to the tents and shot whoever ran.

"Come inside," Mama said. She sat on the piano bench. The hobo pulled a chair close, twanged his ukulele, and sang about a train that didn't carry gamblers. By the second verse Mama's piano had figured out the tune. By the third verse she'd memorized the refrain. Although she was a natural soprano, she sang alto, letting him lead. From the sofa Daddy whistled his meadowlark's song, the only tune he knew.

Luke and I stayed up past our bedtime. The hobo seemed to be making up songs on the spot. He would sing a few words, strum some chords on his ukulele, listen to Mama repeat the chords on her piano, then they would take off again.

When my eyes got droopy, I crawled into bed and listened to Mama and the hobo. Sometimes they would stop playing. I'd hear indistinct talk for a while, and the music would start again. The last song I heard was about someone waiting for a train. "He'll have a long wait if he's a gambler," I mumbled just before I fell asleep.

Next morning Mama made waffles, a treat usually reserved for Sundays. When she ran out of batter, she gave the last waffle to the hobo. She packed him a big lunch, using a loaf of her homemade bread for bacon sandwiches.

Mama and I watched from the porch as he slung his bedroll over his shoulder and slouched down the lane. When he reached the highway he waved, and we waved back. We watched the small figure shrink until it disappeared around a bend of the road.

She went into the kitchen. On top of the piano lay an envelope, scribbled front and back with cramped, unfamiliar handwriting. Lines were crossed out and reworded, grouped into stanzas. It took me awhile to decipher the mess.

I handed you up to the fireman,
You sat on the engineer's lap.
The engine chugged and the whistle blew,
And you left in a cloud of steam.

I don't know where you're going, my love,
I don't know when you'll return,
But I'll wait here by the railroad tracks,
Till your train comes rolling home.

You'll jump from the cab straight into my arms,
We'll dance round the depot stove.
I'll buy you a chocolate ice cream cone,
You'll tell me the wonders you've seen.

Then you'll climb back onto the engine,
I'll climb up right behind,
We'll ride like the wind across this great land

The stanza's last line was missing because the hobo had run out of space at the bottom of the envelope. I put it back on the piano when Mama came into the room. She lifted the lid of her piano bench and tucked the envelope among the sheet music and song books.

"Just a scrap of paper," she said.

"Why doesn't Uncle Jacob believe in God?" I asked Mama as I dried a cup with a towel.

She lifted a dripping plate out of the sink and scratched at it with her dishcloth. "This soap doesn't get things clean. Maybe I'll switch brands."

"I'll ask him."

31

"I don't think that's a good idea." She rinsed the plate and set it in the strainer. "Some things are private."

Uncle Jacob's car was parked in their driveway. I pushed open the door without knocking. Aunt Bea was swatting flies in the kitchen.

"Got any oatmeal cookies?" I said.

"Go pester your uncle. He's upstairs in his office."

Uncle Jacob sat at his desk writing in a red ledger. Mama had told me he kept the farm's books. Shelves lined three walls, all of them stuffed with books. One thick book, *On the Origin of the Species,* caught my eye because of the author's name. Charles Darwin was the man Reverend Taylor had denounced in last week's sermon because he invented evolution. If we were ever tempted to read that book, Reverend Taylor told us, we should remember how the snake tempted Eve to eat the forbidden apple.

I pulled out the book. Uncle Jacob swiveled his chair to look at me. He had dark pouches under his eyes. "You won't find that book in your school library," he said.

"Is that why you don't believe the Bible? Because you read this book?"

"I stopped believing the Bible because I read the Bible." He slid a three-legged stool toward me and took a familiar black book off a shelf. He thumbed its pages. "This is God talking to Moses, Leviticus twenty, verse nine. 'For everyone that curseth his father or mother shall surely be put to death.'"

I'd never said a cuss word, but I'd heard plenty from hired men and the boys at school. Two years ago, when I was riding behind Daddy's saddle and holding onto his waist, he couldn't find our cows in the canyons where they usually grazed. He'd said, "Damn it," shocking me. People who swore were bad. But Daddy couldn't be a bad man, could he? I'd been afraid to ask Mama.

Uncle Jacob set the Bible on his desk. "I don't want to shake up your faith, Mark. The God of the Old Testament was a pretty angry guy, but Jesus was a good man. You won't go wrong if you

32

follow his advice." He smiled, jiggling his mole.

"If you don't believe in God you'll go to hell," I said.

Uncle Jacob's chuckle was as deep as his singing voice. "If there is a God," he said, "I don't think he gives a hoot in hell what we believe. But I don't think there's a God. Why would a loving God let bad things happen to people?"

"They'll be happy in heaven."

A train whistled far to the west. Uncle Jacob looked out the window. "I'm afraid we'll have to settle for happy memories."

If he was recalling something happy right now, his face didn't show it.

"What about bad memories?" I said.

"Ah, there's the problem, Mark. Bad memories crowd out the good ones. There's a time in our lives when everything's perfect, only we don't realize it till later. But that time passes, and we're living in a new time. We want to go back to that perfect time but we can't. And the more time that passes, the more they slip away, our feelings, our memories, the people." He leaned toward me. "I want another chance," he said, his face intense, as if I could grant it to him.

When I got home I said, "Mama, why does God let bad things happen to people?"

Her eyes narrowed. "Who have you been talking to?"

"Uncle Jacob."

"I might have known." She lifted the lid of her aluminum pot and poured in a cup of water, dousing the aroma of cooked beef. I'd once overheard Aunt Bea tell a church lady, "Lola thinks you need to drown a roast in water. Her chuck roasts taste like mush."

"Why *does* God let bad things happen?" I said.

"Maybe there aren't enough angels to go around," Mama said. "Maybe they do their best, but they can't be everywhere at once."

"But isn't God everywhere at once?"

"You ask too many questions. Go find your father and tell him Grady's Machine Shop called."

Snow deadens my footsteps. The searchers' flashlights illuminate the sides of buildings. I hear a woman's voice calling. I touch rough wood. This must be the butchering shed. Its door is closed. If they'd already searched it, they'd have left the door open. Why haven't they searched this shed? I feel like a ghost, willing the searchers to look here for my body. I open the door and see only blackness. The floor is sticky under the soles of my shoes. I smell blood. I remember the last time the men butchered. A squeal, sudden silence, a hog hanging from a hook, Uncle Jacob staggering through the doorway and vomiting in the snow.

I back out of the doorway and trip over something.

The afternoon sun hammered down on my head as we stood in the back yard, surveying the parched boysenberry bushes Mama had planted to remind herself of the Rogue River valley. "Everything's turning brown and it's only June," she said.

Timothy squealed, "Look!" and pointed at the south hills across the river. Huge clouds rolled toward us, the shape of black widow spiders.

"What is it?" I asked.

"I don't know," Daddy said. "I've never seen anything like it."

"Maybe it's a wheat fire," Mama said. She looked at the shirts hanging from our clothesline. "I'd better bring those inside."

"Rain's coming!" Timothy yelled, clapping his hands.

"If those are rain clouds," Daddy said, "we'd better build an ark."

We watched the clouds boil toward us, blotting out the sun. Birds stopped singing. Our collie whimpered. I got impatient and took a forked stick out by the gas pump to make up a new adventure for Uncle Wiggily. The sky got dark.

The first blast of wind almost knocked me over. I opened my mouth and gagged on dust. I could see only a whirling gray haze.

My eyes stung, and I shut them tight. They felt gritty, but I didn't dare open them. There was a steady roar, like barley whooshing down an elevator shaft.

I stumbled into the wind. Something whacked my face, and I sprawled in the dirt. I touched my forehead—wet and grainy. My nose plugged up. I turned my head away from the wind and sucked in a big breath. Dust filled my lungs. I began to cough and couldn't stop. Gasping, I curled into a ball. The roar inside my head got louder. Something brushed my shoulder. With my eyes shut, I pictured a white-bearded figure bending over me.

"No!" I flailed my arms, grabbed a bony thing that raked my palm and thrashed free.

Something was clenched in my fist—leaves, big leaves. I'd walked into a branch of the maple tree. That meant the house was east, but which way was east? The clouds had come from the south, so if I kept the wind to my right... Gasping and coughing, I began to crawl, fingering each weed for clues, wind pounding my right side. Stickers jabbed my face and hands. Russian thistle. Too far south, veer left. My hand flattened against smooth wood. The porch. I crawled up the steps.

"Stay inside," I heard Daddy shout. "I'll go out again and look for him."

I touched his shoe. He scooped me up and carried me into the house. Other arms circled me. Inside, the haze was yellow. Luke and Timothy crowded close, trying to pat my head.

"Give me room to breathe," I croaked.

I shut my eyes and flinched while Mama dabbed iodine on my forehead with a cotton swab. My hacking had dwindled to a burp of a cough every few seconds, like hiccups. I opened my eyes and saw Mama's father looking at me from the photo on top of the piano. The corners of his mouth turned down into his long white beard, but his eyes crinkled. This piano had been one of the few possessions saved when the bank foreclosed his mortgage after he died, scattering his family.

Mama pressed adhesive tape over the gauze on my forehead.

"There's dust all over your piano," I said.

"Might make it play better," Daddy said. He winked at her.

"Let's find out." Mama swiped her hand over the piano bench, raising a puff of dust, and sat down. She sang, "Wait till the sun shines, Nellie, and the clouds go drifting by."

Mama had started giving Luke and me piano lessons two years earlier, gambling that we had inherited her musical talent instead of Daddy's. She broke even. After a year and a half of lessons, I would entertain Timothy with "Chopsticks," then wander into the orchard so I couldn't hear Luke play Haydn's "Surprise Symphony."

But Luke had to think about what he was doing, mashing the keys so hard the tips of his fingers would whiten. Mama just looked at the music and played, her fingers skipping over the keys like water bugs. To Luke the piano was a mule that had to be spurred, to me it was a bucking bronco, but to Mama the piano was a winged horse that carried her across continents and time, away from our treeless hills.

When she played "Home to Our Mountains," she again would feel the Rogue River's spray on her face as she picked blackberries with her sisters.

As she played "Little Mother of Mine," singing along with the piano, she would brush egg whites over a pan of steaming scones and watch her mother slide it into the oven.

She would sit once more on the piano bench alongside her father as he tapped the keys with one finger and sang "The Ninety and Nine" in a quavering tenor.

"Loch Lomond" would whisk her to a Scotland she had never seen, where she and her grandma would climb a hill of purple heather at dawn to watch the loch light up in gold.

"Let Me Call You Sweetheart" would find her sitting in Daddy's car at the Whetstone Depot, waiting for the train that was supposed to take her home to Oregon, a train she would miss because Daddy, watching the engine's light far down the tracks, would clear his throat and say, "Think you'd like it up here?"

Mama lost track of time when she sat at the piano, and like all children of addicts, we suffered. We would wait patiently at the table twenty minutes past the six o'clock supper hour, listening to our stomachs rumble, reporting each minute as it ticked off the clock, while Mama scurried around the kitchen rolling pie crust and shucking corn. Luke and I never offered to help because we didn't want to encourage any more six-thirty suppers. Also, we knew Mama would have supper ready by the time we figured out whose turn it was.

She'd say, "I'd rather do it all myself than listen to you kids quarrel." But of course she didn't understand that we were helping her most by not helping.

Daddy would spoil our therapy by asking if there was anything he could do to help. He fueled her addiction in other ways, too. When he came in for supper after feeding the pigs, he would pause on the back porch with one boot off, listening to Mama. Somehow she always knew he was there, because her next song would be "Let Me Call You Sweetheart." Then she would jump up from the piano and say, "Where did the time go?"

Daddy would put his arm around her shoulder and give her a squeeze and say, "I'd rather listen to you play than eat any day."

It seemed strange that a man could farm all his life and not appreciate the value of food.

The morning after the storm, we plodded through mounds of dust into the field south of our house. Daddy rubbed a shrunken head of wheat between his thumb and forefinger. The husks at the top were missing their kernels. "Wind shattered it," he said.

We all watched Daddy. There was no expression on his face. Mama laid her hand on his arm. He looked at her, and his eyes twinkled.

"You've got to look at the bright side, Lola," he said, jostling her shoulder like the calves did to each other when they felt playful.

"Stop it," Mama said, trying to look cross. "What on earth could the bright side be?"

"You might not have to get up at four to feed a harvest crew."

The smell of fresh-baked bread woke me the first morning of harvest. In the kitchen Peggy Foster, the high school girl who lived across the road, was washing the men's breakfast dishes. She helped Mama every harvest, and sometimes she stayed with us kids when our parents were gone. She'd been hanging around Mama as far back as I could remember. Lately she'd been helping Uncle Jacob in the shop, getting harnesses ready for harvest.

Mama loaded my plate with sausage, scrambled eggs, fried potatoes, and two pancakes. I liked harvest because we ate even better than usual. She once said Daddy was so hard to work for that the only way they could keep harvest hands from absconding to a neighbor's crew was to provide better meals than they could get anywhere else.

When I finished breakfast I walked to the harvest's staging area, a clearing near the asparagus patch that was partly shaded by locust trees. Uncle Jacob was adjusting a mule's harness. Thirty-two mules and horses were already hooked up to the combine, six abreast except for the two lead mules. Three young hired men were currying the animals. Daddy was arguing with Andrus, the combine man, a huge guy with a pot belly.

"It's frayed," Andrus said. He slid his hand over a belt, part of a mind-boggling system of chains, sprockets, belts and pulleys that ran the combine's sickle bar, header reel and thresher.

"It's fine," Daddy said. "Let's not waste any more time."

The combine man squirted grease onto a sprocket, shaking his head. Daddy walked over to join me. "That belt will last longer than he does," he muttered.

Every harvest Daddy had to make a couple of trips to Lutcher's Tavern in Walla Walla to replace crew members who quit or got fired. Once I asked him why so many hired men didn't pan out. "They don't have the brains God gave a chicken," he'd said.

Uncle Jacob saw it differently. "Everything's got to be done his way," he'd told me. "If a hired hand figures out a smarter way, he'd better shut up if he wants to stick around."

Because Uncle Jacob got along better with hired men, I wondered why Daddy was the boss.

The four new men got on the combine, and Uncle Jacob climbed the shaky wooden ladder that slanted from the combine out over the back rows of horses and mules. At the ladder's top he sat in the driver's seat, holding one rein, and the team started moving.

"Doesn't he need a whole bunch of reins?" I asked Daddy.

"Just the one. It's attached to the jerk-line mule."

"Which mule is that?"

"The leader on the left. A steady pull on the jerk-line tells him to turn left, and the whole team follows him."

Uncle Jacob twitched the line and the team swung to the right, heading for the first hill.

"Did you see what happened?" Daddy said.

"No."

"When the mule feels two jerks, he turns right, pulling the rest of the team with him."

"That mule must be strong," I said.

"Smart, too. The smartest animals go up front."

"Aren't horses smarter than mules?"

"When a mule gets overworked in the heat, he stops. Won't move no matter what you do. You've heard of a balky mule?"

"Aren't balky mules bad?"

"Some farmers think so till they have a horse drop dead in its tracks."

39

Daddy mounted Blackie. I climbed onto the water trough so he could swing me behind the saddle. I wrapped my arms around his stomach, and we followed the combine. Blackie was a big horse, and under my legs I could feel his muscles strum as if he could hardly bear to go this slow. Daddy wouldn't let Blackie gallop when I rode behind him, but trotting was what I hated. I'd bounce high with each trot, coming down so hard my teeth rattled. When I was younger, Daddy had to hook one arm behind my back to keep me from falling off.

The team started around the bottom of a hill. The header angled uphill from the combine, its spokes turning, pushing wheat stalks onto the sickle bar as the header tender spun his wheel, raising it to avoid patches of tarweed, lowering it when heads of wheat reappeared. A cloud of dust and chaff enveloped the combine. Although we were ten yards behind, chaff settled on my face and wriggled down the collar of my shirt. It itched something fierce because of the tarweed, but I knew if I scratched my neck it would itch even more.

The combine man worked the leveler that kept the combine from tipping over, but the two men on the sacking platform weren't doing anything. Maybe they couldn't see because of the dust.

After a while the sack jig attached an empty gunny sack to one of the bin's two spouts, took a loaded sack of wheat off the other spout, bounced it a few times, and set it in front of the seated sack-sewer, who tied it, his hands a blur. The sewer then dumped the sack down a chute.

The team went up a draw. Blackie seemed glad to exert some of his pent-up energy going uphill, and Daddy tightened the reins to keep him from outrunning the combine. As the lead mules disappeared over the top of a ridge, the first five sacks fell out of the combine's chute. Daddy looked behind us at the swath of headless stubble. His shoulder hitched up and down. "We've cut well over an acre," he said. "That's less than five bushels an acre."

"Because of the dust storm?" I said.

40

"What the drought didn't get the wind did."

The combine was still going downhill, but the mules in front were starting up the next rise. The end of the ladder dipped lower, almost touching the animals, until Uncle Jacob dropped out of sight. I held my breath, afraid he'd fall off and get trampled. Then he reappeared, and the combine followed the team up the hill. He took a clod out of the box by his side and threw it at a horse that must have been lagging. He threw two more in the same direction. Last harvest Daddy had told me that Uncle Jacob was too gentle to fill the box with rocks as most drivers did, so he often had to throw several clods to get an animal's attention. "Takes a lot more effort to throw a clod," he'd said.

The sack sewer still hadn't dropped the second batch of loaded sacks. "Looks bad," Daddy said, "real bad."

The temperature rose as the hills grew steeper. Tarweed inched down my back, carried by rivulets of sweat. The men on the combine took turns drinking out of a jug, making me thirsty. Blackie's flanks glistened, but he seemed as energetic as when we'd started. Mid-morning the team started around the steepest hill yet. A few feet to the combine's left, scabland dropped off in a cliff to Whetstone Creek far below.

The combine stopped. Uncle Jacob's ladder shook as he climbed down. Daddy dismounted and helped me off Blackie. Andrus was on his hands and knees, inspecting the ground just ahead of the combine's left wheel.

"Dirt's too soft," he said.

"We've got no choice," Daddy said. "We can't back up."

"This ground is too steep to farm," the combine man said. "I've got the leveler set at its limit."

"Sixty degrees isn't that steep," Daddy said.

"Are you crazy? Ninety degrees is straight up. Sooner or later you're going to get someone killed." Andrus pointed toward Uncle Jacob's empty perch high above the team. "Usually it's the driver."

Daddy bristled. "We've never had an accident."

41

"We did once," Uncle Jacob said. "Remember the time—"

"Different situation," Daddy said. "The leveler was faulty."

The combine man blew his nose on a red bandana. "I've never worked for a farmer this stubborn. If you quit farming this hillside you'd only lose a couple of acres."

A vein on Daddy's neck bulged. "We need the income."

"So a little money is worth risking the lives of your crew?" Andrus stuffed the bandana into his back pocket.

I looked at the three men still on the combine. The header tender's mouth hung open.

"If you're scared I'll take over," Daddy growled.

Andrus shrugged. "We've got a better chance of coming out alive if I handle it." He tried to swing his bulk onto the combine's short ladder, but the hillside was so steep Uncle Jacob had to boost him up. Daddy grunted, as close to a chuckle as he could manage.

Uncle Jacob climbed his wobbly ladder. Daddy mounted Blackie and turned the horse so its left side was uphill. It took hardly any effort for him to pull me high enough so I could plant my foot on the stirrup and swing behind the saddle.

Uncle Jacob shook his single rein and the team started forward. The combine began to slide sideways, toward the cliff.

It was going to tip over.

I felt Daddy's stomach muscles stiffen. I gripped him tighter around the belly and pressed my face into the collar of his shirt so I couldn't see.

I counted the seconds, one, two, three. I could still hear the combine's roar, so it must not be hurtling down the cliff. I peeked around Daddy's neck. The header tender jumped off the back of the combine. Its big iron wheel slid to the edge of the cliff and stopped.

The header tender almost collided with Blackie. He ran along the swath of cut wheat stalks and vanished around the curve of the hill.

Daddy laughed. "Too bad we don't have a stopwatch. That

fellow's going to set a world's record."

He rode close to the combine. "Hit a patch of soft dirt is all," he yelled, loud enough so Andrus could hear him over the engine's racket. "Wheels couldn't have slid more than six feet."

"That's all, huh?" Andrus scowled at him. "One more foot and we'd be dead."

Uncle Jacob crawled under the hitch that separated the combine from the team. "Looks like the ground ahead is solid," he shouted.

The sack sewer volunteered to handle two jobs so the sack jig could tend header. "We weren't getting enough grain to keep busy," he said.

Uncle Jacob flicked his rein, and the combine shuddered. I gritted my teeth, watching the iron wheels rotate, until they began moving uphill.

It was after noon when the combine finished its first swath around the hills. Twenty yards short of the staging area, the team stopped and the combine's motor shut off.

"What's he up to now?" Daddy said. When we rode close, Andrus silently held up a busted belt so Daddy could see.

The two young men helped Uncle Jacob unhitch the animals and lead them to the feed racks and water trough. Uncle Jacob checked them for sores they might have got from the hard pulling. He rubbed salve onto a raw patch on a mule's shoulder. He flexed his right elbow. "Feels like I just pitched a nine-inning game."

Daddy said, "We're not getting enough grain, Jacob."

"Look any better near the hilltops?"

"Worse."

The two brothers watched their horses and mules munch hay from the feed racks. Uncle Jacob scratched a horse under its chin. "Well, Henry," he said, "guess I won't have to throw any more clods at you."

Back at the house I washed up at the outside faucet along with the men. I could smell cherry pie through the open kitchen windows, and my mouth started watering. Mama had put an extra leaf in the dining room table, which was loaded with baked ham, mashed potatoes, green beans and strawberries from our garden.

The hired men plowed into the food, knowing it might be the last home-cooked meal they'd get for a while. Daddy said he would ask farmers to the east if they needed harvest hands. Crops closer to the mountains would have gotten more rain. The sack sewer told Mama he'd rather work here for free and eat her cooking than get paid somewhere else.

The combine man pulled Uncle Jacob aside, out of Daddy's earshot, and said he already had a backup job in mind because he guessed he'd get fired before the week was out. "When he wouldn't let me replace that belt, I knew it'd be one thing after another."

"That's just Edward's way," Uncle Jacob said. "He'll let a worn-out part go until it breaks. Thinks he's saving money."

Andrus drove away, and the two young men waited on the front porch while Daddy phoned farmers who hadn't started harvest yet. I walked down the lane to get the mail. When I came back, the sack sewer and sack jig were comparing the checks Daddy had written them.

"He paid us for a whole day's work," the sack jig said.

Daddy came out on the porch. "Sorry," he said. "I couldn't get ahold of anybody who needs harvest hands." The men got into his pickup. I watched it turn west at the end of the lane, heading toward Lutcher's Tavern.

Mama was washing dishes. She wouldn't have to cook for a harvest crew anymore, but she didn't look happy. Peggy arrived, and Mama told her harvest had been canceled.

"I'm going to move the team back to the corrals," Uncle Jacob said to Peggy. "Want to help?" They walked past the chicken house, talking animatedly.

"Why does Peggy talk to Uncle Jacob so much?" I asked Mama.

"He's like a father to her," she said.

44

"What's wrong with Peggy's own father?"

"Burke drinks. I told her I'd rather she didn't get married at all than marry a drinker."

Please keep going. Please don't slow down. The gray car with "Sheriff" on its side turns into Uncle Jacob's lane, coming straight at me, spraying slush. I freeze, hoping the driver hasn't spotted me. He stops. Too late to climb the barbed-wire fence and hide behind the tumbleweeds. I glance at the dried blood on my palm. His car door slams. He's coming toward me through the snow. I see footprints between us, made by the searchers, I suppose. I recognize him. He's Daddy's friend, the sheriff.

"Mark, isn't it? Or Luke? I get you boys mixed up."

I nod.

"Which is it?"

My tongue won't work.

He bends over, hands on his knees, so we're face to face. He has a kind face, like Doctor Harvey but with more wrinkles. He lays a hand on my shoulder. "Why are you shaking? Something you saw?"

"No!" I said it too loud. "I'm cold." It's the truth. I can't feel my toes.

"Been down at the river?"

"No," I say, softer this time. Too late I realize I looked away as I said it.

"What did you see?"

"Nothing."

He looks below my chin.

Reflexively I touch the top button of my coat. Goo. The vomit hasn't yet dried. Can he smell urine?

He pats my shoulder. "It's okay. Whatever you saw, you can tell me. I'm here to help."

"I didn't see anything." I can't tell anybody what I saw for the rest of my life. Especially you.

He straightens up and looks at the cars and trucks parked among the locust trees in front of the house. "Come on, I'll drive you home."

"I'll walk. Thanks anyway." I plod through the snow, past his car, aware that he's watching my back. Act nonchalant. I cross the railroad tracks and

turn left on the highway, relieved that I haven't heard his car come after me.

On the last Saturday of August, dozens of trucks with rickety sideboards clattered into the field south of the house, mashing tumbleweeds and raising dust so thick I couldn't see the road. Other years gunny sacks full of wheat would have dotted the field, but this year the wheat stalks, their shriveled heads still attached, lay tangled in every direction, like my hair when Mama forgot to comb it.

By late afternoon the trucks' owners were bunched in front of me, squinting into the sun. Their necks were burned leather-brown, even though their hat brims slanted low all the way around instead of curling up over their ears like the hats of real cowboys in the movies.

It was so hot the flies on the hats had quit crawling to save their energy. I stood on top of an upside-down apple box and listened to an auctioneer I couldn't see.

"Lot number forty-six, blue mare name of Susie," the auctioneer said. "Got thirty thirty now five now five now two fifty, going at thirty... sold for thirty dollars to Sam Woods of Waitsburg."

Uncle Jacob appeared from in front of the crowd, leading Susie, the last of the horses and mules that pulled our combine. A gaunt-faced man threw a rope around her neck and knotted it. Uncle Jacob untied his own rope, patted Susie's neck, and watched the man lead her into the loading chute.

Daddy listened to the auctioneer's chant from the porch. A rancher came out of the front door, walking gingerly, as if his glass were brimful of nitroglycerin instead of lemonade. Daddy stepped aside to let him pass. Through the kitchen window I could see Mama pour lemonade from a pitcher into a row of glasses on the table. A platter of cookies sat alongside the glasses. Peggy dried her hands on a towel and brought more glasses to the table.

"Lot number forty-eight," said the auctioneer. "Clarendon piano."

Daddy rocked on the balls of his feet, his thumbs hooked under the straps of his bib overalls.

"Got eighty now five now five, got eighty-five now seven fifty now eighty-seven fifty now seven fifty, going at eighty-five..."

The auctioneer waited. I stood on tiptoes, and the apple box under me creaked. Between two men's hats I could see the top of Mama's piano. Beyond the piano, along the river half a mile away, cottonwood trees shimmied in the heat like a mirage.

I looked back at the house. Daddy stood motionless on the porch, overall straps clenched in his fists. Inside the kitchen, Mama reached up and pulled down the blind.

"Sold for eighty-five dollars to Dick Drumheller," the auctioneer said.

I heard a wail from the front of the crowd, and a moment later Timothy ran past me toward the house. Daddy came down the steps, squatted, and took him in his arms. Timothy tried to tell him something between sobs. Then he pulled away and ran into the house. The door slammed. Daddy looked at the door, then at the kitchen window with its closed blind.

He walked toward the loading area, where a truck was backing up to the chute. The chute trembled, and the truck stopped. I caught up to Daddy as a man with a handlebar mustache climbed down from the cab. Timothy trotted toward us from the house.

"What would you take in place of that piano?" Daddy said.

"I don't know, Eddie. Mae Belle's been wanting a piano a long time."

"You know my saddle horse?"

"Blackie?" Mr. Drumheller set the gate against the truck's side panel and pulled a sack of Beechnut tobacco out of his hip pocket. "Well now, Blackie's a real good horse."

"Would you take Blackie instead of that piano?"

47

Mr. Drumheller tucked a pinch of tobacco between his gums and cheek, then worked his mouth until the tobacco settled where he wanted it.

"Reckon I would," he said.

"But Daddy," I said. "How will you find the cows—hey!" I bent to rub my ankle where Timothy had kicked it.

I expected Mama to be happy when Daddy and Uncle Jacob rolled her piano into the living room, but instead she scolded Daddy for giving away Blackie. Daddy and I went out on the porch to watch the auction. I couldn't decipher the auctioneer's drone because Mama started playing the piano.

"Let's move closer," I said.

"Soon as this song is over," he said, although he must have heard "You Are My Sunshine" a thousand times before.

The auction only brought in a fraction of what we owed the bank, so Daddy and Uncle Jacob used the proceeds to buy a used crawler tractor to pull the harrow and seeder. It would also pull the combine next summer if they still owned the farm. They planned to seed the fall wheat and hope for a miracle.

The tractor arrived September twenty-eighth, two days after the first fall rain, perfect timing to seed fall wheat. The problem was that neither brother had ever driven a tractor with metal treads. The morning it arrived Daddy experimented with the levers, acting as if he'd just got a new toy.

"Think I've got the hang of it," he yelled at Uncle Jacob over the tractor's din. He shifted gears and the tractor pitched forward, headed toward the barn.

"Uh-oh," Uncle Jacob said.

Daddy looked up and saw the side of the barn approaching. He pulled two levers back as if they were reins. "Whoa!" he shouted. He ducked just before the tractor smashed through the barn's wall and disappeared. The engine stopped. Dust poured through a gaping hole in the wall.

I peered inside, coughing, and saw the tractor, bales of hay jumbled on its engine and treads. One bale lay across the driver's seat.

A few feet away Daddy sat on a hay bale, grinning. "Got it stopped," he said, "with a little help."

While we were eating dinner I heard an engine start up. I reached the back porch in time to see Uncle Jacob driving the tractor toward the hills, harrows trailing behind. I hadn't seen him practice on the tractor, but he must have learned what not to do by watching Daddy operate it.

A letter from the bank arrived the next day. That evening I got out of bed to listen at the kitchen door.

Mama's voice sounded weary. "What's going to happen?"

"We'll lose the farm unless Jacob or I drop dead."

"What on earth are you talking about?" Mama said.

"Remember how we almost lost the farm when Father died? Jacob and I took out key man insurance on each other's lives so it won't happen again." Daddy's chuckle sounded hollow. "Maybe we should play Russian roulette."

On December first Mama said she had to go to Walla Walla. Saturday trips to town meant stopping for ice cream cones at the Shady Lawn Creamery's takeout window. After the last of the ice cream had dribbled through holes in the bottoms of the cones, and Mama had wiped our sticky hands with a towel, she would drop off Luke and me at the Roxy Theatre. We'd watch a double feature, two cowboy shows plus a serial, until Mama came to get us.

"You boys can't go with me," she said. "Peggy's coming to babysit."

Babysit! What an insult. Peggy was sixteen, only six years older than me.

"Why can't we go?" I said.

"I've got too many things to do. Raisin cookies are in the breadbox."

Something was up. Mama must have made the cookies last night after our bedtime. If she'd baked cookies today we would have smelled them.

Her parting instructions were, "Don't you dare give Peggy a hard time." But how else could we punish Mama for leaving us?

After gorging ourselves on cookies, we sneaked out of the house while Peggy was vacuuming the living room rug.

"I'm cold," Timothy said. We hadn't put on coats, probably a result of confused thinking caused by our sugar highs.

"You can't be cold," I said. "See? The frost is gone from the weeds."

Beyond the cook shack I spotted the old water tank. "We escaped from a German prison camp," I said. "There's a British submarine waiting for us offshore."

We squeezed through the spout. The inside of the tank was so cramped we had to sit with our knees rubbing our chins. I felt claustrophobic. I shouldn't have let Luke sit under the spout. It was the captain's job to man the conning tower.

"Mark?" Peggy's voice came faintly from outside. "Timothy? Luke?"

"We're in here," Timothy said, not loud enough for her to hear.

"Shh," I said. "That's the captain of a Nazi destroyer."

"You boys come here," Peggy yelled, trying to imitate Mama. When she added, "Right this minute," her voice faltered.

All the oxygen was gone. I was breathing pure carbon dioxide. "The sub got hit by a depth charge," I said. "This is your captain speaking. Abandon ship."

Luke went first. Timothy tried to crawl out. "I'm stuck." He began to cry.

I grabbed his legs to boost him through the opening. He shot upwards like a rocket. Wow, I thought, heroes really do find an unexpected reservoir of strength.

I poked my head above the conning tower's rim and sucked in fresh air. Peggy was setting Timothy on the ground. "Do I have to lift you out, too?" she said.

I scrambled out. Didn't this Nazi know that the captain is always the last to leave a sinking ship?

"You're shaking," Luke said to me.

"It's the bends," I said. "The sub sank another hundred feet after you got out."

Uncle Jacob walked toward us from the barnyard. "I heard you calling the kids," he said to Peggy. "Everything all right?"

"It's fine," she said. Her voice sounded funny. Her long, thin face looked scared, as if we were still missing.

Uncle Jacob must have noticed her expression, too, because he took her arm and led her away, out of my earshot. They stood by the chicken house, talking. Peggy did most of the talking. Her shoulders trembled, and I realized she was crying. Uncle Jacob hugged her. The top of her head barely touched his chin. They unclasped, and Peggy hurried toward the house, wiping her eyes. Uncle Jacob watched her until the back door closed. His face looked grim, as if whatever bothered Peggy was bothering him, too.

Peggy left when Daddy finished work, an hour before Mama's headlights turned into our lane. "I couldn't believe it," she said as she set two paper bags full of groceries on the kitchen counter. "We just got over Thanksgiving and the stores are already decorated for Christmas."

Daddy said, "They're afraid if they wait a week they won't get all of our money."

"It's got so commercial," she said. "Everyone's forgotten the true meaning of Christmas."

"Do you have more things in the car?" I said. "I'll bring them in."

"No, this is all." She looked at me suspiciously. "That's the first time you've ever volunteered to help."

"You might have forgotten something. I'll go look."

Luke followed me to the car. The living room windows didn't shed much light, so I felt along the back seat and the floor.

"What are you looking for?" Luke said.

"Remember this, Watson. Sometimes it's not what's here that matters, it's what's not here."

"I never know what you're talking about."

"The body must be in the trunk," I said, but he was already halfway to the front door.

At bedtime I lay on top of the covers until I heard Daddy's footsteps in the hall. After his bedroom door closed, I waited long enough for him to fall asleep. I hopped out of bed and opened our door a crack. The only light came from under the closed kitchen door.

"Wake up, Watson," I hissed in Luke's ear. "The game's afoot."

"What?" he was still half asleep.

"Hurry! Time is of the essence."

He sat up. "What are we going to do?"

"We're facing a dangerous adversary, Watson. Bring your pistol."

"My cap pistol?"

We crept barefoot down the hall in our pajamas, past Mama's and Daddy's bedroom into Timothy's room. Luckily, he was asleep. He hadn't yet learned to keep secrets from Mama. His west window had a view of the driveway, and Luke and I pressed our noses against the glass. In the starlight we could see the outline of our car.

"We may have a long wait," I said.

"What are we waiting for?" Luke said.

"Keep watching the car."

A dark figure glided from the corner of the house and

disappeared behind the car. Its trunk rose. After a moment the trunk came down and the figure went back toward the house.

"That was the ghost of Christmas presents," I whispered.

I heard soft footsteps in the hall and the rustle of paper just outside Timothy's door.

We waited until the kitchen light went out, then the light in Mama's bedroom. I dragged Timothy's chair from his room, opened the hall closet's door, and stood on the chair. It was too dark to see the objects on the top shelf, but I could feel them.

Sharp-edged corners indicated boxes, but there were other shapes I couldn't identify. A delicious feeling spread through me, as if I'd just taken the wrapping off a candy bar and was sniffing the chocolate. I purposely hadn't brought a flashlight. Feeling the objects was legal but peeking wasn't. What fun would Christmas be if we knew for sure what we were going to get?

After Luke stood on the chair, we put it back in Timothy's room and tiptoed down the hall toward our bedroom. As I passed our parents' closed door, I heard voices and stopped.

"Same thing happens every year," Daddy said. "We get so we're almost making it, then we go under again at Christmas."

"I want them to have a nice Christmas," Mama said. She sounded like she was about to cry.

During our school lunch hour on Wednesday, I ate fast, hardly tasting the peanut butter and honey sandwich Mama had fixed me. We'd had heavy rains since Monday, and I wanted to see how high the river had risen. I hurried along the railroad tracks toward the crossing at River Road, jumping from tie to tie. As I approached the depot I saw Uncle Jacob's Model T park in front. He got out, reached under the back window, and pulled the rumble seat's handle away from the window until the lid was pointing straight up. He took out a suitcase. The passenger door opened and Peggy got out. She looked up and down the street, but because I was on the railroad track, she didn't see me. Uncle Jacob took out his wallet and gave her several bills. He watched her tug the suitcase through the depot's door. Then he got in his car and left.

I looked in a depot window. Peggy left the ticket counter and sat on a bench, hunched over. She was facing away from me, so I couldn't see her eyes, but her shoulders shook.

I headed back to the school, not caring anymore whether the river was high. Why did Uncle Jacob give her money? And why would she go somewhere she didn't want to go?

It was after dark when Mrs. Foster drove up. From our front yard I could see her sitting on the sofa, talking to Mama, her shoulders hunched like Peggy's had been inside the depot. I knew how to come in from the back noiselessly, by not pushing the door all the way shut. I sneaked through the kitchen and opened the door a crack. Mrs. Foster's voice was barely audible, just above a whisper.

"She'll stay with my sister. She had to leave before she started showing."

Showing what? I pushed the door open a few inches farther and winced when I heard it creak.

"Is someone in your kitchen?" Mrs. Foster said.

When Mama opened the door I was getting a water glass out of the cupboard. She stood in the doorway, hands on her hips, as I filled the glass and drained it. I went out the back door, aware that she was still watching me.

"I'm going to drive Jacob to the depot," Mama said a week later. "Bea's shopping in Walla Walla."

"Where's he going?" I said.

"Oregon, to visit his mother and sister."

"I want to ride along."

She shook her head.

"Why not?"

She sighed. She knew I'd keep pestering her till she gave in.

We waited on a depot bench for the train. Mama and Uncle Jacob usually talked a lot, but today he replied with one word to whatever she said.

He waved goodbye from a passenger car window as the engine huffed steam and its three big drive wheels churned. The couplings between the cars clanged and buckled as if the cars couldn't make up their minds whether to go or stay. We watched the caboose get smaller until it disappeared behind a stand of cottonwoods. Mama kept watching the empty tracks.

"Can I get a gumball?" I said.

She looked startled, as if she'd forgotten I was standing beside her. "My goodness, I've got to start fixing supper." She rushed through the depot, past the gumball machine and the ticket counter, and held the street door open for me.

After she finished washing the supper dishes, she said, "Let's go caroling." She helped Timothy put on his coat. "You too," she said to Daddy, who was hiding behind his newspaper.

Outside, the crisp air felt good. Mama looked at the sky and said, "The lights in Whetstone will be too bright. We wouldn't be able to see the stars."

"We could serenade the hogs," Daddy said.

Mama made a face. "We could if we put clothespins over our noses. We'll sing for Bea. She'll be lonely with Jacob gone."

Daddy drove us the half mile to the old homestead. When we turned into the lane our headlights revealed two cars instead of the one that was normally there.

"That looks like Reverend Taylor's car," I said.

Daddy backed up and turned around.

"Aren't we going to serenade them?" Luke said.

"We don't want to interrupt their Bible lesson," Mama said.

We parked in front of our house. Daddy and Mama sat staring out the windshield as if they could see something in the dark that I couldn't.

"Who are we going to sing Christmas carols for?" Luke said.

"The stars," Mama said.

We stood in the driveway and sang "Silent Night." At least

Mama and Luke and I did. Timothy made up his own lyrics, and Daddy didn't sing at all. Mama's vibrant voice seemed to echo among the hills. Although the night air was getting colder, I felt warm and safe, as I did whenever I heard Christmas carols.

Next we sang, "Oh little town of Bethlehem, how still we see thee lie. Above thy deep and dreamless sleep, the silent stars go by."

Mama stopped singing, and so did we. She thrust her head back, looking at the Milky Way. "My father used to tell us the stars were angels," she said, "loved ones who have passed on, watching over all the people on earth." She scanned the sky from the Big Dipper to a greenish star above the southern hills. "I wonder which one is hers."

"Whose?" Luke said.

She didn't answer. As I gazed at the thousands of stars sprinkled all over the sky, I got scared.

"Mark, you're shivering," Mama said. "We'd better go inside. It's past Timothy's bedtime, anyway."

The next week was foggy and cold, so Luke and I spent a lot of time indoors poring over the Montgomery Ward Christmas catalog. I begged Mama to somehow find the Uncle Wiggily books I didn't have. She explained that she'd tried everything she could think of, even writing to the publisher, but the books were too long out of print.

"Where did you get my six books?" I asked.

"From Aunt Ethyl. She gave us Uncle Wiggily's bungalow, too."

The papier mache bungalow I'd inherited had no door. Worse, one of the ten cardboard figures had been missing as far back as I could remember.

"Someone lost Jackie Bow-Wow," I said.

"Look in the mirror, Mister. You and Anna were playing with the set before you could crawl."

December twentieth, the day before Uncle Jacob was due to

arrive on the train, the weather changed. By noon it was seventy degrees, like a spring day except the countryside was gray instead of green. After supper it was still balmy, so I went outside to play.

I decided it was December sixth–two weeks ago–and I had just swum to Japan's shore from a United States submarine. My orders were to infiltrate the War Office, which happened to be Uncle Jacob's house, and learn if the Japanese were planning a sneak attack.

The porch light was on to make sure sentries could spot approaching commandos. I crossed the railroad tracks and entered the locust grove that surrounded the house. A moving light illumined the trees to my left. Did the sentries have a searchlight? I heard a car's engine and hid behind a tree trunk.

The motor shut off. Aunt Bea came out on the porch. Reverend Taylor got out of his car and hugged her, the way he hugged all the church women as they filed past him out the door. Shame on him, a Baptist minister collaborating with the enemy.

The porch light went off. I headed for the back of the house, to the living room window where I'd overheard Aunt Bea and Reverend Taylor last spring. Listening to Bible talk would be boring, but they might leak a clue about whether a sneak attack was planned. The window was closed. I pushed on the bar halfway up the window but couldn't raise it.

A light came on in the bedroom. Aunt Bee must have gone in there to get her Bible. The blind was drawn shut, and this window was locked, too.

My only chance to learn the Japanese' plans was to sneak in the front door and listen from the entry way. To be caught meant death before a firing squad, but I was brave. I turned the knob. The door was locked.

As I crossed the railroad tracks on my way home, I asked my colonel for transcripts of messages our code-breakers had failed to decipher. Within minutes I broke the Japanese' code and learned they planned to bomb Pearl Harbor the morning of December seventh.

I stopped on the highway and stood erect as President Roosevelt pinned the Congressional Medal of Honor to my uniform. "Thanks to your warning," he said, "Our fighter planes intercepted the Japanese bombers without the loss of a single warship." The pin pricked my chest, but I didn't wince. Behind the newsreel cameramen I spotted Daddy. He was hitching his shoulder up and down, proud of his son but uncomfortable about being this close to a Democratic president.

A figure took shape in the darkness ahead. For a second I was caught in limbo between the White House and the highway, as if I were struggling to come out of a dream. Then I recognized Uncle Jacob. He was carrying a suitcase.

"Mark?" he said. "What are you doing out so late?"

"It's a nice night, so I went for a walk."

Uncle Jacob put down the suitcase and wiped his cheeks with a handkerchief. "Warm enough to work up a sweat lugging this thing. I decided to come home a day early."

"Why didn't you phone Aunt Bea to come get you?"

"I thought I'd surprise her."

I didn't tell him Reverend Taylor was there because then he'd know I'd been snooping.

After he walked on I tried to pick up where I'd left off, but President Roosevelt had vanished, taking my medal with him. A few minutes later I heard a car rev up behind me. I turned but saw no headlights. The engine's noise grew louder, and I jumped into the ditch just before the car roared past. Farther down the road its lights came on. Reverend Taylor must have been too preoccupied with the Bible lesson to notice his lights were off. Maybe it wasn't a good idea to think about God too much.

The date I'd been dreading arrived: December twenty-third. After an early supper Daddy drove us to the church and took Timothy in through the front door. Mama and Luke and I went to the basement, where mothers were helping kids into costumes. My classmate Bill, Luke and I put on the robes Mama had made for us out of gunny sacks.

Joseph and Mary left first, up the back staircase, followed by the angels and shepherds. Then we wise men went up the outside stairway and into the cloak room, carrying trays. I took my gift to the baby Jesus out of my pocket. It was imitation myrrh, a bottle of cheap perfume some lady had given Mama last Christmas. Luke's tray held a brick that Mama had painted gold. Bill had a bowl of runny fudge. As usual, Mama's fudge had failed to harden, so she'd renamed it frankincense.

We lined up in the entry way. The foyer doors were low enough for me to see the raised platform up front, where angels and shepherds sang "Away in a Manger" so softly I could barely hear them. Jenny Stewart sat by the crib that had once held Mama's babies. She smiled down at Jesus. On the wall behind Jenny, Mama had taped foil-covered cardboard, shaped like a star, around a light bulb.

Then it was our turn. We began singing the first verse, "We three kings of orient are bearing gifts we bring from afar." Mama had told us the congregation would be surprised by voices coming from behind them.

Luke went first, singing the second verse, "Gold I bring to crown Him again." He took a step every few seconds, because we all three had to still be in the aisle at the song's end. Bill followed him with his bowl of gooey fudge, singing, "Frankincense to offer have I."

I took a deep breath and pushed the foyer doors open with my tray, which made the bottle quiver. I sang, "Myrrh is mine, its bitter perfume breathes a life of gathering gloom." I took another step, and the bottle shook harder. "Sorrowing, sighing, bleeding, dying." The bottle teetered and crashed on the carpet. My shoe crunched on broken glass as I sang, "Sealed in the stone-cold tomb."

A sweet, sickening smell filled my nostrils. I remembered the face Mama made last Christmas when she'd opened the bottle of perfume. She'd replaced its stopper and fanned the air with her hand.

Bill and Luke joined me in the chorus, "O star of wonder, star of night..." My face felt like I had a fever. I took another step, focusing on the light bulb above Mary and the crib. The cardboard's tape slowly peeled away from the wall until the star dangled below the bulb, hanging from a single strip of adhesive tape. We sang, "Guide us to thy perfect light." The star bounced off Jenny's head onto the floor. She kept smiling into the crib.

Luke climbed the two steps onto the platform. He knelt, laid his tray on the floor, and put his gold brick in the crib. Bill followed, giving the baby Jesus his bowl of liquid fudge.

I knelt and placed my tray on top of the other two. I could feel the congregations' eyes on me—*so nervous he dropped his bottle*—as I cupped my empty hands and reached into the crib. The gold brick and the bowl of sludge lay next to a rag doll wrapped in swaddling clothes, linen that Mama had cut into two-inch strips. The doll was bald except for a few strands of red yarn. I felt a shock of recognition. Where had I seen that doll before?

As I stood, Jenny looked up at me and smiled. A second shock went through me, and I smiled back.

All of us, wise men, angels, shepherds, Joseph and Mary, faced the congregation to sing the program's finale, "Silent Night." People in the audience fidgeted, wrinkling their noses and glancing furtively at Mrs. Morgan, who was picking slivers of glass off the aisle carpet and dropping them into a wastebasket. These were farm folks. Couldn't they stand the stench of a manger?

I changed out of my costume in the basement and rushed up the outside stairs to join the line of kids in the center aisle. Up front, beneath a stained glass window, a fir tree was decorated with popcorn balls and Mama's homemade Christmas balls. Under the tree was a pile of mesh bags, each tied with a red ribbon. Uncle Jacob, dressed in a Santa costume, was handing a bag to each kid. Overnight he'd grown a long white beard and gained a hundred pounds.

Most of the adults who remained in the sanctuary stood talking along the side walls, as far from the center aisle as they could get. To my left a woman muttered, "Santa Claus and candy bags. Lola's forgotten the true meaning of Christmas."

A few hours earlier, Luke and I had helped Mama fill the bags, combining chocolate-covered cherries with unshelled peanuts and walnuts. Despite our pleas, she wouldn't let us eat a single candy. Daddy opened the front door and looked at the dining room table covered with candy and nuts. "I didn't want to buy chocolates," Mama told him, "but my fudge didn't turn out." He had wheeled around without saying a word and gone back outside.

Being last in line, I prayed Santa wouldn't run out of candy bags before I reached him. Daddy sat in our back pew, next to the cloakroom, his arms crossed. I guessed he was thinking about how much money the candy had cost us.

Because I stood just inside the foyer doors, I could hear voices from the cloakroom. Its walls ended two feet from the ceiling, which gossipers inside the room often didn't realize. A woman said, "Why would Jacob do such a thing?"

"So she couldn't tell," another woman replied.

I turned to face the foyer doors so I could see the women leave the cloakroom. One was Mrs. Carney, a farmer's wife. I only saw the back of the other woman's head.

Daddy left right behind them. He couldn't stand to watch Santa give away the costly candy bags any longer.

A few minutes later I got my bag. As the church door closed behind me, I saw Daddy half a block away on the sidewalk, coming toward the church. A car backed away from the curb behind him.

He'd probably been talking to another farmer.

Luke and Timothy and I opened our mesh bags in the back seat of the car. Mine held more nuts than theirs, which meant less candy. I sulked for the rest of the evening, and so did Daddy. We each had our reasons.

By dusk the next day, Christmas Eve, no snow had fallen. Mama had gone to Walla Walla for last-minute shopping, refusing to take us kids, which meant more presents for us.

This was a good time to inspect my parents' bedroom. Under blankets on the closet shelf I found three parcels wrapped with red and green paper. Because my rules didn't allow me to loosen the wrappings and peek inside, I only felt the edges and speculated.

I checked the bureau next. Daddy's socks, shirts, overalls, and long underwear filled the top two drawers, and the third held Mama's clothes. So did the bottom drawer, but under a cardboard box and some bras I spotted the edge of a parcel with red and green Christmas wrappings. I took out the box, which contained folded pages of stationery in Mama's handwriting, put it on the bed and felt the parcel. It was soft and yielding, a disappointment. Clothes should be off limits as Christmas gifts.

Daddy opened the bedroom door. "Mailman just now stopped," he said.

As I walked back from the mailbox, I remembered the cardboard box was still on the bed.

The bedroom door was open. Daddy sat on the bed, reading one of the pages of stationery. Other pages lay on the quilt beside him.

After supper Mama got out the popcorn popper while Daddy brought in logs from the front porch and kindled a fire. He read the paper while the rest of us sat around the fireplace, munching popcorn and listening to carols on the radio. From his expression, I guessed he was reading about President Roosevelt's latest scheme to help farmers go broke. His bowl of popcorn sat untouched on the end table by his chair.

Uncle Jacob came by, bringing his usual sack of gifts. Mama greeted him warmly, but Daddy didn't look up from his paper. Luke and I added the presents to the modest pile under the tree. Mama had trimmed the tree, leaving the lower eighteen inches of the trunk bare, but the empty space would be filled by morning.

She handed a bowl of popcorn to Uncle Jacob.

"Where did you hide your homemade fudge?" he asked her.

"There isn't any."

"You shouldn't fib on Christmas Eve, Lola." He turned to me. "Mark, explain to your mother how I deduced she made fudge."

"Uh…"

"I'll give you a hint," he said. "Look in the mirror."

"It's too runny," Mama said.

"That didn't seem to bother Mark. I'm not leaving till I get some of that fudge."

Mama brought a bowl from the kitchen. "You'll need the spoon," she said.

On my way to bed I saw three of Mama's nylon stockings lying on the kitchen table. The hours from now till dawn would be the best time of the year, the only night I wouldn't sleep. Luke dozed off right away, but I lay under the covers listening to the crackle of wrapping paper from the kitchen.

It must have been after two when I heard a faint sound across the room, by Luke's bed. I took shallow breaths, like a sleeping child, as something rustled alongside my pillow. I didn't hear Mama slip out of the room. She would make a good burglar.

I brushed my fingers over the long nylon stocking, trying to guess the identity of the items inside. The orange at the bottom was easy. Mama liked to remind us boys that when she was a girl she only got one orange a year, on her birthday. Just above the orange were two small objects that I guessed from the indentations were packets of gum and Lifesavers. Next I felt the can of cashews that I would nibble all morning until I got a tummy ache. The long cardboard box might contain Fourth of July sparklers. Mama shopped all year for stocking stuffers. Near the top of the stocking I felt the crinkle of paper. The thin, rectangular object inside had to be a small book. An Uncle Wiggily book?

I lay in bed till daylight, fingering my stocking, prolonging its mysteries as long as possible, imagining Uncle Wiggily stories that might fill the thin object at the top.

When Luke woke up we emptied our stockings. My wrapped present was a connect-the-dots book, but at least I'd gained several hours of delicious suspense. Still in our pajamas, we went into the living room to see the wrapped presents under the tree. The stack was big enough to hold the tree upright without its stand. This was the second best part of Christmas, looking at the presents until Mama called from the kitchen to say breakfast was ready. I scarcely chewed my oatmeal and buttered toast, eager to get back to the living room.

Because Timothy couldn't read names, Luke and I handed out the gifts. I gave Mama a package with a tag that read "To Lola from Edward." She tore the wrapping off a box of stationery and said, "Why, thank you, Edward."

Daddy frowned and shook his newspaper.

After we'd opened the last of our presents, Luke and Timothy and I sat lethargically among the piles of torn paper. I felt bloated. Daddy's presents lay unopened by his chair. When Mama left the room to start fixing dinner, I followed her into the kitchen.

"That present Daddy gave you," I said. "The tag was in your handwriting."

"Don't tell Luke and Timothy," she whispered. "I want you kids to learn that giving is just as important as getting."

I still had a sugar hangover the morning after Christmas. I felt too listless to play outside, even though three inches of snow had fallen during the night, one day too late for a white Christmas. Daddy hadn't come home by noon, so Mama let us kids start eating. I was chewing my last mouthful of cherry pie when he came in the back door. His overalls were damp and muddy. He told Mama he'd been repairing a fence and didn't want to quit halfway through.

It was getting dark when Aunt Bea opened the front door, letting in a draught of cold air. "Where's Jacob?" she asked Daddy.

"Haven't seen him all day."

"He went looking for you. He needed help getting the pump out of the river."

"I plumb forgot about the pump," Daddy said.

"Could he get it out by himself?" Aunt Bea said.

"It's a two-man job. Did you check the machine shop?"

"Yes, and the barn and the sheds."

"I'll go look for him." Daddy took his coat off its nail.

"I'll come, too," I said.

"Not this time."

I stood in the front yard, watching the other place for signs of activity, as dusk faded into night. Through the dining room window I saw Mama take the phone off its wall hook. Her lips moved just enough to ask the operator to dial a number. She listened for a few seconds and hung up.

Although the night was moonless, I decided not to get a flashlight from the pantry. Mama might ask why I wanted it. I walked down the middle of the highway, where cars had tamped down the snow. When I reached Uncle Jacob's lane I saw lights flicker among the outbuildings.

"Jacob?" a woman called. Had Aunt Bea heard me? The snow should have deadened the sound of my footsteps. I waited until I heard her call again, this time from farther away.

The first building I reached had no windows, so it must be the butchering shed. I tugged the door open. Uncle Jacob hated butchering hogs and steers. He couldn't be inside.

Unless someone put him there.

I backed out of the shed and tripped on something that rolled under my legs, pitching me backwards onto the snow.

"Is that you, Jacob?" Aunt Bea called.

I got to my feet. A milk can lay between me and the shed's door. I ran clumsily through the snow, past the house and onto the highway, until pain seared my side. I bent over, panting, until the pain went away. Flashlight beams still traveled back and forth among the outbuildings, so nobody had followed me. When I reached our house I slipped in the back door and joined Luke and Timothy in front of the radio. Every few seconds I glanced out the window, hoping to see Daddy's headlights. He would tell us Uncle Jacob was okay, that he'd been walking the hills as he used to years ago. Hours later I lay awake under my blankets, listening vainly for the front door to close.

When I went into the kitchen next morning, Mama said Uncle Jacob was still missing. Her face was haggard, and I guessed she hadn't slept. Daddy was already gone.

I gobbled my scrambled eggs, put on galoshes, and walked to Uncle Jacob's and Aunt Bea's house in bright sunlight, an icy wind at my back. A truck and three cars were parked alongside their Model T. To the southeast, across a field of wheat stubble, I saw Daddy's yellow pickup, partly hidden by the river forest. Near the machine shop Mr. Morgan was talking to Charley Simmons. I slunk toward the river on the Fosters' property, crouching behind tumbleweeds that clung to the windward side of the fence.

I straightened up as I passed the little house where I was born. Paint had peeled off the outside walls, and a front window was broken. A narrow grove of cottonwood and chokecherry trees, a canopy over old wagon tracks, ran south from the house to the river. The path inside was impassable now, a tangle of bushes — elderberry, wild rose, and sumac. Where the bark of the chokecherry trees had peeled off, their trunks were bronze, like the color of old pennies, a startling contrast to the gray and white landscape. My right ear, exposed to the wind, began to ache. I wished I'd worn earmuffs. Wading through the snowdrifts took so much energy that my chest was heaving before I got halfway to the river.

"You're trespassing," a voice yelled behind me.

Burke Foster was crossing his field toward me, carrying a shotgun. I climbed over the fence so hastily I pricked my right hand on barbed wire. I thrashed through prickly bushes until I reached our stubble field. Blood oozed from my palm. The snow was sparse east of the grove, and the trees blocked the wind, which made walking easier. Burke had done me a favor, as long as I didn't get tetanus from the barbed wire. The wind died when I reached the river forest, although the skeletal cottonwoods didn't look like much of a windbreak.

A gunshot made me jump. It had come from my right, near the river. Probably Burke shooting ducks out of season.

The river was high and roily, the color of chocolate milk. Afraid Daddy would see me among the leafless cottonwood trees, I moved upstream along the fringe of the forest, behind a cover of spiky weeds.

I saw him near the riverbank, stepping over a beaver-gnawed log. His bib overalls were soaked. Had he fallen into the river? He headed upstream toward the clearing where his pickup was parked. I reached the clearing first and hid behind a dense elderberry bush.

Holding his arm in front of his face, he pushed through thorny-looking weeds into the clearing. He blew on his hands and rubbed them together. He studied the snow-covered ground near the bank. I couldn't see much from my vantage point, but the snow looked mashed up. He got into the pickup, backed up, went forward, and backed up again. The motor revved three times and went dead. Had the engine flooded?

Between two elderberry branches I could see Daddy clearly. He sat motionless, his shoulder hitching up and down, his pursed lips blowing out a thin stream of white mist that fogged the windshield. Then he got out and took a shovel from the pickup's bed. He must have got stuck in the snow. No surprise. His tires were so worn their treads were gone. He bent near the pickup's tailgate, but instead of shoveling snow away from the tires, he did something I couldn't comprehend.

His back to the river, he sidled to his right, smoothing the snow with his shovel. When he reached the line of irrigation pipes at the far edge of the clearing, he took a step backward and edged the opposite direction, sliding his shovel back and forth over the snow, making a parallel swath. He repeated the process all the way to the bank, a distance of about twenty feet.

He turned toward me, and I ducked. I heard a clang, probably the shovel hitting the tools and pipe ends in the pickup's bed. The engine started, revved higher and ebbed as the pickup maneuvered in the snow.

I watched it crawl along the fence, this side of the irrigation pipeline. A quarter mile north, the dirt road angled away from the fence, toward the outbuildings and house. The pickup stopped behind a row of machinery, the combine, tractor, harrows and seeders. I spotted Daddy in the gap between the combine and tractor. A few minutes later, the pickup disappeared behind the shop.

I left my hiding place. The area where the pickup had parked and turned around was churned up, a mixture of snow and mud. Where the pickup's tracks ended, a broad expanse of smoothed-over slush extended to the riverbank.

On the far side of the clearing, iron irrigation pipes led to the bank's edge, where a short pipe slanted downward into the river. The swirling current was too murky for me to see below the surface. The pump must still be in the river. If it had been pulled out, it would be visible nearby.

I heard engines. The pickup was coming back, followed by a

truck. I hid behind the elderberry bush, inching around it as the vehicles reached the clearing. The engines went silent, and I heard indistinct voices. Daddy, Mr. Morgan, and Charley Simmons came into view and disappeared into the forest, moving downstream.

I waited, shivering, not only from the cold but from a dread I hadn't acknowledged until now. The men's voices and movements had lacked the urgency I would have expected from searchers.

Fifteen minutes later I heard the voices again. Daddy and Charley appeared from behind a thicket of willows. Something heavy sagged between them.

Dangling legs.

I dropped to my knees and retched till only bile came up. I lay down on my stomach in the snow and dead weeds and closed my eyes.

I became aware that twigs were poking my stomach. The shadows of cottonwood trees had lengthened northward into the field. How long had I lain here? I stood up, my knees wobbly, and swatted snow and rotting leaves off my clothes. My pants were wet, and I felt a burning sensation down the inside of my thighs. The pickup and truck were gone.

Wind stung my cheeks as I slogged through snow across the rutted stubble field. The gash in my palm still hurt. I passed the little house. On the highway, a car approached from the west. As it slowed to turn into the lane, I saw "Sheriff" on its side.

I stood still, but the sheriff saw me anyway. He walked up to me and asked where I'd been, what I'd seen. I told him I hadn't seen anything. He acted like he didn't believe me, but my toes were so numb I didn't care.

Luke and Timothy were huddled by the radio. "Uncle Jacob drowned," Luke said. Mama was in the kitchen, covering a plate of sandwiches with waxed paper. I skirted the kitchen by taking the long route through the hall to the bedroom. I got clean clothes out of my bureau drawer, went into the bathroom, and turned on the bathtub's faucet. Mama must have heard the running water because I heard the door open.

"Are you okay, Mark?"

"Yeah. I got muddy playing in the snow."

The door closed. For the first time in my life I took a bath without being prodded. As I lay in the tub, my toes started hurting. During my walk home, I'd let my mind go as numb as my toes, but I couldn't suppress what I'd seen any longer.

Why would Daddy erase his footprints? After he'd parked his pickup, he would have walked to the bank, looking for evidence that Uncle Jacob had been there yesterday. Naturally he'd have left footprints.

What did it matter, anyway? Uncle Jacob had drowned. No one was to blame.

By supper time three church ladies were in the kitchen with Mama, making sandwiches, even though they'd brought baskets of food themselves. From their talk I gathered that other women were up at Aunt Bea's place.

Bertha Warren looked into the dining room, saw me sitting at the table, and shut the kitchen door. Although I pressed my ear against the door, the voices were too faint for me to understand. Whenever I entered the kitchen for a glass of water, the women stopped talking. I made several dry runs to the bathroom, which was opposite the hall's kitchen door, before I managed to sneak into the pantry unobserved.

I heard nothing about Uncle Jacob until the telephone rang. The phone was on the dining room wall, so Mama had to leave the kitchen to answer it. Then a woman said in a low voice, "Is it true his hand was missing?"

"His right hand," another woman said. "Tom told me Jacob's wrist looked as if someone hacked off the hand with a dull axe."

"He deserved what he got," someone said.

"Shh." The women stopped talking, so Mama must have come into the room.

Uncle Jacob's hand chopped off? He deserved what he got? A wave of nausea hit me. I opened the back door and stood on the porch, gulping fresh air until I felt better. Now I was ravenous. I rounded the corner and went in the front door.

Mama brought a plateful of tuna fish and egg sandwiches into the dining room for us boys, and Bertha followed with three bowls of tomato soup on a tray. Bits of tomato, onions, and parsley bobbed in the soup. I swallowed a spoonful. It tasted even better than Heinz tomato soup. I would ask Mama to get the recipe from Bertha.

I scooped my spoon into the rich liquid, already savoring the next mouthful. The spoon never reached my lips. It clattered on the bowl's rim, spattering red droplets on my shirt.

What if Daddy wasn't erasing his tracks? What if he was covering up blood?

The sheriff drove up the next morning as I sat down to eat breakfast. Did he want to interview me again? I considered ducking out the back door and running into the orchard, but that would make him even more suspicious. Daddy went outside to meet him. They leaned against our car, arms folded, talking casually, as they sometimes did when a toolbox went missing. When the sheriff drove off, I realized I hadn't touched my pancakes and ham.

I knew something nobody else knew except Daddy. What was I going to do about it? Pretend for the rest of my life I hadn't seen anything? If not, now was the time to investigate. Our thermometer read two degrees below freezing, and snow still blanketed the ground, but if I waited it would either melt or be covered by more snow. Whatever I found out couldn't be worse than what I imagined, Daddy chopping off Uncle Jacob's hand, throwing him into the river, covering up blood with his shovel.

Snow on the highway was tamped down but not slick, perfect

for walking. The Model T was the only vehicle parked by Aunt Bea's house, so I cut diagonally across the field to the river clearing.

Near the bank, snow was messed up by many footprints, probably including the sheriff's. I found a branch and stirred the snow, covering the area Daddy had smoothed over yesterday. I saw no trace of blood.

That didn't get Daddy off the hook. He could have killed Uncle Jacob somewhere else and driven him to the river. But that would leave blood in his pickup, unless he'd wrapped the body in a tarp. I shook my head, trying to clear away these awful thoughts. Daddy was no monster.

The road along the pipeline had turned to slush, so I plodded north through the field. I passed the row of farm machinery and the enormous pile of scrap iron. Inside the shop I found the axe propped against a wall, alongside post-hole diggers. The windows were too dirty to provide much light. I took the axe outside into the sunlight. No trace of blood on the blade, but Daddy could have washed it off in the river.

I heard an engine. Locust trees blocked off my view of the house and the lane, giving me time to hide behind the pile of scrap iron. The vehicle came close and stopped by the shop. Had Daddy come back for the axe? Its handle felt sweaty.

A minute later the engine started. I peeked around a rusty radiator and watched the pickup disappear among the locusts. I took the axe into the shop, but as I replaced it against the wall, my breath caught. The post-hole diggers were gone.

Tom told me Jacob's wrist looked as if someone hacked it off with a dull axe.

He was getting rid of the murder weapon.

Bile filled my throat. I sat down on the shop floor. How was I going to act around Daddy for the next few years—for the rest of his life—without giving away what I knew? What alternative did I have? Phone the sheriff and describe what I'd seen at the riverbank, tell him about the posthole diggers? Testify at Daddy's trial, visit him in prison?

Something was poking me. The head of a small nail, I realized when I stood up. Metal filings, wood chips, nails and bolts, dead flies and crumbs of coal covered the floor. The place must not have been swept for years. If Daddy cut off Uncle Jacob's hand here, he would have to clean up the blood. I walked the length of the shop, praying I wouldn't find a cleaned-off spot. The whole floor was equally grimy, of course. A clean spot, neatly mopped, would look suspicious.

Same problem with the barn. There was only one place where dried blood wouldn't be a giveaway.

The milk can lay near the butchering shed's open door, where it had rolled after I tripped over it. Had Daddy left the door closed so searchers couldn't smell the odor of fresh blood? The men had butchered hogs in November. Afterward they would have hosed the floor, but I couldn't imagine them mopping with bleach, like Mama did in the house. Would fresh blood smell different from six-weeks-old blood?

I gripped the doorframe and took a deep breath. The stench made me gag.

I trudged down the lane toward the railroad tracks. Across the highway, Daddy's pickup was parked on the primitive road that separated the flatland from the hills. On top of the nearest hill, between a scrawny locust tree and a tombstone, a man wearing striped overalls raised his arms and brought them down hard.

Daddy was gouging out Uncle Jacob's grave with the post-hole diggers.

A stranger came to the door the day before Uncle Jacob's funeral. He wore a suit and tie, a rare sight around Whetstone except on Sundays. He shook hands with Daddy and said he represented an insurance company. They went downstairs to Daddy's basement office. I listened from the foot of the stairs.

"You've got a motive," the man said. "Bank's foreclosing on your farm. If either partner dies, your key man policy pays enough to keep the farm afloat."

"You think I'd kill my brother to save the farm?" Daddy's voice was throaty, the way it sounded when he talked about the Secretary of Agriculture. "It was an accident."

"What do you think happened?"

"Maybe Jacob tried to take the pump out by himself."

"How heavy was the pump?"

"Three or four hundred pounds."

"How could one man pull it out of the river by himself?"

"He couldn't."

"He couldn't?" The agent waited for Daddy to explain, but the only sound was the creak of a chair. "Let's assume your brother tried anyway. How did his hand get cut off?"

"When the river's flooding it can carry one-ton slabs of concrete."

"But the Touchet River wasn't flooding, was it?" He pronounced it "tooshay" instead of "tooshee," so he couldn't be from around here.

After a pause, Daddy said, "Not quite flood stage, but it was high."

"How could a concrete slab sever his hand without leaving marks anywhere else on his body?"

A longer pause. "I don't know."

When the man left, they didn't shake hands.

A classmate of Peggy's stayed with us boys during Uncle Jacob's funeral. While Daddy drove her home, I walked down the lane to get our mail. Mama was sitting at the piano when I came back, the sheet music for "Loch Lomond" above the keyboard. She sang, "Oh, I'll take the high road and ye'll take the low road, and ye'll be in Scotland afore me."

"You've got it backwards," I said. "It's 'You'll take the high road and I'll take the low road.'"

"I'll sing it any way I want," she said, sticking out her chin.

Last year she'd told me the story behind the song. In 1746, during the Battle of Culloden, British troops captured a Scottish soldier and imprisoned him in the Tower of London. While he waited to be executed, he wrote this song for his sweetheart. The high road is the road mortals take, and the low road is the path the wee people furnish for the soul to return home.

Whenever Mama gave me a penny, I would buy a gumball at Warren's Grocery during our school lunch hour. One day their machine was empty, so I went to the depot, the only other gumball source in town. I dropped my penny in the slot, but as I pulled the lever I spotted Aunt Bea sitting on a bench. I was so surprised I forgot to cup my hands under the dispenser. A crimson gumball hit the floor, rolled toward Aunt Bea and bumped her shoe.

Afraid she'd step on the gumball, I knelt and grabbed it. I got up and popped it into my mouth. Although I stood directly in front of her, she looked through me as if I were invisible. I turned to see what she was staring at. It was the blackboard, where arrival and departure times were listed in chalk.

A month after the funeral, Luke and I were building a snowman across the highway from Aunt Bea's house when Reverend Taylor drove up. He knocked on the door, waited several minutes, then got in his car and left. As he turned onto the highway Aunt Bea came out of the house. She stood on her porch and watched the car until it disappeared.

I was taking off my overshoes on the back porch landing when the phone rang. Mama came to the pantry door and said, "Go fetch your father. Tell him it's his insurance agent."

We stood on either side of him as he listened to the agent. I couldn't read his expression. Mama bit her lower lip, making her look buck-toothed.

He replaced the receiver on its hook. "Ready to hear the bad news?" he asked Mama.

"The insurance company won't pay," she said. "When will we have to leave?"

"We won't."

"What do you mean?"

"The insurance company will pay."

"You said it was bad news."

"No, I asked if you wanted to hear the bad news."

"You tricked me," Mama said. "You let me stand there for five minutes thinking we'd got evicted."

"More like thirty seconds."

She stalked into the kitchen.

Daddy shook his head, grinning. "There's no pleasing that woman," he said, raising his voice so Mama could hear from the kitchen.

That night Luke listened to me say my bedtime prayers. Mama had taught us kids to bless every family member when we knelt on the floor, hands clasped on our beds. I resented the time it took to rattle off twenty names, but I was afraid if I overlooked anyone, it would be my fault if they died.

When I finished, Luke said, "You left out Uncle Jacob."

Why should we have to pray for dead people? They were safe in heaven. If I had to memorize the names of all my ancestors, I wouldn't have time to sleep. Then I remembered Uncle Jacob didn't believe in God.

I closed my eyes again. "And bless Uncle Jacob."

TUESDAY, JUNE 17, 1986

A roar from overhead jolts me out of my trance. I pull back the bedroom's curtain in time to see a biplane curl to the left, spewing white mist over a hill. A crop duster hired by the farmer who leases our grain land.

The apparition I saw on the hilltop last night seems unreal now, a ghost produced by lack of sleep. I go out the back door, past the burn barrel to the base of the hill. At the top I see a fence post. It's knobby and crooked, a locust branch, like all the fence posts on the farm. It looks smaller than the figure I saw, but objects look different at night.

I haven't eaten for twenty-four hours. No wonder I'm famished. I remember the tuna fish and egg sandwiches Mama used to fix whenever I was sick. I open a can of tuna, hard-boil three eggs, and chop one of her homemade sweet pickles. At Whetstone's store I find a loaf of whole wheat bread and four more cans of tuna. This little store doesn't carry fresh produce, so I add a can of applesauce and three cans of peas and carrots, enough to last me till the funeral.

The sandwiches don't taste like Mama's. She would blame the whole wheat bread. As I wash my dirty dishes, I glance out the window at the burn barrel. I wish now I hadn't burned her letters.

I need to get some exercise. In the back yard, a redwing

77

blackbird flits from one cattail to another above the pond Luke dug years ago. A robin pecks for worms on the lawn grass, pausing every few seconds to eye me. Birds must be singing, but I haven't heard them for years.

Uncle Jacob said there's a perfect time in our lives, only we don't realize it till later.

If I could go back to a perfect time, when would it be? Age ten was pretty good. On the morning after Christmas I would get up at dawn, run to Uncle Jacob's house and warn him to stay away from the river, to let the pump wash away. But if I saved him then, he would still look sad. I would have to go back to before he looked sad, before he had a nervous breakdown. Did guilt cause the breakdown? Mama said she needed to be forgiven, too.

I find Mama's wide-brimmed straw hat in the hall closet, stroll down the highway, and turn right at the lane that leads to the old homestead. All that's left of the house where Uncle Jacob and Aunt Bea once lived is a hole in the ground where the fruit cellar used to be. Earth and weeds have gradually filled the hole, and only the top three feet of the basement's concrete walls are visible.

The machine shop's door won't budge. I pry apart ivy so I can look through the dirt-crusted window at the harnesses hanging from nails, at the forge where Daddy and Uncle Jacob and their father heated horseshoes till they were red-hot. A hammer and tongs lie in the forge. Waist-high weeds cover the area between the machine shop and the little house. I stumble over a hidden pile of boards, all that's left of the shed where the men butchered hogs, the job Uncle Jacob hated.

How did Uncle Jacob die? I don't believe Daddy's theory that a chunk of concrete washed down the river and cut off his hand. Neither did Daddy, I suspect.

I can't think of any way Uncle Jacob's death could have been an accident.

That means someone killed him.

Daddy had a motive. His wife and brother were lovers. Two

motives. If Uncle Jacob died, their key man insurance policy would provide enough money to pay off the mortgage.

But Daddy couldn't be a murderer. Not my own father. Who else had a motive to kill Uncle Jacob?

Aunt Bea! She gained, even though the insurance went to the farm instead of to her. As Uncle Jacob's widow, she owned half the farm. If the bank had foreclosed, she would have lost everything, including her house.

Did she have a second motive? A few minutes after Uncle Jacob passed me on his walk home from the depot, Reverend Taylor's car came tearing out of their driveway. I was no longer a naïve kid. If Uncle Jacob told anyone he'd caught his wife in bed with Reverend Taylor, the scandal would ruin Aunt Bea's reputation. She could never again show her face in church.

It's been so long since I've driven to Aunt Bea's Whetstone home that I turn on the wrong street. Her tiny house looks as if it hasn't been painted this century. Weeds grow fender-high around her ancient Chevy car.

The front porch steps are missing, but the back door is open. I see her inside, mopping the kitchen floor.

She looks up. "Don't step where I've mopped."

The area under the table and chairs is wet, so I stand just inside the door.

"What's on your mind?" she says, sliding the mop within an inch of my shoes.

"What happened the day Uncle Jacob died?"

"He went looking for Edward. He said the two of them could get the pump out easy." Aunt Bea plunges her mop into a pail of water and twists it as if she were wringing a chicken's neck. "Can't say I blame Edward. Many a time I felt like killing Jacob myself, but two wrongs don't make a right."

"You had the same motive my father did."

She stops mopping. "What did you say?"

If she gets defensive she'll clam up. "If Uncle Jacob hadn't died, the bank would have foreclosed. My father would have lost everything, and so would you."

She shakes the mop. Drops of water splatter my face.

"That's not why Edward killed him."

"Why, then? Because he thought Uncle Jacob was having an affair with my mother?"

"Yes."

"What about your own affair?"

"What are you talking about?" Aunt Bea looks so puzzled I wonder if my theory is wrong. I've assumed Reverend Taylor left in a panic because Uncle Jacob showed up, but maybe he gunned his car to get out of the mud. It had been a wet winter.

"That night, sometime before Christmas..." I hesitate.

"The night before Christmas?" she says. "Christmas Eve?"

Christmas Eve. Something about Christmas Eve gnaws at my brain, but I can't grasp it. A train hoots far away, and Aunt Bea's mop handle smacks the floor. She rushes past me out the door. From her weed-choked yard I watch open-mouthed as she lopes downhill. Almost ninety and she's running? At the bottom of the hill she veers left and disappears behind a row of houses.

If that's not the act of a guilty person, what is? I start my car and follow her. When I turn left, she's nowhere in sight. I cruise past the depot, boarded up these last twenty years. Beyond the depot, three circular grain bins and a wooden elevator block my view of the railroad tracks.

The train hoots again, louder. I slip between the elevator and a grain bin. Boxcars wait on a siding, blocking my view of the main track. Could she be on the other side of the cars? I crawl under the couplings that connect two boxcars. The main track is only a few feet away, and the engine looks like it intends to run over me. The next blare is loud enough to cause ear damage.

After the caboose rattles past, I look south across the tracks. Fields of wheat stretch for a quarter mile on both sides of the road to the bridge. The road is empty. Is Aunt Bea hiding in the wheat?

Does asking that question make me as crazy as her?

I head back to the ranch. As I approach our mailbox, I see a woman pushing a lawnmower in front of the house where the Fosters used to live.

They moved two months after Uncle Jacob died. One day they were there, and the next day they were gone. Mama felt bad because she never learned their new address. She wanted to write to Peggy. Why did they move so hastily?

I think back to the day after Christmas. Balmy weather has been melting the mountains' snowpack, and the river is rising fast. Uncle Jacob remembers the pump is still in the river. Waiting one more day might mean losing the pump. Getting it out is a two-man job, and he can't find Daddy. He asks Burke Foster to help him. Burke has been nursing a grudge for thirty years, since the morning Uncle Jacob pinned him to the floor of the school wagon. The Fosters' small farm was on the market for over a year. I remember Daddy shaking his head at what a low price it brought. But Burke came out ahead. Taking a financial beating was a bargain compared to hanging for murder.

How could I trace a man who moved away forty-four years ago? Burke was older than the Roundtree brothers, so he'd likely be dead. At least I can relax now. I have a murder suspect to replace Daddy.

Or a scapegoat.

The year our voices changed, the other eighth-grade boys proved their manhood by smoking cigarettes, while I proved mine by singing bass in the church choir. One Sunday as we began "Love Lifted Me," I heard Mama hit a wrong note and quickly shift upward to the right key. I wondered if she'd been making mistakes for years that I hadn't noticed, and now that I was an adult I'd become more perceptive. Each time she played a wrong note, I edged backward so the sopranos blocked me off more from the congregation. After the sermon, instead of joining the people in the aisle, I slunk out the back door, hurried to our car, and crouched low in the back seat.

During the drive home Mama said, "It's my arthritis. I can't move my fingers fast enough anymore."

"I've never heard you play better," Daddy said.

"How would you know?" Mama said. "You're tone deaf."

Luke said, "The piano sounded great," and Timothy agreed. I snorted and looked out the window.

"Maybe we could move Aunt Mary's old organ up from the church basement," Mama said.

"Maybe it's time Jeannie took over the piano playing," I said.

Daddy turned around in the driver's seat and gave me a look. Then he patted Mama's shoulder and said, "We'll move the organ up tomorrow."

Switching to the organ wouldn't faze Mama. She'd been playing it all along for the beginners' Sunday school class. The week before, our juniors' class discussion was drowned out by "Amazing Grace" surging up from the basement as I was explaining why a murderer could never achieve redemption.

"'Amazing Grace' isn't a kids' song," I'd complained to Mama after we got home from church.

"It's my favorite song." She pulled her frying pan out of the drawer under the stove. "I need to know I'm forgiven."

"Forgiven for what?"

"Would you run down to the fruit cellar and get me a jar of peaches?"

As I went down the stairs, I ticked off Mama's wrongdoings, the ones I knew about. There were the wrong notes she'd played this morning. Twice cops had stopped her for speeding, and last Thanksgiving she had mistimed how long it would take the turkey to roast. Instead of eating at one, we'd waited till a quarter past three, which probably gave me an ulcer.

I set the jar on the counter. "What did you do that was so bad?"

"You're in my way. Go find something to do."

"You brought it up."

"Out!"

Although the organ blurred Mama's mistakes, it magnified mine. Singing along with the piano had been like sitting down in a wooden chair, straight-edged and hard, but trying to follow the organ was like sinking into the sofa Aunt Agnes broke when she went off her diet. I had no choice but to ignore the organ and follow the rumbling bass of Mr. Langley, the high school math teacher. He was pleasant enough after the service, but up in the choir he wore a fierce scowl, which I attributed to his belief that only a hundred forty-four thousand preordained souls would be allowed into heaven. Because he understood the laws of probability, he knew what odds we were bucking.

Since Mama's switch to the organ, Mr. Langley had been singing half a note flat and pulling me down along with him. Once I tried to strike out on my own, but the minister looked up from where he'd been studying his sermon notes behind the pulpit, so I went back to Mr. Langley's key, whatever that was. The sopranos sometimes narrowed their eyes at us, but since we were in tune with each other, they probably assumed we were singing the printed notes and the fault lay with the composer.

One day Bertha Warren came up to Mr. Langley and me after church and said, "It took some getting used to, but I've kind of grown to like hearing you basses sing in a minor key."

A year later, after the choir disbanded, I confessed to Mr. Langley, "I never could hear the organ's bass notes. I had to follow you."

He did a double take. "Are you kidding? I was following you." He shook his head, and the scowl came back. "Boy, did I get mad when you'd stray off key and drag me with you."

Before Uncle Jacob died, Daddy would join the rest of us in the living room after supper, where we'd listen to radio programs. My favorite was *The Shadow*, with its creepy introduction, "Who knows what evil lurks in the hearts of men? The Shadow knows." I would try to imitate the maniacal laugh that followed, but my voice was too high to scare anyone.

After Uncle Jacob died, Daddy spent evenings in his basement office working on the farm's ledgers. What he couldn't do was Uncle Jacob's field work. He had never learned to tame the tractor. Also, he was no mechanic, even though he understood the intricate system of pulleys on the combine.

During the six years since Uncle Jacob died, he'd hired dozens of workers. He would go into town and choose someone from the crowd of hopeful men who hung around Lutcher's Tavern. He would act jolly for the next couple of days, telling Mama he'd found the right man at last. By the third day his jaw would stiffen, and he'd sit at the kitchen table with Mama late at night, rehashing everything the idiot had done wrong. On the fifth or sixth day, he would drive to Walla Walla with the disgraced hired man slumped beside him and return with someone new.

The spring I turned sixteen, rain had delayed barley planting, and by early April all the experienced cat drivers had either been hired by other farmers or fired by Daddy or both. We were eating dinner when I saw a strange contraption enter the lane. Mattresses were strapped to its roof. Above the mattresses, an upside-down table, chairs, and a wash tub swayed in the wind. Stuffed gunny sacks hung from the roof, blocking my view of whoever was inside. The running board was lined with kegs and apple boxes. The vehicle stopped behind our car.

"He's got his own tools!" Daddy said, as if the metal box that sat on the car's rear bumper were a treasure chest.

A husky man got out of the car and met Daddy on the porch. "I hired him," he told Mama when he came back inside. "He owned a wheat farm in eastern Montana. Lost the crop to locusts last summer. I figured any man who'd bring a toolbox a thousand miles has got to be worth hiring."

"He must have a family with all those belongings," Mama said.

"Wife and three kids. I told him they could stay in the bunkhouse for now."

From the back porch Mama and I watched the driver unfasten ropes and remove boxes from the running board. A woman got out of the car and ducked under the gunny sacks, followed by two boys younger than Timothy and a girl about my age. The girl looked at me. I felt ashamed, as if she'd caught me eavesdropping. Mama glanced from the girl to me, frowning, her lips pinched together.

An hour later I heard Daddy and Mama arguing in the kitchen.

"We've never let hired hands use our bathroom," Daddy said.

"You've never hired a family before."

Daddy rubbed his chin. "Maybe we can get the little house in shape."

They were talking about the house where we'd lived till I was four. It was south of the homestead, which had burned to the ground last summer, forcing Aunt Bea to move to Whetstone. She claimed a hired man had started the fire, but Daddy said she'd been burning weeds in her back yard.

"There's only an outhouse," Mama said.

I'd hated that outhouse and its splintery toilet seat. I was afraid a black widow spider would climb out of the dark hole and bite my bottom. By the time I'd worked up the nerve to sit down, my bowels had tensed up. Then Mama would make me swallow a tablespoon full of Milk of Magnesia, which gave me stomach cramps.

Mama invited the family to eat supper with us. Because there wasn't room at the kitchen table, they ate in the dining room.

Whenever I glanced through the doorway, the girl's eyes met mine, and I looked down at my food.

Before breakfast the next morning, I took a bucket out back to hunt for eggs. I was on my knees, peering under the chicken house, when I heard a voice behind me.

"I saw a hen in the crotch of that tree."

I stood up. The girl pointed at a locust tree. She was barefoot and wore baggy jeans that I guessed belonged to her father because the cuffs were rolled up. I could see skin through holes in the jeans. She had wild hair the color of mustard and blue eyes that looked huge because her face was so thin.

"Chickens don't lay eggs in trees," I said.

"Come and look."

The crotch where branches split was ten feet off the ground. "A chicken would never lay eggs up there," I said. "Baby chicks can't fly."

"Look anyway," she said.

"I can't reach that high."

She dug her toes into the bark and shinnied up the trunk. She reached into the crotch and held up a brown egg. "Catch." She dropped the egg.

I lunged for it, but it slipped through my fingers and broke on the ground.

"Butterfingers," she said. Back on the ground, she smirked at me. "You don't know much about chickens, do you?"

My face felt warm. I couldn't think what to say.

She began to giggle. She pressed her fist to her mouth until she finally busted out laughing.

"You put that egg up there," I said.

She nodded. "While you were in the chicken house. Come on, I'll help you look."

She found eggs in places I'd never considered, behind a rusty plow, between two hay bales in the barn, under last year's raspberry vines.

"How do you know where to look?" I said.

"I can smell the eggs."

"No you can't."

"Yes I can."

The bucket was half full when I went inside. "My goodness," Mama said. "Where on earth did you find so many?"

"I checked some new places."

When Mama cracked the first egg, a smell filled the kitchen that would have routed a skunk. Some of the other eggs were also rotten, but we had enough good ones to feed two families. After they finished breakfast, the mother and daughter carried dirty dishes from the dining room to the kitchen counter. Mrs. Weaver offered to wash the dishes, but Mama wouldn't let her.

"At least let Donna dry them," Mrs. Weaver said.

Mama rinsed a plate and handed it to the girl, who wiped it with a dish towel.

"I'll put them away," I said.

Mama looked at me. "Did I hear correctly?"

"She doesn't know where they go," I said.

After I tucked the last glass into the cupboard, I followed Donna out the back door.

"Why don't you show me around your farm," she said.

I looked back at the house. Mama was watching us through the kitchen window.

"Do you know what kind of weed that is?" Donna said.

"No."

"Round leaf mallow. It's a nightmare to hoe."

Tomorrow I'd ask Daddy the names of all the weeds on the farm. We crossed a field of summer fallow.

"Wow!" Donna stopped. "What a beautiful view of the mountains. See how the blue contrasts with the snow on top? I can't wait to see the shadows in those canyons when the afternoon sun hits them. Which canyon does your river come out of?"

"Um…"

"I think it's that one," she said.

"Which one are you pointing at?"

"Come closer. Look down my arm."

I leaned so close my cheek brushed her forearm. She had freckles on her arm. I forgot to look at the mountains.

"We have lots of mountains in Montana," she said, "but none where we lived. We lost our wheat farm. We ran out of money yesterday. We don't have a penny."

"We almost lost our farm."

"Really? How did you save it?"

It came out in a rush, the dust storm, the auction, Uncle Jacob's drowning, his missing hand, the insurance settlement. I didn't tell her about Daddy erasing tracks near the riverbank, nor did I mention the insurance adjuster's visit.

She listened wide-eyed, her face grave. "I want to see the river."

On the way I showed her the hole in the ground where the homestead used to stand. We toured the little house. "My father's going to fix it up for your family," I said. "He'll put in a bathroom." He hadn't said so, but Mama would work on him.

"We've always had an outhouse," Donna said.

We walked to the river along the fence, the western boundary of our field. A few elderberry bushes were all that was left of the canopy of trees that once covered the wagon trail from the house to the river, the path Mama and Daddy took when they'd strolled to the river during their courtship, the jungle where Frank Buck and I caught tigers and orangutans for zoos. When I was twelve, a hired man had bulldozed the trees. "Two more acres we can put into wheat," Daddy had explained.

We gazed at the river a long time. It was high from spring runoff. "I'll like living here," she said.

I could replant the trees, and some day Donna and I might walk to the river under the canopy.

"What do you think happened to your uncle?" she said.

88

Sherlock Holmes had been trying to figure that out for years. "I don't know."

"Let's you and I solve the mystery."

She sounded more like Miss Marple than Watson, but maybe it was time to consult another detective. Luke had been no help at all. The value of sidekicks was way overblown.

"Show me where the pump was," she said.

Our pump lay on matted weeds under the pole that held the light meter.

"You told me one man couldn't take the pump out by himself," Donna said. "So what was your uncle doing here?"

I shrugged.

"How do you know he drowned?"

"My mother said so."

"When did she say it?"

"Right after they found him."

"She couldn't have known for sure. Maybe he died from loss of blood."

"What difference does it make? If a chunk of concrete hit him—"

"Maybe someone killed him and threw his body in the river. Was there blood anywhere on the bank?"

"No."

"You looked away just now. Are you holding something back?"

"No."

We walked north along the pipeline, toward the highway and the grain hills beyond.

Donna pointed to a patch of scraggy locust trees on the nearest hilltop. "Is that a woman?" she said.

"It's our guardian angel. That's what my mother says."

Donna ran toward the white specter. Although she was barefoot, I had a hard time keeping up. She crossed the railroad tracks and stopped in the middle of the highway.

"It's a tombstone," she said. "What's a tombstone doing up there?"

"That's where Uncle Jacob's buried."

"A graveyard on top of a hill?" She looked incredulous. "There's wheat planted all around it."

She beat me to the hilltop. I stopped short of a low strand of barbed wire at the edge of the cemetery. She was already inside, checking tombstones.

She looked back at me. "Afraid it will scratch you?"

I gritted my teeth and stepped over the wire. She laughed.

"What's so funny?"

"Your face. You looked like you were stepping on thumbtacks."

Morning glory vines and dead weeds had been cleared away from Uncle Jacob's headstone and the small one nearby, replaced by bouquets of wildflowers. A gnarled locust tree lay between the two graves, broken off from its stump. Green leaves sprouted from one branch. The bottom of the trunk must still be attached to the stump some way I couldn't figure out.

"The flowers are fresh," Donna said. "They must have been picked this morning."

Had Mama brought them before I got up?

"Can you name the flowers?" she said.

"Uh…"

"The tiny ones are violets, and the bell-shaped flowers are Johnny jump-ups." She stooped to read the inscription on the small headstone. "Who's Anna?"

"My sister."

"She died when she was three years old. Do you remember her?"

"No."

"What did she die from?"

"I don't know."

"You don't know? Why not?"

90

"My mother won't talk about it."

"Are you all right?" Her voice seemed to come from far away.

When the nausea passed I opened my eyes.

"You don't like the graveyard, do you?" Donna said.

"Must have eaten a rotten egg."

"Let's leave."

"Give me a minute." My legs were so shaky I was afraid I'd fall down.

We took the long way home, up and down alternating hills of wheat shoots and last year's stubble. On top of the highest hill Donna looked at the valley, entranced, her straw-colored hair blowing in the wind. A greening, narrow forest meandered along the valley floor, following the whims of the river. Fences ran in straight lines, north and south, a comforting symmetry. Houses and barns looked small enough to pick up between my thumb and forefinger. I felt proud, as if I'd arranged the landscape. We lay on our backs and looked for hidden animals in the clouds. Spotting the same elephant or lion seemed to cement our friendship. When we reached the chicken house, Mama came striding toward us.

"Where on earth have you been?" she said. "It's two o'clock."

My stomach growled, and I realized I was hungry.

Mama took two platefuls of hash from the oven. "Your mother's up at the little house," she told Donna. "I'll drive you up there when you finish eating. She must have her hands full, trying to clean and look after those little boys."

"I usually watch them," Donna said, looking guilty.

"The house doesn't have electricity," Mama said.

"Ours didn't either. We used lanterns and candles."

"So did we," Mama said. "You can't imagine what it's like, Mark, pumping water by hand and chopping wood."

"Builds muscle." Donna flexed her elbow. "Feel."

I touched her bicep. Tonight I would hunt through a copy of *Boys' Life* magazine and find the ad that showed a bully kicking sand on a ninety-seven-pound weakling. After six weeks of Charles

Atlas's exercise program I'd challenge Donna to an arm-wrestling contest.

Mama carried our empty dishes to the sink. "We'd better get up there before those boys drive your mother crazy."

Donna's family moved into the little house the next day. She told me they'd lived in their car long enough, and the bunkhouse wasn't much better.

Monday morning Donna rode the school bus with Luke and me. She wore a blue cotton dress and too-big shoes that were coming apart at the seams. She saw me looking at her shoes and said, "They're hand-me-downs from my mother. But I made this dress myself."

I expected her to show up for sophomore English after she registered at the office, but I didn't see her till lunch hour. She was eating at a table with three junior girls.

On the bus ride home I learned she was a junior, although she was two months younger than me. She had started school when she was five, while Mama had held me out until I was almost seven, worried that I was too young to mingle with other kids. She might have been right. The day I started first grade, I'd cried through the noon hour on the school's front steps because Joan Brumbach had told me she was going to marry me.

Except during bus rides, I didn't talk to Donna all week because she had to help her mother after school. Her father was out seeding from dawn to dusk, and Daddy regained the whistle he'd lost when Uncle Jacob died.

"Milan should finish seeding by noon," he told Mama at breakfast on Saturday. "Just in time. Looks like we'll get a good rain. If we had a headlight on the tractor, I think he'd work all night." He paused while Mama slid an egg off the frying pan onto his plate. It landed sunny side up, matching his mood. "That's the good thing about hiring a man who's owned his own farm. He doesn't stop for lunch. Eats out of his lunch box while he's driving."

Mama cluck-clucked. "He's not giving his food time to digest."

"I bought a refrigerator," Daddy said. During the week he'd piggybacked a wire from a light pole by the shop to the little house, so the Weavers would have electricity for the refrigerator. They didn't have light bulbs or plug-in sockets, though.

After breakfast, I walked to the little house, helped by a strong wind at my back. The wind had been blowing all week, but now dark clouds were hurtling toward me. Donna was hanging damp trousers on a clothesline stretched across the living room. Clothes flapped in the wind because the west window only had a few shards of glass. The two boys ran back and forth under the clothes, slapping them. A shirt jerked free from its clothespin, and Donna refastened it.

"Doesn't do any good to tell them to stop," she said.

One of the boys got tangled in a pair of long underwear and the whole clothesline collapsed.

Donna got some lead soldiers out of a cardboard box and lined them up on the floor. The boys knelt by the soldiers.

She went into the kitchen and came back with a claw hammer. "Nail came loose," she said. "Can you hold it for me?"

I pressed the nail against the wall.

"A little higher," she said.

"Let me hammer it."

"Don't you trust me?"

"Sure I do." I held my breath while she drew back the hammer.

She giggled. "You look like you're sucking a lemon." She swung, and the nail fell on the floor. "You let go too soon."

"I did not. You swung crooked." I picked up the nail. The head was slightly bent, but not enough to need straightening.

"Give it to me," she said. "I'll hold it while I hammer."

"No." I stuck the nail against the wall. "Go ahead."

I vowed not to yelp if she hit my thumb. I could handle pain. Hadn't I taken Japanese bullets without a whimper five years ago when John Wayne and I had fought to the death with our fellow

Marines, defending Wake Island?

The nail held firm as she pounded it in. I watched her hang up the rest of the clothes.

"Want to see our pictures?" she said.

We ducked under the wet clothes. Two mattresses were spread on the floor, each covered by a blanket.

"This is where the boys and I sleep," she said.

There were two beds, weren't there? Mine was under that broken window. The other bed–a shadowy figure filled the doorway. Someone moaned.

Dangling legs.

The shadow dissolved in sunlight. A cloud had passed over.

"What's the matter?" Donna said.

"Nothing."

"You moaned. And you're shivering."

"It's cold in here." I touched a jagged point of glass that protruded from a window pane. "Your brothers could get hurt on this."

She knocked out the remaining shards with the hammer. Then I followed her outside and watched her shovel dirt over the slivers.

"My father will buy a new pane," I said.

"There's another broken window where my folks sleep."

"Two panes."

She shrugged. "Fresh air is good for you."

She spread sepia photos on a mattress's blanket. I knelt on the floor alongside her. She handed me photos one by one, explaining the relationship of each person, even when a picture included a dozen people. The houses behind the people were small, the surrounding land bare and flat. Did they all live on a desert?

"You can see why I love it here." She motioned out the south window. "The river, the forest, the mountains."

Her mother came in from the kitchen, "Would you like to stay for dinner, Mark?"

I hesitated. Dinner would be ready at our house, too.

Donna touched my sleeve. "Please."

In the kitchen, Mrs. Weaver pulled out a chair for me. Donna rolled a keg toward the table. "We could only bring three chairs," she said. She sat on the keg, and the boys took the other chairs.

Mrs. Weaver placed bowls in front of us and dished baked beans out of a can. She put another bowl on the counter and scraped the last few beans from the can. She smiled at me. "I'm used to eating standing up."

I noticed two halves of an empty toothpaste tube on the counter. "Why is it cut in half?" I said.

"So we can squeeze more out," Donna said.

I picked up my fork. There were no other utensils, but apparently there would be no other food. No wonder Mr. Weaver could eat his lunch without stopping.

Mrs. Weaver took a canning jar out of the refrigerator and spooned half a peach into each of our bowls. Mama had made sure they wouldn't starve.

It didn't take us long to eat. Donna and I walked to the river, silently because the wind had picked up. I was glad when we reached the shelter of the forest. The cottonwoods and willows were greener than they'd been last week.

Donna said, "I can only think of one way your uncle could have lost his hand."

"There's lots of ways. The river was high—"

"Someone cut it off," she said.

"Big slabs of concrete come down the river."

"Have you seen them?"

"No, but my father has."

"Your father." She cocked her head at me. "He was supposed to help your uncle take out the pump."

"He didn't know Uncle Jacob was looking for him."

"So he says."

I tensed. "He wouldn't lie."

"He had a motive. You said the insurance settlement saved the farm."

"He'd never murder his own brother to save the farm." My voice sounded hoarse. I unclenched my fingers.

Donna's face softened. "I'm sure you're right. We'd better head back. Mom needs my help."

She took my hand. In spite of the wind, the warmth of her hand spread through me as we walked toward the house, swinging our arms in a semi-circle.

The wind died and big raindrops spattered our faces. When we parted at her house, rain was coming down hard.

Mama stood on the front porch. "You're soaked," she said, "and you missed dinner again." She looked toward the little house, nibbling her lower lip. "Better get out of those wet clothes before you catch pneumonia."

In the living room, a Christian Herald magazine lay on the end table by the sofa, opened to an article urging teenage chastity.

Before we left for church the next morning, I rummaged through my bureau drawers until I found the unopened jar of hair crème Mama had given me last Christmas. She had invited the Weavers to church, but they didn't show up. After the service Mrs. Morgan said to Mama, "My, Mark looks nice."

"When he was little, we thought he'd be so handsome." Mama shook her head. "We should have got him braces."

Back home I bared my teeth in front of the bathroom mirror. My incisors stuck out, crowded by other teeth. The bottom row was also uneven.

I went into the kitchen. "Do I have buck teeth?" I asked Mama.

"Mark, no woman will ever be attracted to you. To get a good woman, you'll have to be a good provider and a good person. But I'm sure you will be." She tried to hug me, but I pulled away.

During the next few days I spent a lot of time in the bathroom, checking my reflection from different angles. My upper lip jutted out a fraction of an inch over the lower lip, but if I pressed my teeth together, my lips looked even. Maybe I could learn to talk without moving my lips, like a ventriloquist.

It took me till Thursday to work up the nerve to approach Donna's house. She was digging holes with a shovel. "For our garden," she said. I tried to return her smile, a tough thing to do with clenched teeth. She let me dig holes while she dropped in seeds and smoothed over the soil. She told me what she'd done at school that week, which girls she was getting to know. When she asked why I was so quiet, I mumbled something unintelligible, my hand covering my mouth.

"Have you got a canker sore?" she said.

"No."

I held a bucket while she ladled out dippers of water for the seeds we'd planted. I wanted to talk, but my two front teeth felt like a vampire's fangs.

"Did you tell your father what I said? That I thought he killed your uncle?"

"No."

"Why won't you look me in the eye?"

"I've got to milk the cows," I said. As I neared Aunt Bea's house, I looked back. Donna was standing on her porch. I waved, and after a moment she waved back.

Friday I saw Daddy and Mr. Weaver standing in a newly-seeded field. Mr. Weaver knelt and brought up a handful of dirt, which he held in front of Daddy's face. Daddy turned away.

He came in through the back door, his jaw tight. "Durn fool wants to reseed," he told Mama. "Says the barley won't break through the crust." After last Saturday's rain, wind had blown all week, drying the topsoil. "What does he know about rain?" Daddy said. "Eastern Montana never gets more than a spoonful. That fellow's more stubborn than any mule I've ever owned."

"The pot calling the kettle black," Mama said, shaking her head.

"I told him I'd been farming this land for forty years. The

barley will come up just fine."

During the next week only a few green shoots broke through the crust. When I got off the bus Friday afternoon, I heard the tractor somewhere in the hills. But Mr. Weaver hadn't won the argument. The one thing Daddy hated worse than a dumb hired hand was a smart one.

Mama was kneeling in her begonias by the front porch, digging out weeds with a trowel. I bounced my fuzz-less tennis ball off the opposite side of the house, playing a baseball game. If I caught the ball on the fly, the Red Sox batter was out. If it bounced back to me on the ground, I had to throw it against the wall and catch the rebound, playing both infielder and first baseman. Phil Rizzuto, the Yankee's shortstop, had just caught a line drive for the third out when I heard Daddy's growly voice by the back porch.

"Took off in the pickup this morning without a word. For all I knew he might have headed for Idaho."

"Where did he go?" Mama said.

"Waitsburg Hardware to get a bolt."

"Did we need the bolt?"

"That's not the point. He should have told me where he was going. Stubborn fool acts like he owns the farm."

Mr. Weaver reseeded our last hill on a Tuesday. That night I heard faint voices from the kitchen. I got out of bed and listened, my ear against the closed door.

"Blame fool argues about everything I tell him to do." Daddy said. "I can't put up with him any longer."

Mama was silent, thinking how to talk him out of firing Mr. Weaver, I felt sure.

"I'm going to let him go tomorrow," Daddy said.

Say it, Mama. Don't fire that poor man. Think of his family, all the work they've done making the house livable.

"It might be for the best," she said. "I like Hilda, and they've fixed up that house so nice. But I'm worried about Mark."

What? Did I hear right?

"They're both sixteen," Mama said.

So that was it. I wanted to burst into the room and shout, "For Pete's sake, all we ever did was hold hands one time. I'm too ashamed of my teeth to even talk to her!"

Instead, I slunk into my room and lay on the bed open-eyed, feeling helpless.

Thursday morning Donna sat in the front of the bus, as far from Luke and me as she could get. A classmate told me that Sam Herring had hired Mr. Weaver.

Luke and I were playing catch Saturday morning when I saw the Weaver's car come down the highway. As it passed our mailbox, Mrs. Weaver waved at us from the passenger seat. The back seat was packed with belongings, which meant they'd left Donna and the boys at the house. Daddy's pickup passed the mailbox a few seconds later. In its bed was the refrigerator he'd bought for the little house.

Donna came out on her porch before I reached the little house. "Stay inside," she called to the boys.

I'd been practicing what to say in front of a mirror, trying to hide my crooked teeth, but when she came close I forgot it all. The sun lit up her hair, as it had the morning we first walked to the river.

"You did tell your father," she said.

"I never told him a thing."

"Don't lie to me. The next time you came over, you wouldn't look me in the eye."

"That wasn't the reason. I—" How could I admit I was ashamed of my teeth?

"What I said got Papa fired."

Tears streamed down her face. I'd steeled myself to take a punch if necessary–if I was lucky, she'd knock out my incisors–but she was blaming herself. She ran into the house and shut the door before I could think what to say.

I rapped on the door and waited. After a few minutes I walked home.

TUESDAY, JUNE 17, 1986

I should go up to the cemetery and look around. At Daddy's graveside service Mama pointed to the ground and said, "I want to be buried here," but I wasn't paying attention. When Luke and Timothy arrive Friday, we'll dig her grave.

Most farm families bury their dead in the Whetstone cemetery, but a few diehards still dig graves by hand in Lost Cemetery. They want their loved ones to look out over their beloved valley until Christ returns to take them to an even finer place–if such a place exists.

I'm out of breath by the time I reach the hilltop cemetery and step over the sagging barbed wire. Weeds have been pulled away from Daddy's, Uncle Jacob's, and Anna's graves, replaced by Mama's long-stemmed roses. The flowers are wilted but still colorful. How did she climb the hill with osteoporosis and a bad heart?

As I look at Anna's little marker, I remember Donna's question, "What did she die from?"

Mama never told us. Aunt Bea would know. I also want to ask her why she ran off this morning when she heard the train whistle.

This time I ignore the front door and go around back. As I raise my hand to knock she says, "Come in."

She's taking a teapot off the stove. "Black tea okay?"
"Sure."

"Good thing. It's all I've got."

She pours hot water into two cups and sets them on the kitchen table. Two teabags nestle in each cup. She sits down across from me, drinks from her cup and blows out steam. She hasn't provided saucers, so I helplessly watch the water turn dark inside my cup. A magpie shrieks, so close I wonder if it's in the house.

Aunt Bea doesn't do small talk and I've forgotten how. "My mother never talked about Anna," I say. "Do you know why?"

"Back then people didn't talk about their dead. Too painful." She touches her cheek in the same spot where Uncle Jacob used to rub his mole.

"How did she die?"

"She drowned."

Dangling legs. I feel a sick headache coming on.

"Drink some tea," Aunt Bea says. "That might help."

I sip and scald my tongue, chasing away the headache.

"How did it happen?" I say.

"Anna wandered to the river. They thought she was playing right outside."

"They? My mother and father?"

"Your father? Maybe." She cackles. "I meant your mother and my husband."

The magpie squawks again, closer. I glance around the kitchen.

"How do you know they were together?"

"That morning Jacob told me he was going to start seeding. It was the day after Palm Sunday, and they didn't want to wait any longer for rain. I packed him a lunch, but he came home at noon. He said Edward had to go to Walla Walla for some parts. After he ate he left the house, and he didn't take the car. Where else could he be?"

"He might have gone to the corrals. Or the machine shop."

"How many times had I heard that? I'll be up at the machine shop, he'd say. I'd go up there and he'd be gone. Wouldn't take a detective to figure out where."

101

Her laugh sounds like the magpie's. Maybe she's lived alone so long she's learned to mimic magpies.

"I was emptying garbage on the compost pile, and I heard Lola calling Anna. She was frantic, running all over the place. Jacob was already up there, searching for Anna. Quite a coincidence, wouldn't you say?"

"That doesn't prove he'd been in the house with my mother."

"Oh yes it does."

"How?"

"His shirt was buttoned wrong."

The headache comes full blast, right between my eyes. I slump in my chair.

"Want to lie down?" Aunt Bea says.

"I'm all right."

Try not to think. Focus on what's going on around you. Something is ticking. Is it my pulse or does she have a wall clock in the kitchen? I want to open my eyes to look, but I don't dare. I hear Aunt Bea's voice.

"I remember the wind blowing. Lola kept smoothing her hair, as if it mattered how she looked. The men lowered the casket, and Jacob tamped down the last shovelful of dirt. We all just stood there. The sparrows stopped chirping, and all I could hear was the wind. I remember thinking he won't be spending any more time at that woman's house. What happened next was worse. He came apart."

The pain ebbs. I hear a clink from across the room and open my eyes.

Aunt Bea is refilling her cup at the counter. She adds a third teabag and sits down. "Breakdown, everyone said. Take care of him, Bea. They didn't know what I went through. I'd fix him a delicious supper and he wouldn't touch it. He'd get up from the table and walk out the door. Pitch black, without a coat in freezing weather, and he'd be walking the hills somewhere. I'd sit in the living room watching the clock. Three hours, four hours. I was the one deserved to have a nervous breakdown. You think anyone worried about me?" Her mouth twitches.

"Reverend Taylor, he was the only one I ever told, and that was years later. He understood what I'd gone through. Jacob was a sinner, but we were going to bring him back to Jesus. We would have, too, if we'd had more time."

She drains her cup. As her chin tips toward the ceiling, three strings dangle from her lower lip, as if she's swallowed the teabags. She sets the cup down. "The Lord punished him but not her."

As I drive to the ranch a pickup approaches with a "Wide Load" sign in front. Behind it a combine hogs the road, and I pull onto the shoulder. Another combine passes, followed by four grain trucks. A roustabout's pickup brings up the rear, its bed full of grease pumps and oil drums. Three weeks till harvest. I park behind Mama's car and gaze through the windshield at the hills where I used to tend header on the combine. A horse fly lands on my windshield, and I close the windows. The sun warms me. I feel drowsy.

On the last day of harvest I washed up before supper. I'd been driving an old Chevy truck without a cab, and I was coated with dust and chaff. I'd acquired a tan that I hoped would draw attention away from my teeth.

Next month I would start my freshman year at Washington State College. I would miss playing football because my pads made me look as muscular as the other boys, but I wouldn't miss basketball season. My jersey exposed my thin shoulders with their bony points. Besides, Luke had outscored me last winter as a sophomore.

Washing chaff off my face, I noticed a red pimple on my chin. When I looked in the mirror next morning, another pimple had sprouted near my lower lip. In the pantry I selected a fine-grained sheet of sandpaper and applied it to the pimples. Ten minutes later, I admired my face in the mirror. The pimples were masked by drying blood. People would think I'd got in a fist-fight, which was okay with me.

Mama gasped. "You cut yourself shaving," she said. "Go wash your face."

I washed off the blood and looked in the mirror. The pimples looked larger and redder. The sandpaper must have nourished a growth spurt.

"It's all that chocolate," Mama said.

Giving up chocolate wasn't an option. Behind a loose board in the attic I'd stashed enough Hershey bars to last me through a world war. Even if the acne disappeared, I'd never have a girlfriend because of my crooked teeth and puny shoulders.

Our family always looked forward to the Walla Walla fair, especially the exhibits in the pavilion, where the women of each farm community arranged wheat, barley, peas, and berries into colored maps. But this year I stayed in the hog barn with my Hampshire pigs, a place I hated because I couldn't avoid stepping in manure when I cleaned the pen. I wore a bandana over my lower face. "Because of the dust," I told anyone who asked.

On the last day of the fair, I went out the barn's side entrance to get a bucket of water and came face to face with Donna. I hadn't expected to see her again because she'd graduated the year before. In high school we'd attended different classes and only said hi when we passed in the hallway.

At last year's Junior Prom, standing alone in my usual spot against the gym wall, I'd watched Donna dance with Archie, the bully who had nicknamed me "Shoulders." That night I dreamed she was walking along the river with Archie when a grizzly reared up on its hind legs. Archie ran away screaming. I leaped in front of Donna and wrestled the bear until it loped away–in Archie's direction, I was glad to see. Donna praised my courage as she tore off strips of her dress to bandage my hands. She shouldn't have acted surprised. I'd previously rescued her from an avalanche, stage coach robbers, and a mutiny led by Long John Silver, who resembled Archie except for the peg leg.

"Pigs need water," I mumbled.

She smiled. "I haven't been to the pavilion yet. Want to come with me?"

After we'd gone a few steps she said, "Better leave the bucket." When I rejoined her, she said, "You won't need your bandana."

I took it off, half expecting Donna to change her mind when she saw my pimples.

Other years I'd walked past the clothing exhibits without a glance, but today they fascinated me. Donna explained the intricacies of sewing. "I've been making our clothes since I was nine," she said.

At the food section we studied each jar of pickles, each cupcake, each cookie, shaking our heads at the judges' incompetence.

"I wonder if they taste the entries," I said.

"If they did, by the time they got to the last one, they'd be so full nothing would taste good."

"I've never been that full," I said.

She laughed. "You should be the judge next year."

At the carnival we entered a tent full of mirrors that turned us into alien creatures. I liked the one that gave me broad shoulders.

We rode side by side on the merry-go-round. "Are you going to college this fall?" I said. Last summer Donna had won a hundred-dollar scholarship as valedictorian, but my classmates said she'd been working all year as a waitress.

"I haven't saved any money. By the time I buy groceries for my family there's not much left."

The Ferris wheel stopped while we were at the top. "This is how cats must feel," Donna said as we surveyed the stock barn's roof and the tiny people below. "Do you know why cats always look down when you carry them? They're seeing everything from a new angle."

So was I, this afternoon.

Our car swayed downward a few feet.

"People ought to be as curious as cats," she said.

"Curiosity killed the cat."

"Give me an example." She looked at me.

I turned my head to hide the pimples. "Say a cat climbed a power pole and stepped on a hot wire."

She giggled, the sound I'd been hearing in my dreams for two years. "You're confusing cats with squirrels. Cats have nine lives." Our car jiggled downward again. "I wish people did. My grandma died last month."

We stepped out of our car and watched a red balloon drift above our heads. Beside us a little boy wailed.

"I told you to hang onto it," said a heavy woman with sunburned cheeks. "Come on." She yanked the boy's arm, and he stumbled after her, bawling.

I craned my neck, watching the balloon shrink. When it disappeared I realized Donna had, too. A minute later she came running toward me, holding a red balloon by its string. "Where did they go?" she said.

"I don't know." Why hadn't I thought to buy a balloon?

"I think I hear him crying," she said.

We weaved through the crowd, Donna leading the way. Near the American Legion's food booth, the mother was munching a hamburger. The boy's chest heaved, but I couldn't hear a sound.

"He's sobbed out," Donna said. She tied the balloon around his wrist.

He sniffled and showed the balloon to his mother, who, aware of onlookers, gave Donna an angry smile.

"How could you hear him crying with all the noise?" I asked as we walked away.

"Years of experience." She looked at the big clock on the pavilion's wall. "I'm supposed to meet my family at six."

"Are you going to the rodeo tonight?" I said.

"I can't afford it."

I'll take you. I've got my harvest money. The words stuck in my throat. She'd seen my acne and my crooked teeth.

She waited a few seconds, then sighed and said goodbye. I watched her walk away. At the pavilion's entrance she looked back at me and waved. I didn't think of waving back until she'd turned around.

There might be a slim chance... Inside the pavilion I pushed through the crowd, looking around wildly. I saw her standing by the farm communities' exhibits, flanked by her brothers and parents. No way could I ask her in front of her family. I hurried back to the pig barn, feeling my cheeks flush as if she'd actually turned me down.

I told my college advisor I wanted to be a senator. I'd considered aiming for President but decided the job would require too much responsibility. He suggested I get a bachelor's degree in business administration and transfer to a law school. I signed up for Business 101.

On the first day of class, the buzzer had already sounded when I opened the classroom's back door. I saw row after row of young men with husky builds and crew cuts. They sat motionless, placidly listening to the teacher up front, like beef cattle waiting to be slaughtered.

I closed the door and left, aborting my political career. Back in the freshman dorm, I pored over the school catalogue, trying to decide what I wanted to be. Nothing looked good. Mama wanted me to become a minister, which was reason enough to reject the idea. Daddy hoped I would farm, but I got glum thinking about a lifetime of trudging through manure, coughing from dust, trying to figure out the unsolvable mysteries of the combine's pulleys and belts.

College classes were so easy I didn't have to do much homework. One Saturday night my roommate, Bill, hosted a poker game. Three other guys from the dorm laid their pocket change on the table. Bill sat on the lower bunk, and I sat alongside him, curious. Gambling ranked just below drinking on the sin scale. The only cards allowed in our house were decks for Pit and Authors.

I watched, trying to figure out the hierarchy of winning hands. One boy lost all his coins and left.

"Fourhanded is better," Bill said.

They all looked at me. They each had a beer on the table, breaking dormitory rules, which made me feel even more of a prude. For a few seconds the room was so quiet I could hear my heart racing, as it had a year ago when I'd sat in Bill's parked car near the principal's house. We had just dropped off Nancy, the principal's daughter. Bill's girlfriend was in the car along with Sam and Judy, who were sort of going together, and Sandra Klein. A car rolled past us and stopped in front of the principal's house. Mama got out. She stood on the porch talking to the principal's wife, then went down the steps. I hunched low in the front seat, but she didn't look our way. I could feel the others' eyes on me. *Mama's boy.*

"I can't believe she came looking for me," I said.

Nobody spoke for a while after Mama drove away. Then Bill said, "We're going down to the river. Want to come along?"

Two six-packs of beer were wedged between my feet and Sandra's. Everyone in the car knew I didn't drink. Here was my chance to join the in crowd. I might even get to neck with a girl for the first time. But Mama was worried about me. "What time is it?" I said.

Judy looked at her watch. "A quarter till nine."

I pretended to think about it some more. My heart was thudding so loud I thought sure the others could hear it. "I'd better not," I said. "I've still got to write that English paper for tomorrow." Too late, I remembered Bill had been sitting alongside me in study hall when I'd written the paper.

Bill shuffled the cards. "You in or not?" he said.

"Okay." I dug out every coin in my pocket. The game was penny ante, nickel limit. I learned the hard way that two kings beat two queens and a flush beats a straight. It took them twenty minutes to get my seventy-eight cents.

"Can I get change for a dollar?" I said. They were happy to oblige.

I won back what I'd lost plus another thirty-three cents by the time the game broke up.

"When can we play again?" I asked Bill.

"Maybe next Friday," he said.

"Why not sooner?"

"We've got homework."

"I'm done by seven o'clock," I said.

He looked at me with a sour expression. He'd lost sixty cents. "We're not all geniuses."

By November I was hosting poker games Friday and Saturday nights. I had no trouble recruiting players throughout the dorm. Weekends, good-looking guys like Bill went out on dates, but boys outnumbered girls at WSC four to one.

To lure players, I stocked our room with potato chips and bottles of pop. Even at penny ante poker, I won enough to break even after buying the provisions. I began promoting poker games on week nights. I could usually find a few fellow degenerates.

At the end of our first semester, freshmen were separated into two social classes, those who pledged at a fraternity or sorority and those who didn't. During pledge week Bill's cousin invited us to dinner at Sigma Phi Epsilon. Their building looked like a mansion. Bill and I wore cords, but the fraternity members wore suits and ties. Were they all business majors? A thumbs-down by one member would blackball a potential pledge, and I broke into a sweat trying to decide which forks to use for the shrimp cocktail, the salad, and the prime rib. I discovered my shirt sleeve was coated with salad dressing. I tried to brush it off with my napkin under the table but got some on the tablecloth. The members politely looked away.

A week later Bill got a letter from Sigma Phi Epsilon inviting him to pledge, but I didn't. Too mortified to stay in my dorm with the other rejects, I rented a room off-campus. It was close to downtown Pullman, where one tavern had a twenty-five-cent-limit poker game that started at noon. I quit going to afternoon classes. Because the games ended at midnight, I stopped going to my morning classes, too.

Back home for summer vacation, I haunted the mailbox until my spring semester grades arrived. I shredded the unopened envelope into the burn barrel.

With six weeks to kill before harvest, I got a job at the Walla Walla Cannery that paid $1.49 an hour. I pushed steaming tubs of peas past conveyor belts where women picked black balls of deadly nightshade from the peas. A woman at the end of a belt picked frantically, like an angel charged with saving a fleet of rafters before they plunge over a waterfall. She had a purple bruise on her swollen left cheek. Sweat dripped from her chin, and her belly stuck out like a pumpkin. She shouldn't be here, I thought. I remembered Mama rubbing shirts up and down the washboard, her stomach bulging with Timothy.

"What if they miss some nightshade?" I asked my boss.

"Symptoms resemble a heart attack. The coroner won't suspect a thing." A machine shrieked behind us, and he raised his voice. "Don't you have two tubs of peas stacked up over there?"

That night he told me to wash out the tubs, pointing to what looked like a fire hose. When I turned the faucet's handle, the nozzle twisted in my hand and water blasted my face, snapping my head back as if I'd been punched. The hose leaped out of my hand and writhed on the floor like a python. With blurred eyes and stinging nostrils, I dropped to my knees and groped for the hose. My knees skidded on wet cement, and I splashed onto my stomach as the hose whipped away. By the time I got the nozzle aimed at a tub, the women at the conveyor belt had forgotten about the peas. It was the first time all day I'd heard anyone laugh.

Behind me my boss said, "Why didn't you just turn off the faucet?"

My shirt and pants were still wet when I parked outside Shep's Smoke Shop and squished into the poker room, past the "No one under 21" sign. I handed the house man a soggy five-dollar bill and held my breath. He glanced at my wallet as if about to ask for ID, saw more bills, and counted out chips.

"Fresh blood," said a man with matted hair and a bulge in his cheek. Spittin' Joe, someone had called him a week before when I'd watched all afternoon from the doorway. The game was dead spit, which I'd never played, and the limit for each bet was a dollar, enough to buy five gallons of gas. "One seat open," he'd said to me then. Now he licked his lips.

What he didn't know was that I'd figured out which hands usually won pots, and they weren't the cards he most often turned over at the showdown.

Another man I'd pegged last week as a poor player was also in the game tonight, a burly man with tight neck muscles and angry eyes. Last week I'd given him plenty of room when he'd passed through the doorway on his roundtrips to the bar.

As I sat down alongside Spittin' Joe, the burly man cursed and threw his cards into the muck. He took out his wallet and handed a ten-dollar bill to the house man.

I threw away eight hands in a row without playing a pot. So did a gray-haired player who had three stacks of yellow chips. He was watching me out of one eye. The other eye had a patch over it. His face looked as if sore losers had periodically gone after him with beer bottles they'd broken off at the necks. The fingers of his right hand moved constantly, shuffling two short stacks of chips into one stack, separating them, clicking them together again, like a hawk flexing its talons as it waited for a field mouse to scamper into the open.

"Professional gambler," the busboy had whispered the week before when we'd stood in the doorway and watched the one-eyed man turn his hole cards face up and drag in a huge pile of yellow chips.

"Professional gambler," I'd echoed, feeling my cheeks puff and hollow.

"They call him Mack the knife behind his back," the busboy said. "He's been in prison."

I looked at my hole cards. A five and a deuce, trash. I pitched the cards toward the discard pile, but Spittin' Joe picked them up and ran a forefinger over the backs of both cards. He shook his fingers as if he'd dipped them into a toilet.

"Get a new deck," he said. "Somebody here must be awful nervous."

While the house man broke the cellophane on a new deck, I wiped my palms on the underside of the table. I took out my Lucky Strikes and jiggled the pack–I'd practiced this move for weeks–until one cigarette shook out far enough for my lips to clamp onto it. I let it droop while I fished in my pocket for a matchbook. The match didn't light. I struck it harder, and the tip broke off. One-eyed Mack threw me his matchbook. I held a burning match under my cigarette and inhaled. All I could taste were flakes of tobacco. I took the cigarette out of my mouth. Damp. My face got warm.

"Try my brand," Mack said, tossing me the pack of Camels that had been lying by his chips.

As I lit up, I said out of the side of my mouth, "Been thinking of switching to Camels anyway."

"Jack?" said a soft voice. A dark-haired woman stood in the doorway, her stomach protruding into the card room. Except for the purple splotch under one eye, her face looked even paler in the card room's light than it had over the conveyor belt.

"Jack?" she said again.

The burly man shifted his chair so his back was to the woman, sending a whiff of second-hand beer my way. When I looked up again, the doorway was empty.

I squeezed my cards, and my scalp prickled. Two queens in the hole with another queen face-up on the board. I pitched a yellow chip into the pot. Spittin' Joe said, "Up it a buck," and raised me. Across the table Mack had two chips in his hand, ready to call, but now he looked at me and threw away his cards.

The burly man hesitated, checked his small stack, and called the raise.

"Raise it again," I said, hoping the two men couldn't hear my heart thudding. Both men called. The dealer turned more cards face-up, and the pile of chips in the center grew. The burly man tossed in his last chip. I turned over my queens.

"Beginners' luck," grumbled Spittin' Joe. He flipped his cards into the muck and shot a stream of tobacco juice toward the spittoon and my shoes.

The burly man tore up his cards and flung them into the air. I sat still, looking straight ahead, as bits of pasteboard fluttered onto the table. He stood up, kicked his chair backward against the wall, and stalked out of the room. I heard a whang and guessed he'd kicked one of the counter stools on his way through the bar.

"Well, his wife wanted him to come home," Mack said.

I rose from my chair, banged my head on the brass lampshade that hung over the table, and raked in the pot.

Mack pushed out his ante for the next deal and said, "You may look like you shouldn't be shaving yet, but you play poker like a man."

I'd arrived in heaven sixty years ahead of schedule.

In two hours I won eighteen dollars, more than I'd earned all day at the cannery. After my shift was over the next night, I won twenty-six. The third morning I didn't show up for work. My cannery career had ended. Two weeks later I came home at dawn.

As I sat in the car counting grainy bills—I'd won exactly thirty dollars—the smell of frying bacon seeped through the car's open windows.

I sat down at the table and pried a waffle loose from the waffle iron. "Night shift pays twenty cents an hour more," I said.

"You'll have Sunday mornings free again," Mama said. She forked bacon from the frying pan onto my plate. "Everybody misses you at church."

"Can't make it to church anymore. I'll need to sleep."

"Pea season's about over, anyway," Mama said.

"They want to keep me on after pea season." I turned to Daddy. "You'd better get another truck driver for harvest. My hay fever's got worse." I dabbed a handkerchief at my dry nose.

He looked out the window toward the orchard. Twelve years earlier, his father had gone out there in a drizzling rain to pick pears, wanting to help the family some way even though he was just getting over the flu. There had been no antibiotics to fight pneumonia in those days.

"Well," Daddy said, "you've got to do what's best for your health." He picked up his plate and carried it to the sink. The creases of his fingers were black with grease. Last summer I'd changed the cylinder teeth, curled on my back inside the combine's womb in hundred-degree heat, sweat dribbling into my eyes, wheat chaff falling on my face. Even though I'd scrubbed my hands with Lava soap, I couldn't get them clean.

I admired my white fingernail tips. One-eyed Mack and I wouldn't get our hands dirty the rest of our lives.

Daddy took his hat off its nail by the pantry door. "When Luke gets up, tell him I'll need help on the combine," he said to Mama. From the kitchen window I watched dust rise behind his pickup as he headed out the lane.

"They want to keep me year around at the cannery," I said.

Mama carried dirty plates to the counter. "What about college?"

"I'll take a year off. This job's too good to pass up."

She sloshed dishes in the sink. I picked up a dish towel and dried a plate. She looked at me in surprise.

"My, those people at the cannery smoke like fiends," she said. "I hope I can get the smell out of your clothes."

I dropped the last knife into the silverware drawer and followed Mama into the living room. She sat at the piano and began to play her father's favorite song. She sang, "There were ninety and nine who safely lay in the shelter of the fold..."

"I better get some sleep," I said.

"But one was out on the hills away, far off from the gates of gold..."

"Could you have my dinner ready a little before noon?"

Mama sang louder, "Away on the mountains wild and bare, away from the tender shepherd's care..."

"I've got to be at the cannery by one," I shouted.

She stopped playing. "That new job sure has you working long hours."

"Pays better, though."

"What is it you do?"

"Oh, different stuff."

"Well, I'll tell Bea she ought to scold whoever told her that nasty lie."

It was mid-afternoon when Mack followed me into the men's room. He opened the stall doors and looked inside. I stood in front of a urinal, so tense I couldn't pee. The game had just broken up, and on the next-to-last hand I'd beaten his three nines with a straight.

"Come up to my room," he said. "I want to talk to you about something."

"Can't we talk in the parking–out front on the sidewalk?" Where people can see us.

"No."

Cigarette stubs and candy wrappers littered the second-floor hallway of McNealy's Hotel.

Spools of flypaper hung from the ceiling, so black with the husks of flies that a live one would have trouble finding a vacant place to die.

Mack stopped in front of a door that had a second lock above the keyhole. His room stank of urine. It had no toilet, just a sink. A narrow bed, a bureau, a small table, and a chair filled the room. The bed sheets were rumpled and grainy, as if they hadn't been changed for months. There was no window and no closet. Shorts, pants, and shirts were piled in one corner of the room. On the bureau stood an open can of Heinz pork and beans, its lid jagged enough to cut my throat. He bolted the door. A hotel that allows residents to bolt their doors?

"Installed it myself," he said. "I've been here a long time, so they give me some leeway."

He took a deck of cards from a bureau drawer and pulled the table close to the bed. He sat on the chair and gestured toward the bed. It sagged in the middle, and I put my hand on the pillow for support.

"Don't touch that pillow!" he yelled.

I jerked my hand away. He couldn't be worried about germs. The pillowcase was filthy.

"What's it been, four months since you started playing at Shep's?" He shook cards out of their packet onto the table top. "Done pretty good, huh?"

"You've done better," I said.

"I'm what they call a mechanic. If you want to make a living at this game, you can't depend on the natural run of cards."

"I don't want to cheat."

"You already do. You like to sit alongside Joe because he doesn't shield his cards."

I'd never turned my head, so I didn't think anyone knew I

116

peeked at Spittin' Joe's cards. "That's not cheating. It's his responsibility to protect his hand."

"We're both taking advantage of losers. If we don't get their money, the house will."

What he said made a weird kind of sense. Players hardly noticed the rake-off. The house man palmed a chip after each round of betting while the gamblers watched the dealer turn up the next card. I estimated the house raked about twelve dollars an hour. That was why Mack and I were the only long-term winners. Ernie won a little during the day but lost it back at night after he'd had a few beers.

He spread the cards face down on the table. "Mix them up, like the muck after a hand's been played."

I stirred the cards with my fingers.

"It's my turn to deal," Mack said. He gathered the cards the same way he did at Shep's. He was the clumsiest dealer I'd ever seen, fumbling cards as he squeezed them together. I'd wondered if he had arthritis until I saw him shuffling two stacks of chips together with one hand.

He dealt eight hands of two cards each, face down. Then he turned up his cards. The ace of spades and ace of diamonds.

My mouth must have fallen open because he chortled. "I'll go slower this time."

We repeated the process. He awkwardly collected the cards. "I've lifted them just enough to locate two aces," he said as he jammed the cards together. "One ace is three cards from the top of the deck and the other is seven cards down. So there's four cards between the aces, right?"

I nodded. He started coughing and spit a yellow glob into his wastebasket.

"First I'll slip three more cards between the aces." He shuffled. The lower part of the deck spliced together evenly, but higher up chunks of cards stuck together. "Next I'll put four cards on top." He shuffled again. "Now one ace is eight cards down and the other

117

is sixteen cards down. Who's going to get them?"

"You, if the deck isn't cut."

"What do I do when the guy on my left is dealing and he plops the deck down for me to cut?"

"You say, 'Run 'em.'"

"I'm training the players so when I'm dealing, it'll look like they don't trust me if they cut the cards."

"Ernie cuts the cards every time."

"That paranoid bastard wouldn't trust his own mother. You always cut the deck, too. I want you to sit on my right every chance you get and say, 'Run 'em.'"

So that's why Mack was showing me his secret. I'd suspected he wasn't driven by altruism. He dealt and turned up his hole cards. Sure enough, he had the ace of clubs and the ace of diamonds.

As we walked back to Shep's I felt superior to him. I won almost as much as he did without cheating.

Just for fun I began practicing at home after breakfast. My bed was in the basement, and if I heard Mama coming down the stairs, I shoved the cards under my blanket. It took me a week to realize my fingers weren't nimble enough to stack the deck in a real game. Instead of feeling bad, I felt relieved.

In December I hit a bad run of cards. I lost seven days in a row. Mack, thanks in part to my sitting on his right, won big every day.

I resumed practicing at home, while my losing streak continued. By Christmas I could stack the deck about half the time.

The morning of my debut as a mechanic, I got diarrhea. At noon the house man broke the seal of a new deck. I decided the new cards were too slick to manipulate, but I wouldn't have to wait long. Most players, anxious to get back to the card table, didn't wash their hands after using the toilet. I hadn't warned Mack what I was planning. I'd purposely taken the seat to his left. He'd raised his eyebrows at me because the seat to his right was also vacant.

Now was the time. Mack was dealing and the cards were grimy.

After he turned up the last card, the house man shoved the rest of the deck toward me. While everyone watched the betting and the showdown, I had fifteen seconds to pull the cards toward me and lift them enough to spot two aces.

The houseman pushed the pot to the winner. The loser bought more chips. That gave me more time to arrange the cards, a lucky break because my hands were sweating.

I shuffled three times and placed the deck in front of Mack. He said, "Run 'em." After I dealt, I squeezed my hole cards. Two aces. I'd pulled it off.

Three players called a quarter. Mack picked up a blue and a yellow chip, ready to raise the pot. I banged my knee against his leg. He glanced at me and threw away his cards. I raised a dollar, and all three men called.

I bet each of the next three rounds. One player dropped out but Ernie and the Bogger called. After I dealt the last card, the king of diamonds, Ernie bet. There were now three diamonds face up, so he'd probably made a flush, but the pot was too big for me to fold. I tossed in a yellow chip.

Ernie turned over the king and jack of spades. He only had two kings. I'd won!

I stared at Ernie's cards. The players and house man waited, wondering why I was taking so long to act. I wondered why, too. I cleared my throat, rehearsing how to explain that I wasn't slow-rolling—letting Ernie think he'd won, then turning over the best hand just to rile him. *Sorry, Ernie, I thought for a minute you had two pair.* He would believe me. I didn't have a reputation for slow-rolling.

I'd waited too long. I sailed my aces into the muck, face down, and ran into the men's room, where I vomited into a urinal.

The door creaked open. "What happened back there?" Mack rasped behind me. "I had king queen. I'd have won that pot."

My hands against the wall, I retched again. Nothing came out. I straightened up. "I stacked the deck. Two aces."

"Two aces? Why the hell did you throw them away?"

119

"I don't know."

I silently read the obscene messages scrawled on the wall above the urinal.

"You couldn't cross the line," Mack finally said. "You got lucky. There's one thing I forgot to tell you. Ernie can spot a mechanic."

The game broke up at five-thirty. I was eating a hamburger at the bar, waiting for the night crew to arrive, when Ernie sat down on the stool beside me. He'd told me he once played shortstop for his high school team, but now his torso looked like a pear. He ordered a beer.

After the bartender moved away, Ernie said, "That big pot I won, you shuffled kind of funny. Hurt a finger?"

"Yeah." I rubbed my right index finger. "Pinched it on the restroom faucet."

He nodded. "Mack must do that pretty often."

I chewed a mouthful of hamburger but couldn't swallow it. The bartender set a glass of beer in front of Ernie. He sloshed beer around in the glass, raising foam that dripped on the counter. "I drink too much of this stuff," he said. He took a gulp and wiped foam off his mouth with the back of his hand.

My hamburger was now the consistency of mush, but I still couldn't swallow.

"Mack's lost his card sense," Ernie said. "He relies too much on his... let's call it his dexterity. He's lost his edge. So will you if you go down that path."

He drained his glass. "Might be a good idea to cut the cards from now on."

He ambled toward the poolroom in back. I went into the men's room and spit my mouthful of hamburger into a toilet.

TUESDAY, JUNE 17, 1986

My eyes open. It's so warm in the car I'm sweating. Through the rearview mirror I see the postman stop by the mailbox.

At the end of our lane I wait for a car to pass before I cross the highway to get Mama's mail. Rose Carney waves as she drives past. Her husband George farms the old Carney place, two miles upstream.

George's mother was one of the women I'd overheard in the church cloakroom the night of the Christmas program, a few days before Uncle Jacob died. One woman had said, "Why would Jacob do such a thing?" The other had answered, "So she couldn't tell."

Could Mrs. Carney still be alive? George was about fifteen years older than me, so she would have to be in her nineties.

Mama's only mail is a seed catalog. Right up until she died she'd planned to expand her garden. I toss the catalog onto the passenger seat and start the car.

Rose answers the door. I say, "Does George's mother still live here? I wanted to ask her a question."

"She died several years ago."

I thank her and turn to leave, but she says, "Maybe George could help. He's irrigating." She leaves the porch and points to a far-off figure near the river. "You won't have to climb any fences. There's a gate just past the shed."

I can't leave after she's been so nice, so I open the gate. Angus

121

cattle graze in the pasture. I watch my feet to avoid stepping in manure.

George is carrying a thirty-foot aluminum pipe on his shoulder. He drops it and beckons to me. When he takes off his hat to rub his brow I see gray hair, but his face looks tan and smooth, younger than the face I see when I shave. He must be almost seventy. What would I look like if I'd spent my life farming? More important, what would I be like? Probably bored to death.

"Sorry about your mother," he says. "She was a nice lady. I was in her Sunday school class. I think of her every Christmas when we decorate our tree."

Every year Mama made Christmas balls for her Sunday school students, past and present, using Styrofoam balls, beads, colored fabric and pins. I've got some in my apartment, but I don't put up a tree anymore.

Holding the pipe in the middle, George shoves one end into the opening of the pipe at my feet. "Fasten it, will you?" he says. The pipes are easier to snap together than the heavy iron ones Luke and I strained to fasten when we were teenagers.

He rubs his cheeks with a bandana. "What's up?"

"I overheard your mother and another woman talking when I was a kid."

"What did you hear?"

I tell him what I overheard from the cloakroom.

George walks to the line of sprinkler pipes that drenched a sixty-foot wide swath of his field during the night. His boots sink two inches. He brings back a pipe, but it wavers when he tries to jam it into the other pipe's opening. I guide it in and snap the fastener. He kneels to examine the sprinkler head. "Clogged," he says. He takes a strand of baling wire out of his hip pocket and pokes it into the sprinkler's tiny hole. He reaches for his shirt pocket and pats it. "Can't break the habit. I haven't smoked a cigarette for thirty years, but I still reach for the pack. You still smoke?"

"I quit when I started coughing." Is he trying to avoid the subject? Or is he just being sociable, doing farmer small talk? "Sorry I bothered you, George. There's no way you would know what they were talking about."

I start toward the fence, but I've taken only a couple of steps when he says, "I do know." He watches a chicken hawk circle above us. "Don't know if I ought to tell you."

I wait. The hawk circles lower, over the river. It disappears behind the cottonwoods.

"I was fishing for trout," he says. "Out of season. I started fishing downstream. It was maybe three in the afternoon when I reached your property. They were standing by the riverbank, holding hands."

Mama and Uncle Jacob.

George's lips are still moving, but whatever he's saying is drowned out by a roar from the highway a quarter mile north. A semi is passing, and my hearing aids magnify background noise. The truck sounds like a jet taking off.

The noise fades. "I went back upstream so they wouldn't see me," George says. "I was fishing out of season."

I hear a shriek from the river forest. A small animal or a bird has been caught by a predator.

George heard it, too, because he's looking at the river. "Sometimes I wish I hadn't told my mother."

But he did tell her, and what he saw spread through the community. Daddy was probably the only adult who didn't know about the affair. Or did he learn about it the night of the program? He was sitting in the back pew, next to the cloakroom. Was it a coincidence he left right after the women? I saw him again a few minutes later as I left the church with my bag of candy. He was coming toward me on the sidewalk, half a block away. He'd been talking to someone because a car had backed into the street just as I spotted him. Mrs. Carney?

I walk back along the fence, thinking hard. Suppose Daddy had learned from Mrs. Carney that Mama and Uncle Jacob were holding hands by the river. That information wouldn't prove they were having an affair. It would make him suspicious, but not enough to kill Uncle Jacob three days later. I remember something else. The day after the church program, Christmas Eve, I saw Daddy sitting on his bed, reading a letter. Beside him were other letters–letters he'd taken out of the box I'd forgotten to put back in Mama's bureau drawer. Her love letters to Uncle Jacob.

I'd been playing against rocks and shills one afternoon, not a live one in sight, when Shep's busboy beckoned to me from the card room door. Frank pulled me a few feet into the poolroom.

"You don't have a girlfriend, do you?" he said. "You play poker every day from noon to midnight."

I shook my head. Donna had married Archie a year after we parted at the fair. I wanted a girlfriend, but I'd never approached a woman because of my crooked teeth and pointy shoulders.

"Why don't you ask my cousin out?" Frank said.

Sue worked behind the counter at Shep's. Frank had noticed me looking at her when she fixed me lime phosphates–I'd learned the hard way that beer messed up my poker game. Most days Frank joined the game as soon as his shift ended. He yearned to be a pro like me, and during the last four years I'd tipped him off to holes in his game, mainly his tendency to play trash hands after he lost a big pot.

"Sue wouldn't go out with me." As if my physical deformities weren't enough of a handicap, Sue had an oval face, long blond hair, and a figure that drew the attention of every man in the bar.

"Wait here," Frank said.

I blew smoke rings as I waited. My neck muscles tensed when Frank came back. How could I look Sue in the eye from now on? I'd have to get my lime phosphates from the Book Nook fountain two blocks away.

"Pick her up at six," he said, handing me a scrap of paper with an address.

A man in a rumpled suit got up from his bar stool and staggered into the card room. He was a salesman who dropped a hundred every time he hit town. I took a step toward the card room.

Frank grabbed my elbow. "Forget it."

"But it's only four-thirty."

"Go home and take a shower. Your hair looks like a magpie's nest." He hustled me past the pool tables toward the parking lot in back. "I get off shift in fifteen minutes. I'll take care of the drunk's chips."

When I drove up, Sue was waiting on the porch of a small house. I took her to the most expensive restaurant in town. I had plenty of money in the bank because I still lived at the farm. Between bites of prime rib she talked about her previous husbands, her eyes flashing. Barry was a drinker and Ralph was a yeller.

"I made up my mind I'd never marry another drinker," she said.

I was about to sip my glass of wine, but I set it back down. Sue had ordered water.

"Ralph was the sweetest man when we were going together. He'd bring me roses and chocolates. He fell for me the instant he saw me."

Who wouldn't?

"He'd phone me at work. I told him I'd get in trouble with my boss, but he said he just had to hear my voice. When we went out, he wanted to know everything I'd done since our last date. He got jealous if a man so much as looked at me." Sue smiled, her eyes distant. "We never argued once until we got married. Then every time I opened my mouth he'd yell at me and storm out of the house."

I didn't care what she said as long as I could look at those

125

long-lashed eyes and lush lips. When Sue ticked off the awful things her husbands had done, I'd say "Huh!" and shake my head. When she explained how she'd tried to cope, I'd nod and murmur, "Uh-huh," the last syllable rising to encourage her to keep talking. Four years playing poker had taught me how to deal with bad-luck stories. Gamblers' attitudes toward me followed a pattern, friendly at first, becoming resentful as I won more of their money. After watching a hothead go after a gleeful winner with a pocket knife, I learned to grimace in fake sympathy and say, "Tough hand to get beat," as I dragged in a pot.

Sue saved half her meat for her daughter. "Karen's never eaten prime rib," she said. The waiter brought her a cardboard box. He'd been glancing at her as he cleared tables. I felt proud, not jealous like her ex-husband Ralph. The most beautiful woman in the restaurant was sitting across from me.

"The worst thing was not having enough money," she said. "Neither of them had a good job."

What job was I qualified for? Maybe a carnival freak because of my narrow shoulders. Sue knew I played poker throughout her shift. Frank had probably told her I was a professional gambler, yet she'd agreed to go out with me.

When I stopped in front of her house, she opened the car door part way. "Thank you for the nice dinner," she said.

"You're welcome." Would you like to go out again? I couldn't get the words out.

"When are we going out again?" she said.

On our second date, a woman with disheveled, graying hair came to the door. She squinted at me as if I'd come to steal her silver. No surprise. After dealing with two rotten sons-in-law, she couldn't have much faith in Sue's choice of men. She turned and called, "He's here," in the voice of a two-pack-a-day smoker. The sun had set an hour ago, but the living room was dark. She went into a hallway and muttered, "He's a worthless piece of crap."

Sue must have told her what I did for a living.

126

"Tracks up my rug with manure," the husky voice continued.

Had I stepped in dog poop on the sidewalk? I checked the soles of my shoes. They were clean, as they had been since I'd quit farming.

Sue came out of the hallway and said, "Come meet my family."

In the lit-up kitchen she introduced me to her father, a shy, bald man who was fixing a sandwich at the counter. Dust rose from his overalls as he shook my hand. I sneezed. Sue had told me he worked for a farmer.

"We've been seeding in the dust," he said apologetically.

"This is Karen," Sue said, smoothing the hair of a girl two or three years old who sat at the kitchen table.

The man spread mayonnaise on a piece of bread, added a lettuce leaf to a slice of bologna, and placed the sandwich in front of the little girl.

Outside the room the hoarse voice muttered, "That damn Otto. Never leaves me enough money. He's totally worthless."

As we walked to my car, I asked Sue, "Who was your mother talking to?"

"Herself. She gripes about my father from the time she gets up until she goes to bed."

"He seems like a nice guy."

"He's a saint. When he gets home from driving tractor his back is killing him, but he still gets down on the floor and plays with Karen."

On our third date, while Sue was getting her purse and coat, her mother came into the dark living room, approached me, and said, "That damn Otto isn't worth a nickel. He won't do a thing about that cougar."

"What cougar?" I said.

Ella pointed at the ceiling. "The cougar on the roof."

"There's no cougar on your roof."

She glowered at me and went into the kitchen.

In the car I asked Sue, "What's this about a cougar on the

roof?"

She laughed uneasily, "Mom imagines things. Where are we going tonight?"

Two nights later, Sue answered the door and said she'd be a few minutes because she'd just got off work. Karen was lying on the living room floor, coloring a sheet of paper. In the kitchen Ella was reciting her husband's faults to the appliances.

Karen showed me a crayon drawing.

"That's good. Is it a house?"

"It's an elephant."

"Oh, yeah. I can see its trunk now."

Ella rushed into the room, snatched up Karen, and carried her into the kitchen, eyeing me warily over her shoulder. She closed the door. "That's the bad Mark," I heard her say. "He wants to kidnap you."

In the car I told Sue what had happened. She sighed. "My mother thinks there's two Marks, a good one and a bad one. The bad Mark showed up tonight."

"You've got to get that little girl away from your mother," I said.

She covered her face with her hands. "I can't afford a babysitter. I work all day, and my father doesn't get home till dark."

The whole picture crystallized. In her innocence, Sue had fallen for an abusive alcoholic. She had fled with her infant daughter to her parents' house, aware that living with a crazy mother was preferable to living with a drunk. Then she'd married a man who treated her like a princess until they got married. After the wedding, he yelled at her every time she opened her mouth. Both men had returned her love with disdain. Left with no child support, she had pinched pennies, probably sewn her family's clothes, as Donna had done. Now this good woman–I only had to look at that beautiful face to know she was good–was trapped, unable to protect her daughter from her mother's poison.

"I can think of one solution," I said.

We eloped two weeks later, giving the Pasco justice of the peace fictitious addresses. We registered as Mr. and Mrs. John Franklin at a cheap motel under the Pasco-Kennewick bridge.

Late that night we lay on our backs watching *The United States Steel Hour* on a jittery television screen. I couldn't believe my good luck. Despite my crooked teeth I was married to a gorgeous woman. I could see into the future, one joyful day after another, fifty years together, sixty, seventy. After we died we'd spend eternity together in heaven.

I touched Sue's bare shoulder, but she pushed my hand away.

"What's wrong?" I said.

"Nothing."

I could guess what the problem was. I'd felt awkward making love, but I couldn't admit this was my first time.

"I won't let you adopt Karen," she said.

Where did that come from? "The idea never occurred to me," I said.

"See? You don't care about her."

"Sure I do."

She rolled onto her side, away from me. "You never hold her."

"I didn't know I was supposed to."

"My father holds her all the time."

I couldn't recall my father holding me or my brothers. I sat up, trying to figure this out. We'd never had an argument.

"He plays with her and fixes her supper. You don't even talk to her."

"I tried to, but your mother yanked her away."

"Leave my mother out of this!"

"Are you kidding? She's the reason we got married!"

Someone thumped the wall behind our heads.

"I've got a knack for picking losers," she said.

She was calling me a loser? Last year I'd won more money than one-eyed Mack. "You don't even know me!" I said.

129

Our neighbor banged the wall again.

"You're yelling at me, just like Ralph." Sue got out of bed and turned off the television. She sat in a chair, facing the dressing table.

Through the closed curtain the motel's neon sign gave her silhouette an orange glow. She stared into the dark mirror. Things were out of whack here, and I didn't know why.

I lay awake all night. Next morning Sue silently ate ham and eggs at a truck stop diner. I had buttered toast. My stomach felt roily, as it did whenever the poker game lasted till dawn.

I dropped Sue off at Shep's and drove to the ranch, dreading what lay ahead.

My parents listened quietly when I told them we'd got married. "It's the best thing for Karen," I said.

"How will you support a family?" Daddy said.

"I make good money." We'd never talked about how I earned it, but they knew.

"It'll take more than you think," he said.

"I've got a couple jobs in mind."

Mama hugged me. "We'll treat Karen like our own granddaughter."

I borrowed Daddy's pickup, and Frank helped me move furniture from a department store into the apartment Sue and I had rented two days earlier. Then I returned to the ranch, swapped the pickup for my own car, and waited at Shep's counter for Sue to finish her shift. She brought me a large lime phosphate, a sign she wasn't mad at me. I itched to check the card room to see who was playing. I resisted the urge, knowing I'd kick myself if the game was full of suckers.

"The walls are too thin," Sue said when we entered our apartment. "The other day I heard people talking next door."

"You should have said something before we rented it."

"I did. You wrote a check to the landlady anyway."

"You didn't act like it was important," I said.

She began filling the refrigerator with groceries we'd bought at

Safeway. "Everything's my fault, isn't it?"

"I didn't say it was your fault."

"That's what you're thinking."

"You don't know what I'm thinking!"

"You're just like Ralph. He blamed me for everything that went wrong."

"I don't blame—"

"You never listen to a word I say. You think I'm an airhead."

Was that a knock? I opened the apartment door. A young woman stammered, "I'm so sorry to bother you, but my husband works graveyard, and he's a light sleeper."

"I'll see that my husband keeps his voice down," Sue said behind me.

"Oh, thank you so much." The woman darted toward her apartment.

I closed the door. "You made it sound like it was my fault," I growled.

"You were the one yelling."

"No, I wasn't. You were yelling!"

"Ssh." She put a finger to her lips.

We drove to her parents' house without saying a word. Karen came out of a bedroom, holding an armful of stuffed animals, ready to go. Sue laughed, and I felt better.

Back in our apartment, Sue cooked a big pot of goulash that included beans, hamburger, chili, onions, and canned tomatoes. We sat at the table, the three of us talking as if we'd been a family all along. I ate four helpings of goulash. Things would be all right after all. Sue had been stressed out, but this was her last day behind Shep's counter. From now on my crazy mother-in-law would have no more influence on Karen.

While Sue washed the dishes I drove to Shep's, determined to make up for the two days' wages I'd missed. I drew good cards, but when the game broke up, I'd won only six dollars.

"I can't understand it," I told Frank as we headed for our cars.

"I hit three flushes and two full houses, but the pots were tiny."

"You played too tight," he said. "You never bluffed, so after a while they realized you had the nuts whenever you bet."

Frank was right. Usually I bluffed now and then. Poker players can't stand to get bluffed, so they would call me with mediocre hands. Tonight I must have felt the pressure, not wanting to waste money on a bluff because I now had to support a family.

We'd been married eight months when I opened a small envelope from the bank. It contained a notice of insufficient funds and a returned check for $186.63, made out to the Bon Marche, a high-priced department store that we never patronized. The signature was a clever forgery of Sue's name.

I'd never looked at our bank statements because I knew we had thousands of dollars in our joint account. The forger had probably been writing checks for months.

"I'm going to the bank," I told Sue. I didn't explain why because her mother was in the room. Ella's eyes were slits, a sign she was watching the bad Mark again. The good Mark hadn't shown up since she'd told me about the cougar.

Last night I'd complained to Sue, "Your mother's been here every day this week."

"At least she spends time with us. You never get home before midnight."

"The best games are at night."

"You never go to the park with us."

"I can't leave the poker game. I'd never get my seat back."

Sue didn't understand why I had to slave away in Shep's stuffy card room, missing a beautiful spring, summer, and fall. Why couldn't she appreciate my sacrifice? Besides, I did take them to the park, one afternoon when the game broke up early. Compared to the thrill of playing a big pot, watching Karen throw peanuts to a squirrel had felt pretty tame.

"A forger cleaned out our bank account," I told a teller. "The bank will make good, won't it?"

She looked at the overdrawn notice. "Did you ask your wife about the check?"

"I'm sure she didn't write it."

"Go home and ask her."

I approached Sue in the kitchen. "You didn't write a check to the Bon Marche, did you?"

"I had to buy Christmas presents."

My stomach felt as if I'd swallowed a load of buckshot. "Let me see your checkbook."

She took it out of her purse and slapped it on the table. The check register was blank.

"Look, you're supposed to list who you write each check to and the amount." I showed her my check register.

"You write checks, too." She ran her finger down my list of check recipients.

"Those were checks I had to write."

"So were mine."

"You'll have to take back those presents," I said.

"I won't! I want Karen to have a nice—" She put her hand over her mouth.

I wheeled and saw Karen toddle into the room, dragging a stuffed elephant by its trunk. Behind her, Ella glared at me. She took Karen's hand and led her out of sight.

Sue gazed at the empty doorway. She seemed more troubled about Karen overhearing us than about her own reckless spending, which infuriated me.

"I'm going to take your name off our checking account," I said in a voice so harsh it irritated my vocal chords.

Her eyes widened. "You can't do that. I need to buy groceries."

I drove to Shep's, rolling through every stop sign. At eleven that night I bought more chips with my last twenty-dollar bill. After

I drew to a heart flush and missed, I pushed in my remaining chips on a bluff. I expected Chi to fold because of my tight reputation, but he called. He knew I was stuck, playing loose. Not that it mattered. There was no way I could have won enough to cover the bounced check in one night.

Another letter from the bank arrived next morning. Three more checks had bounced. I phoned Daddy. "Could I borrow some money?" I said.

When I reached the farm, Doctor Harvey's car was parked in front. Daddy lay on his bed, shirtless, clutching his chest. His face was pale and tense. The doctor stood by the bed, filling a syringe.

"He thinks Edward had a heart attack," Mama said.

Doctor Harvey injected the needle in Daddy's upper arm. I had to turn away.

"Mark," Daddy said. "Would you get me my checkbook?"

I found it in the pocket of his bib overalls. He sat up with an effort.

"You should lie still," Doctor Harvey said.

Daddy wrote in the checkbook and fell backward onto the pillow, exhausted. He handed me a check. After the medics arrived and carried him on a stretcher to the ambulance, I looked at the check. He'd made it out for five hundred dollars.

Mama phoned Luke and Timothy, who both taught at Seattle high schools. When she hung up, she put on her coat. "I'm going to the hospital."

As fast as she drove, she'd probably beat the ambulance.

Three nights later, I had to leave a poker table full of amateurs to join the family at the hospital. I walked down a corridor, wishing I was still at Shep's, where the chips would be wandering back and forth among the amateurs like homeless children. I passed a "Keep door closed" sign on room 326. I stopped, remembering. Last year I'd stood inside that room, looking at the oxygen tubes curled into one-eyed Mack's nostrils, listening to the rattles as he breathed.

"You're his only visitor so far," a nurse had told me. "He won't last the night." She fastened an empty plastic bag to the catheter hose under his bed. "He brought all his money in a paper bag, wads of twenty-dollar bills. Wouldn't let us put it in the safe. Said he didn't trust anyone." She checked the IV needle taped to his wrist. "We had to wait till he was sedated to sneak it out from under his pillow."

After the nurse left, Mack raised himself on his elbows and stared past me. "Give me the three of hearts," he croaked. Then he'd flopped back onto his pillow, and the rattling had resumed.

Laughter burst from a room at the end of the corridor. I snubbed out my cigarette on the linoleum and walked toward the laughter.

"Well, the gang's all here," Daddy said. He was sitting up in bed.

"Let's go down the hall and sing Christmas carols," Mama said.

"It's almost nine," I said. "We'd wake people up."

"They can go back to sleep," she said. "None of them have to get up at six to milk cows." Luke and Timothy, less thoughtful than I, sided with Mama.

"I'll stay and keep Dad company," I said.

"Go ahead," he said, perhaps aware that my company would consist of sitting in a chair and thinking about poker hands I'd misplayed that afternoon. Or maybe he wanted to get me out of the room before Mama decided to wheel his bed down the corridor, too.

Outside an open door we began "Angels from the Realms of Glory." Mama sang soprano and Timothy sang baritone. I resigned myself to following Luke's tenor, an octave lower, unless the room's occupant happened to be a bass who felt well enough to join us.

We sang "Joy to the World" outside room 326. A card taped under the keep-door-closed sign read "Whalen, James." How insensitive, I thought. His door's closed because he's so sick he wants to be left alone, maybe dying for all we know, and we're

135

singing about joy.

When we finished I heard a faint tapping, slow and rhythmic like a faucet dripping. It was coming from behind the closed door.

"What's that sound?" I said.

"Mr. Whalen is clapping," Mama said.

We saved "Silent Night" for Daddy's room. At "sleep in heavenly peace" my throat clogged and I stopped singing. I wanted the song to hurry up and be over so we could go inside and make sure Daddy was all right. Then, as the others gathered their breaths for the last verse, I heard his whistle. He was whistling the tune he'd learned from the meadowlarks who sang to each other across our canyons of bunch grass. His tune blended with "Silent Night" about as well as when I rode the school bus to football games, the girls singing "Sweet Alice Blue Gown" while we boys tried to drown them out with "Ninety-nine Bottles of Beer on the Wall."

When we entered the room, Daddy was chinning himself on the trapeze bar that hung over his bed. "I could hear you clear down at the far end of the hall," he said. "You sounded like twenty voices."

By late January, Daddy was feeding the livestock, as spry as ever. His five hundred dollars had covered the bounced checks, but my bank balance languished in the two-digit range instead of four. One evening I spread a newspaper on the table. Reading the Help Wanted ads depressed me. Most of the jobs required experience. Worse, they all required work.

I checked Sales Help Wanted. Magazine subscriptions, waterless cookware, Fuller Brush, cosmetics. I was about to turn to the sports section when the last ad caught my eye: "Help people succeed with the nation's most prestigious home-study school. Salary plus commission. Expense account provided. Must be good at working with people."

The division manager conducted my interview in his motel room. All the blood in his face seemed to have settled in his nose. He wore a white shirt and a loosened tie. Before I'd left for the interview, I stood in front of a mirror for five minutes, trying to tie a Windsor knot. I'd forgotten how because I hadn't attended church for years.

The manager explained that the salary only lasted one month. After that I'd get paid by commission.

"What about the expense account?"

"One-third of your commission will be considered expenses. You'll only have to pay taxes on the other two-thirds." He looked at my resume. "So you've been working on your family farm. Show me your hands."

I held them out.

He grabbed both wrists and turned my hands palms up. "Those aren't a farmer's hands. No calluses, no strength in your wrists. Tell me the truth. What have you been doing?"

I swallowed air. "Playing poker."

He slapped my resume on the desk. "You've got some nerve answering our ad. You expect me to hire a kid who's done nothing for five years except play poker?" He wrote something on his yellow pad. "Get out of here," he growled without looking up.

As I opened the door, feeling as if he'd caught me rifling through his billfold, he said, "Your parents keep you supplied with gambling money?"

"I make money at poker."

"Nobody beats the house rakeoff. What's your secret?"

I wanted to leave, but it seemed important to show this jerk how good I was. "I size up poker players. Bluff the tight players and don't bluff the loose ones. I watch for giveaways. If I get ready to bet and he starts pushing his chips out to call, he's going to fold. If he shakes his head and looks ready to pitch his cards into the muck, he's got a monster."

"So you can manipulate people," he sneered. "Close the damn

137

door. You're letting in a draft."

I tried to slam the door as I left, but it hissed behind me. My watch showed four-fifty, enough time to get to Shep's before the night crew showed up. I got into my car and shifted into reverse. As I backed up, peering over my right shoulder to make sure I didn't run over a bystander, my window rattled. I turned and saw the division manager's red nose.

"Get back inside!" he yelled.

On his desk lay a coupon that had been filled out by a fork lift driver who wanted to be a millwright. "Our appointment's at seven." The manager tightened his tie and took a suit coat out of the closet. "Let's get a bite to eat first."

He selected a table in the restaurant's bar and ordered brandy.

"What would you like to drink?" the waitress asked me.

"Just water."

"You passed that test," the manager said. Halfway through our meal he ordered a second brandy. As he drove away he took a package of breath mints from his suit pocket.

At eight-thirty we left the prospect's house with a signed contract. I'd kept quiet during the interview.

"Think you can do this?" the manager said.

"I sure can." Better than you, I wanted to add.

He reached under his seat and brought up a pint bottle of whiskey. His car straddled the center line as he unscrewed the cap. He took a long swig and swerved back into the right lane. Whiskey fumes filled the air, an aroma I loved to sniff at Shep's. Playing poker with a drunk was more fun than riding with one.

WEDNESDAY, JUNE 18, 1986

In the pre-dawn light I dress, weary from lack of sleep. I put on Daddy's coat of many buttons and go out to the back yard. Between two raspberry bushes a spider's web shines in the morning dew like a fragile sculpture. I learned to love the dew forty years ago because it made the wheat too damp to harvest till mid-morning, shaving two hours from my stint behind the combine's header wheel.

No, I'd loved the dew years earlier, when Daddy and Luke and I would get up before dawn and drive to the Tucannon River to fish for rainbow trout. If dew was still on the bushes when we tossed our first hook-impaled nightcrawler into the current, we'd have a fish fry that evening. If the sun had dried up the dew, warming us, we'd get skunked.

The dew! I dumped those letters in the burn barrel the night I arrived, but I didn't set fire to them till just before dawn.

I run to the barrel and peer inside. Beneath some ashes I see paper and recognize Mama's handwriting. The flames that flared above the rim came from the paper bag. I scoop out the damp letters, carry them inside, and plop them on the kitchen table. Mama won't scold me for getting ashes on the table.

My Darling Anna,

Edward is asleep, and so are you. I'm too tired to sleep, so I thought I'd write you a letter. When you get older you can read it and know all the things we did. These last few months have been the happiest time of my life. I don't understand why English mothers hire a governess. If I could afford one, I'd let her do the cooking and cleaning, and I'd spend all my time with you.

I love feeling your warm bald head against my cheek as I carry you. You jerk your head from side to side, wanting to take in everything, twisting your body so I have to hold you tight. When you get sleepy, you sag against me. It's a heavy feeling, so trusting. I want to protect you forever so nothing bad ever happens to you.

I like to watch you sleep. Your legs and arms are fat, so soft and flabby. You lie flat on your back, knees out, feet together at the heels. You look like a frog.

When you cry, it breaks my heart. Your mouth curves down, your whole face shows misery, and you wail so loud I'm afraid a safety pin is pricking you. It's hard for me to realize you just need your diaper changed. When you calm down and start sucking again I feel so relieved.

I have to be careful what I eat. I love corn on the cob, and when I picked the first batch from our garden I ate six ears, loaded with butter. They were delicious, but you got sick from drinking my milk. I felt so guilty. I wish I'd asked my mother about things like that.

This afternoon you woke up crying and wouldn't stop. I changed your diaper and tried to nurse you, but you only cried louder. It's a wonder I heard Jacob knock. He sometimes comes by after supper to play with you, but he's never come during the day.

As soon as you saw him, he ducked behind the front door. He peeked at you and ducked again. You stopped crying. He did this trick again and again, until you started laughing. Then you held out your arms toward him.

Jacob stayed for two hours, and that gave me time to finish the washing. Once he carried you into the pantry, and he must have seen how tired I was, rubbing Edward's overalls on the washboard. He offered to hang the wet clothes on the clothesline. I told him no, but he insisted, and I was exhausted. I reached for you, but you turned your back on me and wrapped your arms around his neck. I had to pry you loose. I felt so embarrassed. Jacob must think I'm a bad mother.

Edward likes to stand by your crib and watch you. I'll go up to him and put my arm around his waist and we'll both stand there looking at you. Then I'll look up at his face and he'll be smiling.

I love you,
Mama

My Sweetie,

Mark is taking his nap, so I have a few minutes to spare. I had to write you, though of course I can't send the letter. I think about you every minute. This morning I burned the bacon. I was standing right over the frying pan and didn't notice the smoke until Edward came in from the bathroom and asked if something was burning. I ache to hold you again, to feel your hair against my cheek, your breath in my ear.

Last night in bed I heard you laugh from the living room. I thanked God and promised I'd never let you out of my sight again. I opened my eyes and listened, but all I heard were raindrops on the roof.

I'd give anything to live that day over. You were playing outside. Mark had the colic, and I was fixing a mustard patch for him. He's such a sickly baby. I laid him on the bed, but when I put the patch on his chest, he started howling. I should have put another layer of cloth between the patch and his skin. I've fixed enough mustard patches for him, you'd think I'd learn. I rubbed camphorated oil on his chest, but he kept crying. I'm not fit to be a mother.

When I finally got him quieted down, I went outside to check on you. I didn't see you anywhere, and you didn't come when I called. I thought you might be playing inside the canopy. It's surrounded by thick bushes, and you might not have heard me calling. I went to your favorite spot where the path widens, where you pretend you're in a jungle. I used to play with you there before Mark was born, and Jacob still does. Did, I mean.

I got panicky when you weren't there. I never dreamt you'd go all the way to the river by yourself. Jacob heard me calling and helped me search. So did Bea. Neither of them had seen you all day. We looked everywhere. Jacob wondered if you'd gone to the river looking for him. He often took you there. We ran under the canopy to the river and searched every inch of the forest. The river was high, and Jacob looked along the bank. I couldn't bear to go near it.

Edward joined us when he got home from Walla Walla, and we searched all night and all the next day. I went to pieces the afternoon Jacob carried you through the doorway. I'm so sorry Mark was in the room. He saw Jacob standing in the doorway, holding you, and he heard me wailing. I wasn't even aware of him there on the floor. I was hugging you, wishing I could breathe life back into you. Then I heard him screaming. He was looking at us, his red face all screwed up.

I ask God to give me the strength to keep going. It's all I can do to fix meals and take care of Mark. I washed his diapers yesterday, and the smell made me throw up. Mark adored you. He crawls everywhere, looking for you. I decided I won't ever tell him what happened. I don't think he could stand to know. He's only a year old, and I expect he'll forget you after a while.

Edward doesn't talk anymore. Before, when we ate supper he would tell me about everything that happened that day. He used to enjoy what I cooked. Now he eats mechanically, as if he doesn't know what he's eating. He sits by the lantern with his newspaper, but he doesn't read it. I don't think he blames me. Jacob says it wasn't my fault, but of course it was. Can you ever forgive me?

I love you,
Mama

My hand trembles as I put down the letter. Now I know what Uncle Jacob meant when he said, "Mark saw us," the time I eavesdropped on him and Mama from the hallway. He didn't mean I saw them having sex. He meant I saw him carrying Anna's body through our doorway. I also know why Mama said, "It was my fault."

Uncle Jacob was right. It wasn't Mama's fault Anna died. It was my fault.

PART TWO

I turned off my headlights before I reached the house, coasted to a stand of willows, and knocked the car door open with my shoulder. When the radiator stopped gurgling I could hear the rustle of the Wallowa River. That black mass above the willows was not the night sky, I realized, but a mountain, so steep I had to look almost straight up to see stars. I tiptoed across the yard, hoping mud wouldn't ooze onto my socks. A gray and white television flickered in a window. Good. They didn't shut curtains. They trusted strangers.

I wiped my shoes on the doormat. Although I'd been doing this for fifteen years, my pulse still knocked in my ears, the same mix of dread and exhilaration I got when I pushed all my chips into a pot and waited for the last card to fall. I took a deep breath, exhaled slowly, and whispered the low-pressure salesman's creed, "They need me; I don't need them." Right. No sales for a three-day trip, the light bill lurking on my desk, cutoff date circled in red.

The woman who answered my knock had short black hair and friendly eyes that almost wrecked my frown.

"I'm looking for Jim Lang. I'm with ACI."

She waited. I waited, too, long enough for her to decide I couldn't be a salesman despite my coat and tie—no briefcase, no patter, no smile. Bill collector? When her face got anxious I crinkled my eyes. "Sorry. I forget everyone doesn't recognize the initials. American Correspondence Institute."

Her smile came back, wider than before, and she swung the door open. I stepped around two kids sprawled on the floor, a boy stacking crayons on a miniature logging truck and a girl coloring butcher paper. An older girl and a man sat so close to a snowy television screen I wondered how their eyes could focus. One arm of their sofa was scorched brown from a wood stove. Everything was crammed too close together, like dollhouse furniture.

Lang laughed at something on television, a bass-drum laugh that trembled through his upper body. Wide suspenders made his shoulders seem twice as broad as mine. His black jeans looked as if they'd been slashed at boot-top level with a chainsaw, then sandblasted with sawdust. No wonder the room smelled like fresh-cut pine.

"Honey, this is the man from the school," the woman said.

"Mark Roundtree." I held out my hand.

Lang stuck up a hand with only an index finger and little finger. Six to ten months since the accident, I guessed, judging by the reddish scars and the puffy hand, no doubt bumped every day since he'd returned to work.

His wife herded the kids through a doorway, trailing butcher paper. If she wasn't back in two minutes I'd go get her. Too many times I'd pitched a perfect demo to a lone prospect, then heard the death knell, "Got to talk it over with my wife."

I scooted an armchair close to the television set and turned a knob till there was no sound. Lang watched the silent picture.

I threw out my standard icebreaker, "Quite a thing about the My Lai massacre."

"I hope they hang Calley," he said. "All those innocent women and children."

"That's exactly how I feel." I'd responded with the same five words since the court-martial had started, including last night after my prospect had said, "Them Viet Cong, you never know when

148

some six-year-old's going to toss a hand grenade at you. Lieutenant Calley ought to get a medal."

Lang's wife came back and switched off the picture. She sat on the edge of the couch, leaning forward.

He looked at the front door. "Thought they'd just send something in the mail. I didn't know they had salesmen."

"I'm the opposite of a salesman. Ninety-three percent of our students finish their courses, and that's because we're selective about who we enroll. My toughest job is turning a man down once I realize he doesn't qualify." Such as not having the down payment.

I studied his coupon. Woman's handwriting, which meant I had an ally. Occupation: logger. From our list of forty-three courses she'd checked the "Surveying" box.

"Not many loggers left in the Wallowas," I said.

"Starved out," she said. Her eyes were the color of floodwater. I was afraid if I looked at them for more than a second, I wouldn't be able to turn away.

"We're cutting one of the last stands of old-growth ponderosa," he said.

To bond with a prospect, relate an experience similar to his. "My great-grandfather came through this country on the Oregon Trail," I said. "His diary mentioned ponderosa pine two hundred feet high, so thick sunlight couldn't penetrate."

"Sound carries, like you're under a canopy." Lang shoved a bark-covered log into the stove. "This morning I heard the hook tender talking on the next mountain."

He stirred the fire, holding a poker between his two fingers. The fire crackled. Smoke billowed toward me, mountain smoke, not the stale stuff I was used to breathing in Shep's card room.

"We had a canopy like that," I said. "Over an old wagon trail that ran from the barn to the river. My parents used to walk under it the summer they were courting. Cottonwoods, chokecherry trees, sycamores. By the time I was old enough to play alone it was overgrown, like a jungle inside. I'd pretend I was Frank Buck catching pythons and tigers."

"Is it still there?" the woman asked.

"No." I glanced at my watch. Enough bonding. Time to establish his need for a course.

She leaned closer. "What happened to it?"

"My father figured we were losing two acres we could put into wheat. And weeds kept spreading into the field. So he took out the trees and we burned everything. I lit the matches."

"I'm sorry," she said.

"What?"

"I'm sorry you lost your jungle."

My eyes brimmed. I forced a cough, kept hacking nonstop till tears streamed down my cheeks.

"Smoke got me," I rasped, reaching for the glass of water she'd rushed from the kitchen.

High-pitched voices came from the kitchen. The woman stood with her head cocked, gauging the aggression level, then went back to the kitchen.

"She took my crayon," a kid wailed. The woman murmured something. Two kids whined in unison. The woman kept murmuring. I couldn't make out her words, but the words didn't matter; I just wanted to listen to that soft voice. I leaned back into the cushion, closed my eyes, let the warmth of the stove seep in. The kids quieted, and all I could hear was the murmur. My skin prickled. I could hear the Wallowa, the Touchet, all the rivers I'd ever known.

"Mr. Roundtree?"

I opened my eyes. She was bending over my chair.

"Are you all right?"

I stared into her eyes. Pure brown, no flecks of gold or green. I watched the pupils dilate. My cheeks felt hot. I swiped a hand over my face. "Haven't been getting much sleep."

"Would you like some coffee?"

"Apparently I need it."

150

A minute later she handed me a cup of something that looked like road tar. I managed a swallow without gagging. My tongue felt coated with sand. Had she boiled water and coffee grounds together? Lang took a slurp and set his cup on a warped floor board.

"Hits the spot," I said. "This will keep me awake for the drive home."

"Where do you live?" she said.

"Walla Walla."

"That's a hundred miles. Have you had supper?"

"No."

"I could warm you up a plate of spaghetti. It would only take a few minutes."

Homemade spaghetti. I could see her at a stove, pouring grease off the hamburger so her husband wouldn't get heart disease. I could smell onions simmering as she brushed diced tomatoes from her chopping board into the pan. My stomach rumbled.

"Thanks for the offer, but I'll eat when I get home."

"How long have you been away?" she said.

"Three days."

"My goodness. I'll bet your family will be glad to see you."

"Yeah."

Lights will blaze from every window, Sue's attempt to keep the power company solvent. I'll close the front door and hear pots banging in the kitchen. Sue's back will be rigid at the sink. She won't turn around. I'll open the refrigerator.

You won't find anything in there, she'll say.

She'll be right. A stick of half-melted butter in its dish, hardened again. Three French fries in a McDonald's carton, a meatball that was there when I left.

How could there be any food when you didn't leave me any money?

I left you thirty dollars.

That was gone the first day.

If you'd learn to hang onto money—

Don't lecture me about money. You've got money to eat in restaurants while your family starves.

Keep your voice down. You'll wake the kids.

Scared they'll find out their father's a deadbeat? Mom had to buy us groceries again.

We'll argue another hour, taking turns peeking into the kids' rooms to make sure they're still asleep, before we're lying in bed, stiff as those French fries. I'll slide my hand across her thigh. Don't touch me, she'll say, but she won't push my hand away.

"Will your children still be awake?" said Mrs. Lang, a wife who would cook her husband a hot meal no matter how late he got home. She would never watch him fix his own sandwich out of a meatball old enough to kill him.

"I'll see them in the morning." And while Sue walks them to the bus, I'll lay a ten-dollar bill on the table and head for Umatilla, taking Elm Street so I won't pass the bus stop.

"We don't see much of Jim, either. He's gone by four and doesn't get home till after dark."

"Time supper's over I'm ready to conk out," Lang said.

"Some jobs he only gets home weekends."

"I'd come home and the kids would act different," he said. "Changed just in those five days. They were getting older and I was missing out on it."

Were Daniel and Jennifer and Karen changing that fast? I looked at the floor. A nub of white crayon lay near my shoe. Just like home. Hunched over my chips at Shep's card table, I couldn't shift my feet without mashing a cigarette stub.

"What's your job in the operation?" I said.

"Choker setter."

The key to low pressure selling is asking questions when you already know the answers. "Choker setter? What's that?"

"When a tree falls I wrap the choker chain around it. Chain's fastened to a cable that runs up the mountain."

"Then what?"

"I signal the yarder engineer. That's the guy on top who runs the winch."

"How do you signal him?"

"With a whistle tooter. Little box I carry. When I press the button a whistle blows. That tells the engineer to drag the tree up the mountain."

"That's the only purpose of the box? One signal?"

"No. One toot means everybody stop what you're doing. Two toots means go ahead and bring the equipment back down the mountain. The hook tender–he's the boss–he gives that signal."

Lang lifted his cup off the floor with his good hand. Coffee slopped over its rim, and he slammed the cup down in the puddle without drinking. "Whole bunch of toots at quitting time–that means damn the son of a bitchin' yarder engineer!"

"What's three toots? Your signal to the engineer?"

"Yeah. Chain's set. You can haul the tree up."

"Four toots mean anything?"

"I'm having trouble getting the chain around the tree, so give me some slack."

His carotid artery was bobbing. If he played poker he ought to wear a turtleneck sweater.

"Clear enough," I said. "No way the guy on the winch could get mixed up."

Near the house a dog began barking. A chorus answered far away, yip-yip-yowl. Coyotes.

She stroked his arm. "Tell him how it happened, Honey."

"Six months ago. Wrapped my chain around this tree, but I couldn't get it right. So I signaled for more slack."

"Four toots?"

He nodded. "Had my right hand on the chain, ready to yank soon as it loosened. Punched the button three times, but my thumb slipped on the fourth tap. I was sweating."

"So the engineer heard three toots?"

153

"Yeah."

"And the chain tightened?"

His wife closed her eyes.

"Me and that tree went up the hill a ways." He rubbed his right ear lobe. The top of the ear was missing.

His wife took his maimed hand and wrapped her hands around it. "I got sick to my stomach when the phone rang."

"Premonition?" I said.

"If you're married to a logger, you never want to hear the phone ring."

"It's not *if* you're going to get hurt, it's *when*," Lang said.

"Turn around," she said.

Thumbtacked to the wall behind my armchair were snapshots of laughing men standing by fallen trees, by bulldozers, by trucks piled high with logs.

"Can you guess why I circled some faces in red?" she said.

"I think so."

"To remind me I got off lucky this time," Lang said.

She nodded. "Jim's not supposed to be working yet."

"You don't work, you don't eat," he said.

"Surely your employer took care of you." I cupped my hands like the giant hands holding a family in the insurance ad. "Sick leave–"

Lang snorted.

"No sick leave?" I pulled my hands a few inches apart and looked down into the gap. "How about medical insurance?"

"Gypo loggers don't pay for medical insurance," she said.

"They can't," Lang said. "Sam's in hock for his equipment. He misses one bank payment and he's out of business."

"Jenny told me when a truck breaks down it's like the world coming to an end. She buys all their clothes at Goodwill."

"It's not *if* a logger's going to go broke," Lang said, "it's *when*."

"The store lets us charge groceries. But the bills…" she flicked her thumb and forefinger. "Once I flipped a coin."

154

"I know what you mean," I said. "Do we read by candlelight or haul water from the creek?"

"Sounds like you've been there," she said.

"My students tell me what it's like." Did Inland Power's cutoff date say the twenty-seventh? Tonight's sale wouldn't show up on my paycheck till the thirtieth, but I could postdate a check. And if I hit Shep's poker game for fifty this Saturday...

"My mother warned me." She tilted her head at Lang. "Stay away from loggers."

He laughed. She smirked at him, enjoying his laugh, tracing his partial ear with her finger. Had Sue once smiled at me like that?

"Marry a man with a future, Mom said."

A man like me? No salary, credit rating lower than a hobo's, junior colleges springing up everywhere to steal my prospects. A month after I told Daddy I couldn't farm, two mutual fund salesmen got out of a green Cadillac. They minced toward us through four inches of harvest-truck dust, trying not to dull the polish on their oxfords. "Look at those new suits," Daddy had said. "Remember that Bible verse, Mark? What shall it profit a man if he gains the world and loses his soul?" He spat into the dust. "Hard day's work would do those fellows a world of good. I'd put them out forking hay bales, give them a few honest blisters." I'd shoved my hands into my pockets. Shuffling cards and stacking chips had left them smooth enough to pose for moisturizer ads.

I held my coffee cup in both hands, staring at the tarry sludge, wondering how a man could lose his soul. Would it pound against his stomach like an overdue baby, searching for an orifice to escape through? The stove's heat was making my mind wander.

"What's your education, Jim?"

"Tenth grade. I dropped out of high school to work in the woods."

I whistled. "No wonder you wrote us. You can't get into something else without an education, and you can't keep logging."

Mrs. Lang shook her head so hard the cross around her neck

155

swung back and forth. He looked at the stove.

"What's your dream?" I asked him.

"Huh?"

"If you could do anything you want for a living."

He stood and sorted through the stacks of firewood. The chunk he picked up was streaked with dried pitch the color of pancake syrup. He pushed it into the stove and poked at the fire.

She turned toward him, the muscles at the base of her neck taut. "Jim, we've talked about this."

I felt a twinge in my bowels.

He looked into the fire. "I want to be up on that mountain."

"Logging?" I said.

He nodded.

A cramp surged through my gut. "Why?"

He shrugged. "Gets in your blood."

"It's an addiction." She jerked an end cushion off the couch, slapped it with the front and back of her hand, raising dust, then plopped it back on the couch and smoothed it. "I'd be better off married to an alcoholic."

"You're running a rig, you feel the power of the engine. It wraps around you." He spread his arms, circled them over his head till his palms touched. "There's the smell of the earth, the saw, smoke pouring out of a truck. Everything going on and you're right in the thick of it."

The muscles of his shoulders strummed under his shirt as if he'd plugged into a couple hundred volts. Lang had the look Daddy got when he talked about farming before tractors, back in the days of mules and stationary threshers and twenty-man harvest crews who took two-hour lunch breaks so the animals could rest, who slept in their bedrolls under the stars. "I'd never want to go through those times again," Daddy often said, but his twinkling eyes belied his words.

"Four years ago I nagged Jim into moving to Pasco."

Lang's mouth curled. "Sagebrush and houses."

"My brother got him on at Oregon Beef."

"Had me swinging the sledgehammer. You aim right between the eyes."

"He'd come home nights, he wouldn't even talk to us."

"If I didn't swing hard enough, those steers would crumple on their knees. Looked like they were praying."

"No spring layoff. The only time we had enough money."

"That Bible verse," I said. "What shall it profit a man—"

"I got homesick just smelling our Christmas tree," he said.

"We'd come back to the mountains visiting, we'd drive through a logging town and he'd be off looking at stacks of logs, sniffing the air. Like he was passing an old girlfriend, smelling her perfume, and I'd be trying to distract him, keep his eyes on the road."

"My first day back on the mountain, I felt like kissing the saw."

Something exploded like a firecracker. I jumped, but Lang and his wife didn't flinch. I glanced at the stove, half expecting to see its door hanging by a hinge.

"Don't let Lori fool you. She loves the mountains." Lang grinned at her. "Wish I had a picture, you fishing Mirror Lake. Snow up to your butt, Pam strapped on your back. She'd giggle every cast, try to catch the fly when it looped behind you."

Her lips quivered as she tried to suppress a smile.

"We've got a spot picked out, up Lightning Creek." He left the room, came back and handed me a three-ring binder. I thumbed through pencil sketches of a log house.

"Ever since we got married Lori's been putting money into a kitty. For her dream house."

"Not anymore," she said.

"Well, we do keep taking it out."

There were more rooms in the later sketches, more small rectangles labeled "bed." The page after the last drawing was covered with smudges. The sketches had been erased with long strokes that ripped the paper.

"Now that I'm back to work—"

"No!" She went to the window and looked out, arms crossed. "After supper's in the oven I stand here and watch for his truck lights. Every light I see coming down the road..."

"You been getting sick again?" He pivoted on the couch to stare at her.

"I eat antacid pills like popcorn, and you know it."

"I'm afraid we can't help you, Jim." I stood and held out my hand. Lang reached up automatically, still looking at his wife. I shook his limp hand for several seconds, feeling the scars.

"What's the matter?" she said from the window.

"Jim doesn't need a course."

"Yes he does."

Lang rubbed his thigh. "Lori and I need to talk."

"We've talked," she said.

"Maybe you could stop next time you come through."

I shook my head. "That's against our policy. We've found that if a man puts off starting a course, he'll never finish it."

Lang shifted on the couch as if his shorts had wadded up.

"I've enjoyed meeting you both." A crayon crunched beneath my shoe as I walked across the room. I opened the door a crack. Cold air hit my left leg. "You folks will be on my mind." I edged the door open. Door speed is critical. Too slow and it looks contrived, too fast and I'm out the door before he says...

"Wait a minute."

I kept my hand on the knob, knowing better than to close the door too soon. Years earlier at Shep's, I'd pushed all my chips into the pot without a pair, not a dollar left in my wallet. Chi started to throw away his cards, then noticed my hand inching prematurely toward the pile of chips in the center. He'd called with a pair of fours.

"Lori's right. I've got to do something."

"We require seven hours a week," I said.

"Maybe after supper," she said. "I can keep the kids busy so they won't pester you."

158

He nodded, his face glum.

"I'll get my books," I said.

Mud sucked at my shoes as I walked to my car, but I felt like I was bouncing. I could smell a river cold enough to hold trout.

Back inside, I plunked my briefcase on the floor and examined his coupon. "Why did you check surveying?"

"Friend of mine said if I finish that course he can get me on with the highway department in Wallowa."

"How does that sound?"

"Well, they're cooped up indoors all winter."

"Ben's out surveying almost the whole year," Mrs. Lang said. "I asked Sheila."

"You'd work alongside the mountains," I said. "You could afford your dream house after all."

He sighed. "Might not be that bad. Tramping all over, peeking through that telescope."

The smallest kid tottered in from the kitchen, her nose runny. Mrs. Lang wiped it with a tissue and picked up the girl. The older daughter came in and scowled at the dark television set. "I want to watch *The Wizard of Oz.*"

"No television tonight, Pam," her mother said. "Let's put Glenda to bed."

Lang beckoned to me. "Want to see something?"

I followed him into the kitchen. Squeezing past the boy, who was coloring butcher paper at the table, I rattled a wastebasket, knocking an empty spaghetti can onto the floor. I picked it up and balanced it on top of the other cans. The refrigerator was plastered with crayon drawings. So was ours, but Lori Lang's fridge would look different inside, loaded with home-cooked leftovers.

Lang raised the lid of a chest freezer. Inside lay three huge rainbow trout, their stripes faint pink. The biggest had an underslung jaw that made him look mad.

"Wow! Where did you catch them?"

"Few miles upstream. You fish?"

159

"I fished this river when I was a kid."

The one time Daddy got away from the farm long enough to take us camping. As we passed a man fishing from a wooden bridge, his rod arced. Daddy braked, and Luke and I jumped out of the car before it stopped rolling. We ran downstream, glimpsing the battle through gaps in the willows. When we finally got a clear view, the man stood in a knee-deep riffle below the bridge, his thumb hooked under the jaw of a flapping rainbow too big for his creel. We pitched our tent nearby and fished till dusk without a bite, then trudged back upstream along the road, breathing the cool piney air, listening to the rapids, Luke and I trying to convince Daddy that the big ones got hungry after sundown. "They'll be hungrier yet by morning," he'd said.

Lang closed the freezer lid. "Bring your rod next trip. I'll show you where."

Maybe I'd bring Daniel. He was old enough to take fishing. What was he, seven? Eight? He couldn't be nine yet, could he?

When Lang's wife rejoined him on the couch, I pulled out my manual. "If you folks scoot over, "I'll show you what's in the course."

The couch was a tight fit for three people. I held my manual in front of Lang. She leaned over his shoulder to look, her arm across his collar, fingers almost touching my hair. The right side of my neck tingled.

"Algebra," he read. "Geometry. Trig–trig…"

"Trigonometry," she said.

"Physics. Calculus. Holy Hell!"

"I'll show you the first lesson if you promise not to laugh." I handed him a blue booklet. "We're going to start you at the bottom, assume you don't know anything. Hope you won't feel insulted."

He laughed. "Won't hurt my feelings a bit." He opened the book in the middle. His lips moved as he read. He grimaced. "Always had trouble with long division."

I snatched the book out of his hand. "No wonder. You were

160

on page fifty-six." I tucked it safely into my briefcase.

"What if he needs help?" she said.

We looked at each other across the bridge of Lang's nose.

"Any time Jim has a question he can pick up the phone and call ACI."

"We haven't had a phone since he got laid off."

Not like me to make that blunder. I'd checked the phone book. Too little sleep. That lousy motel, logging trucks roaring by all night within a foot of my wall. Word must have spread that the weigh station was closed. After I'd finally fallen asleep the dream had come, the tiny car cradled in my hands, a kid's head poking out of a back window. Then I spread my hands apart and the car plunged out of sight, and I was sitting up in bed, sweating, blinking at sunlight shining through cracks in the blinds.

"I'll help Jim. Every trip I'll stop by."

"Do you visit all your students that often?" she said.

"No." I'd tried, my first year, studying an algebra text till midnight in my motel room so I could help my students. But I found I couldn't earn enough, even back then with just one kid, unless I made more sales demos and fewer student visits.

"I'll stop because I want Jim to succeed." And because I want to sit in this room and drink your lousy coffee and get goose bumps when I listen to your voice, and pretend for an hour that I live here. You see, Mrs. Lang, there's always a student somewhere I visit faithfully because I've got a crush on his wife. Only she never knows it.

Glenda appeared in the doorway, chewing the ear of a stuffed rabbit. Behind her the older girl said, "I read her Goldilocks but she wouldn't go to sleep." Glenda climbed onto her father's lap.

"Jim always reads her a bedtime story," the woman said.

I got home too late to do that, though sometimes I'd close the front door and hear Sue reading from a kid's bedroom in a voice I hardly recognized, gentle and stripped of anger. But it's not what you do that matters, it's what you feel in your heart, what you'd do if you could. Driving home Saturday, I'd missed my kids so much I got an ache in my throat. When I opened the door, they were dancing around because Sue had promised to take them to a drive-in movie.

"Come with us, Daddy," Daniel had pleaded.

"We'll see," I told him. Then I called Phil at Shep's Smoke Shop and asked how the poker game looked.

"Barnburner's shaping up. The Bogger's had a few, raising every pot."

"How many pros?"

"Just Chi. You ought to make a bundle."

I hung up, my heart beating faster, and promised the kids next time I'd go. As Sue pulled away, Daniel stuck his head out the back window and yelled, "They charge by the carload, Daddy. You could get in free."

That kid's a born salesman, I thought as I drove to Shep's. Halfway there I remembered asking Daddy to go to the movies with us kids and Mama, and I'd stopped smiling.

Glenda snuggled against Lang's chest. He rocked her, swaying his shoulders the way Sue used to rock our babies.

"She's almost asleep." Lang carried Glenda out of the room.

His wife and I listened to the drone of his voice as he read from the bedroom.

"He's so patient with them," she said. "Too bad you have to work nights. Do you spend a lot of time with your children weekends?"

"Whenever I can. Saturday they wanted me to go to a movie, but I had an appointment."

"I hope you canceled it."

"I did. The way I see it, they're only young once."

"They grow up so fast."

We sat at opposite ends of the couch, looking at the open bedroom door. I tugged down my shirt cuff to hide the goose bumps.

162

Paper rustled in the kitchen. I pictured Lang at the table working a mixed equation, staring at an example, scribbling, erasing, checking the answers page, crumpling the paper in his big fist.

When he came back I moved to the armchair. I felt drained. The coffee had worn off. I couldn't remember what I'd said last, what I was supposed to do next.

"Jim," she said, "what do you think about the course?"

"I don't know. That math..."

She leaned toward me, palms pressed between her knees. "What do you think he should do?"

Our eyes locked, and my commission didn't matter anymore. I wanted what was best for this trusting woman and her daughters, for the boy coloring in the kitchen, even for Lang himself, who didn't know how lucky he had it with a perfect wife and an hourly wage. How connected we all were, how fragile. The wrong advice from me could start one wave pushing against the next like a soprano's high note, splintering this family like the wine glass in the television ad.

I silently rehearsed my answer. Mrs. Lang, all my good surveying students thrived on geometry. Jim can't fathom long division. He'll struggle for a while, then throw his math book into that fire. You'll call him a quitter. He'll call you a nag. Save your four hundred dollars. Let him stay on those mountains, the saw whirring, the smell of diesel and smoke tickling his nostrils, doing what he loves till the last tree falls. Swallow your antacid pills and watch for his headlights, pray you'll never see blue and red lights flash by and your neighbor hurry across the yard toward your porch.

My hands were shaking. Too much coffee. Had the Langs noticed?

They were looking at me expectantly, and I realized that to them my long silence meant I was pondering her question so I could deliver the wisest possible answer. I'd discovered a new sales technique! And how could I be certain he would fail? What I sold was the idea that dreams can come true, that a man who is mystified by long division can learn to decipher calculus.

I walked to the window and stood with my hands in my pockets. In the dim light I could see only mud.

I turned and said, "It won't be easy, Jim. You'll have to keep pushing yourself. But I see you opening an envelope." My voice sounded strained. Something had risen in my throat. I belched silently, and it was gone. "A brown envelope. Two, three years from now. There's a certificate inside, fancy printing, wax seal. Your family crowds around. What do you think it is?"

She gave me the straight line. "His diploma?"

"No, Jim got that the year before. It's his land surveyor's license. You'll frame it, Mrs. Lang. And you, Jim, you'll show it to your boss. You're working for the highway department, making good money. You'll tell him you're thinking of going into business for yourself so you can survey in the mountains. He'll beg you to stay, show you the pay chart, another five thousand a year now that you're licensed. You tell him you'll think it over."

The air smelled smoky, like when I used to huddle around the camp fire with the other boy scouts, making up ghost stories. I squinted through the haze, trying to bring the Langs into sharper focus. She placed her hand over his and jiggled it. He would do fine on the math. I would help him and he'd do just fine.

Mopping up took a while. She had to get her checkbook, do some pencil work on her budget. The two older kids wheedled their dad into watching television with the sound off. Judy Garland, a child forever, was mouthing a song, "Over the Rainbow." I could read her lips. I knew the words by heart. I'd watched *The Wizard of Oz* in the Liberty Theatre with Mama and Luke and Timothy, told Daddy when we got home how the wizard puffed smoke to mask his trickery. I'd seen it two or three times on television with my own kids. Hey, I must be doing okay as a father.

They came out on the porch to see me off. The porch creaked under the weight of three people.

"Where'd you park?" Lang said.

"By the willows."

"Why so far away?"

So you wouldn't see my car and wonder how a man who drives a junker could show you how to succeed. "So I could hear the river."

He waved as I drove past. She had already gone inside. Would she stand at the window until my tail lights disappeared, wishing she had a phone so I could let her know I'd got safely home?

I started up Tollgate Mountain, the same canyon my great-grandparents climbed on the Oregon Trail. A field mouse skittered across the road, barely beating my tires. The temperature needle crept into the red, but it was a cool evening. I'd make it to the top easy.

Near the summit my ears popped. The radio's static cleared, and I sang "King of the Road" along with Roger Miller. Eight sales for the month already. A good day in Umatilla tomorrow and I might pass Wylie for the division lead.

Always had trouble with long division.

I turned up the radio until the din rattled the dashboard, hurting my ears.

Something swooped above my headlights like a dive bomber. I swerved, hit the brakes, felt my tires shudder on gravel. The car skidded and stopped crossways in the road. I gripped the wheel and waited for my heart to slow. Did I think the owl was about to whisk me into the air, clutching my car in its talons? Field mice were the ones in danger, no match for the owl's cunning. The wise owl, squandering his wisdom in an endless search for prey.

A mile farther I nosed onto the shoulder to admire the view. Walla Walla's lights shimmered to the north. Had my great-grandparents stopped their oxen here to look? In November of eighteen fifty-three, the hills that rippled to the horizon would have been gray with bunch grass. Why had they decided to homestead there? Maybe instead of bunch grass they had pictured apple trees and wheat, whatever they carried in their seed bags. Or maybe they were tired of traveling, happy to settle anywhere before the snow came.

Those lights to the northwest would be Hermiston. What was that faint glow beyond? Umatilla? This whole expanse was my territory, no other ACI rep could breach it, and tomorrow I would drive to Umatilla and capture the division lead.

I put my car in gear and rolled downhill. As I spiraled down the mountain, pressure built in my ears. Every time I rounded a curve and glimpsed the north country, the vista had shrunk. Umatilla's lights vanished first, then Hermiston's, then Walla Walla's. At the bottom the road straightened, flanked by barbed-wire fences.

Ahead, I saw only a hill.

I turned onto our street a little after eleven. For once the porch light was on. The house was quiet. A note on the kitchen counter read "Goulash in fridge."

I relished every bite of the goulash. How wrong I'd been, expecting an angry confrontation with Sue. Instead, she'd fixed my favorite dish. Tomorrow I'd reciprocate. Both of my Umatilla prospects worked swing shift, so I'd get home early. Instead of going to Shep's, I would treat Sue and the kids to dinner at MacDonalds. Afterward, I'd take them to a drive-in movie.

Sue was asleep when I crawled into bed. We would make love tomorrow night.

Next morning I overslept. Sue had already taken the kids to the bus stop. I dressed quickly, worried I'd be late for my ten o'clock appointment. No time for breakfast. I opened my wallet, intending to leave money on the counter for Sue, but I only had eleven dollars. If I left the ten-dollar bill I wouldn't be able to buy lunch, and my stomach was already growling.

I left the one-dollar bill, plus twenty-eight cents in change, all I had in my pocket.

Lunch turned out to be the best part of my day in Umatilla. My morning prospect had no money but promised to mail the down payment next payday. I estimated the odds were five to one I'd never see a penny.

My afternoon appointment was a dud. Although two cars sat in the driveway, no one came to the door.

Back in Walla Walla, I stopped at my bank to get cash for our outing tonight. I wished I'd left a note for Sue, telling her my plans for the evening and explaining why I couldn't leave her more money.

Sue's car was gone, and the house was empty. I sat on a kitchen chair with a view of the street and waited. When her car pulled into the driveway, no kids inside, I began to sweat.

I was halfway between Elgin and Lostine when the Minam River came into view, an inch-wide ribbon a thousand feet below the winding highway. I imagined my upcoming conversation with Lori Lang. This was my first trip to the Wallowa Valley since I'd enrolled Jim seven months ago.

Jim gave up on the course, she'll tell me.

I'm sorry to hear that.

I'm thinking of leaving him. I can't stand the stress any longer. So many times I've got my hopes up.

I've got some bad news myself. My wife left me. The divorce will be final next month.

Lori will look incredulous. How could she leave a wonderful man like you? Is there any chance you can get custody?

Not unless I remarry.

I couldn't live without my children, she'll say.

Me neither.

We'll sit silently, avoiding each other's eyes, thinking the same thing. Six children, one big happy–

A scraping sound? I swerved away from the barricade. No problem. My right fender was already dented.

Lori didn't smile when she opened the door. I sat in the same chair and sipped the same sludge she'd given me before. The room was cold, even though logs were stacked by the wood stove. She must have planned to light the fire when her kids got home from school. What a woman! Sacrificing her own comfort for her family's sake.

"Jim gave up on the course," she said.

"I'm sorry to hear that."

"He got stuck on fractions."

"I was afraid this might happen."

She sat up straighter. "What do you mean?"

"I was afraid he wouldn't have enough willpower."

"He studied every night. You said you would stop by to help him."

"I'll come back tonight. What time—"

"He's already given up."

"If a person doesn't have an aptitude for math—"

"You knew he didn't. I asked you what you thought, and you said he could make it if he worked hard enough."

"Maybe that was wishful thinking. I wanted him to succeed, for his sake and your family's sake. I talked myself into believing he would."

The muscles around her mouth loosened. "I wanted to believe it, too. I'm sorry I snapped at you."

"I wasn't thinking too clearly. I hadn't slept the night before."

She smiled. "I remember. You fell asleep while I was in the kitchen."

I felt jubilant. Now we were on the same wave length. To bond, bring up an experience similar to hers. "I was feeling a lot of pressure that night. I was worried about paying the light bill. Like you were when Jim was off work."

"You're paid on commission!"

168

"No, that's not what I meant. My wife–my ex-wife can't hang onto money, and–"

"You told us you weren't a salesman." Her pupils had shrunk to pinpoints. "You said your toughest job was turning a man down because he didn't qualify."

Just my luck she has a photographic memory. "I almost turned Jim down."

"No, you pretended to turn him down. It was all a performance, going to the door, giving him one last chance." Her eyes bored into mine, and I looked away.

"ACI has a seventy-eight percent completion rate. There was a good chance he'd do okay."

"You told us the completion rate was ninety-three percent."

My armpits felt damp. "Last month I got an update."

"Skip the bullshit. Can we cancel the course?"

"The contract's non-cancellable. If you don't pay, you'll get letters from a collection agency."

"I'll tell the school you misrepresented the course."

I felt like she'd punched me. "Stop paying," I said. "The collection letters come from the home office. They'll threaten to garnish Jim's wages, but they won't."

"You weren't going to tell me that, were you?" She picked up my nearly-full mug and went into the kitchen. I heard the sound of running water. Flushing my coffee down the drain.

She came back but remained standing. "If I hadn't threatened to complain to the school, you'd have kept quiet. You'd have let us pay another three hundred dollars. All for a course Jim had zero chance of completing. And you knew it."

"That's not true. I had a student who was just as poor in math as Jim. Now he's an engineer at Boise Cascade."

"What's his name?"

"David Smith." Did she notice I paused for an instant?

"So if I contacted Boise Cascade, I could locate him?"

"He might not still be there. This was years ago."

"Sure it was." She opened the front door. "Just leave."

She stepped back as I passed her. How dare she treat me like a dog that had pooped on her rug? She should get down on her knees and thank me for saving them three hundred dollars. I'd done the right thing, enrolling Jim. Twelve percent of our students do complete their courses. Who am I to judge? I'm not God.

I tried to peel out, but my worn tires couldn't get any traction. One coupon lay on the passenger seat—filled out in a man's handwriting, thank God. Andy Blake had a rural Post Office box somewhere in the boondocks outside Pendleton, but I would find him.

An hour later I careened down Tollgate Mountain like a drunk, turning the wheel at the last instant, feeling centrifugal force push me outward, as if God wanted me to sail off a cliff. Near the bottom I entered fog so thick I had to slow to a crawl.

My headlights went out the instant the engine died. In total blackness I held the steering wheel steady and pumped the brakes until my car groaned to a stop.

This was unreal. There ought to be some light even in heavy fog. I fumbled in the back seat for the garbage bag that contained my razor and clothes. I could smell dirty socks. This trip I'd forgotten to bring an extra plastic bag, so each morning I'd sniffed socks and shorts to identify the clean ones.

I slung the bag over my shoulder and walked away from the car. This wasn't much more than a dirt road. Worried I might wander off the road into the desert, I focused on the pinch of gravel under the thin soles of my shoes. Fog prickled my nostrils. The temperature was below freezing, but if I kept moving I wouldn't die from hypothermia.

I knew I could flag down the first driver who came along. Although I never picked up hitchhikers myself, those bearded hippies who wore clothes grimy enough to clog a washing machine, the ranchers of eastern Oregon would be more charitable. They knew what could happen if a man stayed outdoors all night in November. Besides, I wore a dry-cleaned suit and tie. No one could mistake me for a predator.

The coins in my front pockets swung against my thighs, enough to cover a motel room and the towing fee. I'd write a check for the alternator.

I smiled, recalling how the Blakes had emptied piggy banks all over the house to make the down payment. My demo had been a work of art. Late in the interview I pulled the trick I'd learned at the Langs. I stared at the floor and silently counted off forty-five seconds. Then I stuck out my hand and said, "Congratulations, Andy. I'm going to recommend we accept you as a student." In two hours I'd transformed a high school dropout into a future electrical engineer.

Weeds crumpled underfoot. I'd strayed off the road. But which direction, right or left? I sidled to my left, listening for the scrape of gravel, but tripped and fell in a clump of weeds. Sagebrush, I could tell from the pungent smell.

I stood up, unsure which direction I'd been moving. What should I do? Stay motionless, waiting for a car that might never come? If I started walking I might be ten miles from the road by dawn, lost in this scabland. Worse, I could step into a gully and sprain an ankle. But if I didn't keep moving I'd freeze to death. I shuffled a few feet, and the damp fog closed around me as if I were deep inside a narrowing cave. I hugged myself, shivering, afraid to take another step.

I heard the car long before the lone headlight appeared, shrouded by fog. Gauging its direction from the moving light, I ran to intercept it. When I felt gravel under my feet, the headlight was almost on me. I dropped my bag and waved, crisscrossing my arms, but the car was coming too fast to stop. I jumped backwards as it hurtled past, brakes shrieking.

A hazy glow and a sputtering engine told me the driver had stopped, so far away his brakes must be shot. I trotted up the road. Smoke poured out of the vehicle's tailpipe, blending with fog to obscure what turned out to be an old van. I'd heard somewhere that hippies liked this kind of van because they could hold sex orgies in the back.

A coatless, black-bearded man leaned out the window.

"Could you give me a ride?"

He grunted something in a foreign language. I pointed at the road ahead. He motioned toward the back of the van.

The passenger's seat in front was empty. I opened the door and started to climb inside, but the driver waved me off with a scowl and thumbed toward the back.

Okay, whatever crazy reason this foreigner had for not letting me ride in front, I'd humor him.

I wrestled the back door open, coughing from the exhaust fumes. There was no back seat. A figure lay in the middle of the floor, head toward the rear of the van. I was too bleary-eyed to make out the face, but long, dark hair indicated this was a young woman. She was covered by a blanket and an overcoat. She didn't move to make room. Her body seemed taut, pulsing with some emotion.

I crawled around her and sat on the floor, facing the front seat, my sack between my knees. Something gouged my hip. I pulled it loose and brought it close to my face. A nude plastic doll.

From the van's smell I guessed the occupants had worn the same underwear for days. I was used to smelly places. Last night I'd walked into a prospect's house and seen dog crap in a corner and a bare-assed toddler wearing a dirty T-shirt. I'd left without giving a demo.

The driver twisted in his seat and spoke gibberish to the woman, his voice tense. She responded with similar nonsense in a high-pitched, strained voice. I guessed the quarrel had been going on awhile. The driver looked at me and pointed to the woman, speaking in short bursts like a dog barking, as if he'd been angry so long he'd forgotten how to talk calmly. Did he want me to take his side in the argument?

I nodded. The man turned, apparently satisfied, and the van lunged forward. He was going too fast for this fog. He must be so mad at his wife he didn't care if he got us all killed.

A cold hand gripped my wrist.

What was going on? Did the woman want to have sex, her husband five feet away? The van wasn't dark enough, but maybe he wouldn't care. These were foreigners. Who knew what their customs were?

Then it hit me—the guy was her pimp! That's why he'd forced me to get in back, why he'd pointed at the woman. It could also explain the tension in their voices. Maybe he'd ordered her to have sex, and she'd tried to talk him out of it.

I couldn't sink that low, of course, but the urge was overpowering. I hadn't slept with a woman since Sue and I split up. I'd never had sex with anyone except Sue, a secret I'd kept even from her. Although I'd trained myself to manipulate sales prospects, I'd never let a woman know I was attracted. If a prospect didn't buy, I could tell myself he was lazy. If a woman rejected me, who could I blame but myself?

Fingernails dug into my wrist. I winced.

The van's interior lightened. A car was coming toward us. I turned so I could see the woman's face, and the lump of coins in my right pocket slid across my hip and thumped the floor.

I recoiled. Her eyes were sunken, like empty sockets. Instead of lips there was a thin line under her nose, as if her mouth had been sewn shut. Blue veins protruded from the back of the hand that clutched my wrist.

I wrenched my hand free.

The other vehicle passed, its roar absorbed by the fog. I squirmed away from the woman till my knees mashed the back of the passenger seat. I felt germs crawling up my left arm like spiders.

The woman clawed at my coat. She writhed on the floor and began to wail. Brakes squealed, and the van stopped. The driver leaned to his right. Something snapped, maybe the glove box popping open. He climbed over the seat. I cringed.

He squatted at the woman's feet, his bearded face illumined in the headlight's pale glow. The tension drained out of my body. I recognized that look. I'd seen the same expression on Daddy's face when he leaned over the crib the night Timothy almost died from convulsions.

There was a small object in the man's hand, banded with the colors of a rainbow. He peeled back paper, revealing a red candy, a miniature life preserver so familiar I could taste the cherry flavor. Only a few candies remained. He separated the top wafer with a fingernail and held it out to the woman. She sucked it into her lipless mouth and snatched the package.

The fingers of her right hand burrowed into the side pocket of my suit coat, tugging so hard I was afraid she'd tear the cloth. The driver pulled her hand loose. He grasped me around the waist and scooted me backward till I was sitting alongside the woman's stomach. He took my left hand and closed it over the back of her hand. The overcoat had slipped onto the floor when she reached for the candy. The man spread it across her legs. He tucked the blanket under her chin.

Her veins felt like nightcrawlers. I had a panicky feeling our blood was mingling, my health pumping into her and her sickness leaking into me.

As soon as the driver climbed over the seat and started the van, I jerked my hand free. The woman raised her head and looked at me. I understood now why she had grabbed my wrist. She didn't want to feel alone. That's why her husband had joined our hands together.

What would it cost me, really?

I placed my hand on hers, palm to palm so I wouldn't touch the bulging veins. Our fingers interlocked. Her hand began to shake, and she squeezed so tightly my knuckles hurt. I grimaced, counting the seconds, as I did when my dentist drilled a tooth. One minute passed, two. Her spasms lessened, though her hand still trembled. I could do her this favor, and I'd be making points with her husband.

The van roared through the fog, its headlight useless at such a high speed. If it plowed into a stalled car it wouldn't leave skid marks. We hit a dip in the road. My stomach fell, as if I were riding the old lurching elevator in Drumheller's hardware store. It was a pleasant sensation except for a hint of nausea.

The woman sighed, and her hand stopped quivering. Maybe I was healing her, like Christ.

I realized with a shock that I felt at peace.

The last time I could recall feeling this peaceful was five years ago when I'd driven my family home from Seattle. As usual, the trip had started badly. I'd argued with Sue over the menu in Issaquah. She wanted to order full dinners for the kids instead of hamburgers. As we neared Pasco, an orange moon rose over the Horse Heaven Hills. The kids were tangled in the back seat, asleep. Sue snored beside me, her head resting against my shoulder as if we were still dating. I steered with my left hand all the way to Pasco. When I stopped for gas my right arm was numb, and I'd flexed my fingers to get the blood moving.

The woman groaned and arched her back. She jerked her hand free. The driver turned, and I saw his anxious eyes.

What should I do? I felt lost, as if I were seven again, slouched against the wall of Grandpa's hospital room, watching the adults for clues about how I should act. Grandma sat quietly in the only chair. Daddy and Uncle Jacob stood at the foot of the bed, talking to each other about the price of hogs and what to do if they didn't get enough rain to seed the fall wheat. Both men wore striped bib overalls with huge pockets in front that sagged under the weight of checkbooks, wrenches, measuring tapes. Why were they talking about farm stuff when their father was so sick? I felt superior to

175

both men. I alone had been thinking about Grandpa, praying even.

As I watched the woman squirm, I realized that my father and uncle had been doing the right thing. What my grandpa needed to hear were their calm voices talking about when to seed.

Maybe talking would soothe her. She couldn't understand English, so I could say whatever popped into my head. "Humpty Dumpty sat on a wall. The quick brown fox jumped over the lazy..." I couldn't remember the rest. "One potato, two potato, three potato, four."

She moaned louder, shaking her head. She must have guessed my words were meaningless.

"All right, I was being a phony. I've been a phony as long as I can remember, since I started selling. Every word you say has to be programmed to influence the prospect, every facial expression. You forget who you are. I don't think I was a phony when I was growing up. Yes I was. There was that time I conspired with this kid, a kid nobody liked. I didn't like him either. We were going to steal a watermelon from our patch. Yeah, right there in front of our house. It was my idea. So this kid—I can't remember his name—he went out there and got a watermelon and started running away. I yelled, 'He's stealing a watermelon!' My father came out of the shop and hollered, 'Put that down!' The kid dropped the melon and kept running. I don't know why I did that. Maybe to make my father proud of me."

The woman stopped moaning and looked at me. The pressure on my knuckles eased. This seemed to be working.

"I miss my kids. Every time I came home from a trip, I brought Daniel one of those little metal cars. We'd play on the floor for hours. I miss playing soccer in the hallway with Jennifer, kicking a tennis ball, and I miss playing gin rummy with Karen. I wasn't home much because I only got paid by commission. That's why I played poker when I wasn't selling. I had to pay the rent. You see that, don't you?"

She squeezed my hand as if she understood what I was saying,

176

as if she wanted to comfort me. Something broke loose inside me.

"Sue and me, things have been bad for a long time. Whatever money I gave her, gone the next day. She phones from California, collect. We're out of money, your kids are starving. And they're right in the room listening. I do send her money, a lot more than the court–God, I can't stand the thought of them listening. This one time years ago, we were driving away from my folks' place and Sue started picking at me. Daniel was on the front seat between us. He couldn't have been very old because he was standing up. Sue and I were going back and forth, and Daniel put one arm around each of our necks, hugging us."

I started sobbing and couldn't stop.

The woman rolled onto her side, facing me, and placed her left hand on top of mine, clamping my hand in both of hers.

I choked off a sob, felt it building up inside.

The driver peered back at us. I tried to get inside his head, as if he were a sales prospect.

His wife's in this awful pain, this hitchhiker's holding her hand and he starts crying–the driver has to recognize those sounds. So what does he think? That I feel so bad about his wife that I'm crying for her. Maybe that's what I was doing. I'd been talking about myself, sure, but I was trying to distract her, take her mind off the pain. I'd got wrought up, feeling so much empathy for her. I exhaled slowly, hearing my breath hiss through my lips.

Mark the altruist. I tried to laugh, but it came out a snarl. Who was I kidding? I had no empathy for the woman. I cared only about myself. Had I ever cared about Sue? I'd never tried to see things from her point of view. A husband who got home late every night, never asked how her day had gone, never talked to her at all, really. Maybe our arguments were the only way she could get me to talk.

For the first time it occurred to me that maybe the kids weren't in the room when Sue phoned from California. At home she used to close the kids' doors before she ripped into me. I'd got it wrong. She didn't want them to think I was a bad father. Maybe we could get back together, be a family again.

The woman shuddered. I gripped her hand and felt her spasm course through my body, the way I'd felt Jennifer's pain when she fell off her tricycle and cut her lip. With each spasm I gritted my teeth.

The van slowed and swung left. We'd reached the highway.

A fuzzy neon sign appeared above a truck stop. The outskirts of Pendleton. Through the windshield I saw a "Vacancy" sign, the blurry outline of a motel's roof. The fog must be lifting.

We ran a red traffic light, then another. Horns blared. We turned onto a side street and climbed a hill, the engine chugging. The driver rounded a corner too fast and the van swayed, barely missing a car parked on the opposite curb.

I saw house lights on the far side of the canyon that split the city of Pendleton. We'd risen above the fog.

The van passed under floodlights in the hospital's parking lot and stopped below a red "Emergency" sign. The driver got out of the van, leaving the motor running.

"Just a few minutes longer," I said. "They'll give you something for the pain."

The back door grated open. I loosened my hand from the woman's grip. I saw some quarters on the van's floor that must have fallen out of my pockets.

The bearded man reached under the woman to lift her. She shook her head, telling him something. He laid her back down.

She turned and groped the floor on the side away from me. Then she rolled over and reached out her hand. She held what was left of the packet of tiny life preservers, its paper peeled almost all the way down, exposing a green candy. I took the package and dropped it into my coat pocket.

Somehow the driver got her out of the van without bumping her head. He carried her through a sliding glass door. I stood outside the door, watching my reflection blend with the man's back and the woman's drooping legs as they moved down a corridor.

The van's engine was still rumbling. I climbed into the driver's seat and shut off the ignition, then reached in back to get my plastic bag. I hopped onto the pavement.

The palm of my right hand felt sticky. I took the candy pack out of my pocket and rubbed my thumb along the outside, feeling the indentations. Three pieces left. I split one off, placed it on my tongue, then folded the paper over the remaining candies and put the roll back in my pocket.

I tossed the garbage sack over my shoulder and began walking downhill to look for a motel. I let the candy melt between my tongue and the roof of my mouth, savoring the tart lime flavor.

Halfway down the hill I re-entered the fog, though I could still see hazy lights across the canyon. Coins bumped my thighs, reminding me of the quarters on the van's floor. Should I turn around and get them?

No, I decided. I'd come too far to go back.

When I reached my apartment the next afternoon, I wrote a letter of resignation to my sales manager. Then I put Blake's contract into an envelope along with my check to repay the down payment. I enclosed a note suggesting he talk to a counselor at the junior college in Pendleton.

I drove to Shep's and sat alone at the poker table, waiting for the night crew to arrive. At least I'd be making an honest living. The gamblers knew I wasn't there to help them succeed.

WEDNESDAY, JUNE 18, 1986

I shake my head to clear away the fog. Two piles of stationery lie on the table in front of me, the letters I've read and the ones I haven't. I reach for a page.

My Sweetie,

I'm so worried about Mark. He quit his correspondence school job six months ago and hasn't worked since. I've been praying he'll come to his senses and stay away from that wicked gambling den. Edward says Mark is lazy. I think he's just depressed. After all, he lost his family. Sue told me she didn't want to move so far away, but she couldn't keep going any longer without enough money. Her sister's husband is a doctor. They own a duplex, and they're letting Sue live there free.

Edward still hopes Mark will come back to the farm. I don't think he will. The pollen gives him hay fever. I sneeze until the rains come in September. My nose is always sore from wiping it. When I look in the mirror I'm reminded of Rudolph the Red-Nosed Reindeer.

I don't see how Mark could make a go of it even if he liked farming. Wheat prices stay low. Timothy and Luke are teaching in Seattle. Before Luke got married he came home every summer to help with harvest. We miss him so much. I always hoped we would travel when Edward retires, but I might be a hundred by then. He never wants to leave the farm.

If you were still alive, I know you could talk some sense into Mark. He adored you so. Whenever you left the room, he'd crawl after you. Never gave you a minute's peace. He expected you to play with him all the time. You were so patient with him. After you left us he would crawl all over the house looking for you. Then he would start crying. I would rock him, but he would keep twisting around, looking for you. He never took a nap after you left. He was cranky all the time. I made everyone promise never to talk about you. I thought he was too fragile to know the truth. He was only a year old when you passed, too young to remember you, but he kept having nightmares. For years he would wake up screaming.

Jacob had a breakdown after you died. I almost did, but somebody had to take care of Mark and do the housework. Sometimes Jacob would come over and we would talk for hours, remembering the happy times with you. Edward was just the opposite. I know he loved you, but he kept it all inside. I felt sorry for Bea, sitting alone in that big house night after night, but I was glad Jacob came over so often. Isn't that wicked of me?

I had to comfort Jacob like I comforted Mark, as if I had two children, one big and one small. I didn't mind. After you died, Jacob was lost. He was so happy playing with you. Whatever you wanted to play, he would go along with it, as if you were his big sister telling him what to do. Your favorite place was under the canopy. You would be a little tiger, and Jacob would be a monkey or crocodile, whatever you told him to be. You would both come into the house laughing. As often as not I had to sweep leaves and dried weeds off the floor.

181

Jacob would bring his books and read to you. He had an illustrated animal encyclopedia. You would point to a picture and say the name of the animal. By the time you were three you knew what a duck-billed platypus was.

I love you,
Mama

I put Mama's letter on top of the pile I've already read and go outside. The afternoon sun glows like a dim bulb behind ash-gray clouds. Teasing clouds, Daddy called them, promising rain that never falls. George Carney won't be fooled. He'll be out in the fields irrigating.

He saw Mama and Uncle Jacob holding hands on the riverbank. That was the last thing I heard him say before his next words were drowned out by a passing truck.

Something nags at me. Did he say "I saw your mother and uncle holding hands"? No, he said, "They were holding hands." He didn't say who.

The woman in the cloakroom had asked, "Why would Jacob do such a thing?" George's mother had replied, "So she couldn't tell." Her answer doesn't make sense if George saw Mama and Uncle Jacob. Maybe George saw someone else holding hands with Uncle Jacob.

Peggy Foster!

"She had to leave before she started showing." That's what Mrs. Foster told Mama after Peggy went to her aunt's. When I overheard her, I had no idea what she meant, but now I'm fifty-four years old.

In the old days, a girl often went to live with a faraway relative until the baby was born and arrangements were made for its adoption. I remember the day Peggy found us hiding in the water tank. She seemed distressed afterward, talking to Uncle Jacob. She was crying, and he hugged her. A few days later he dropped her off at the depot and gave her money.

Uncle Jacob was the baby's father!

If word got out that he fathered Peggy's baby, his reputation would be ruined along with hers. Maybe having sex with a sixteen-year-old was a crime back then, as it is now. He talked Peggy into going to her aunt's. *So she couldn't tell.* That's what George's mother meant in the church cloakroom.

Maybe Burke Foster made Peggy confess who got her pregnant. Now he had a real motive for killing Uncle Jacob.

As I open the Carneys' gate, sprinklers come on in the far field. I spot George leaving the river forest. We meet halfway and stroll toward his house.

He takes a blue bandana out of his hip pocket and wipes his face. "Moving sprinklers is a heck of a lot tougher than it was twenty years ago."

"Yesterday a semi drowned out something you said. The last thing I heard was that you saw them holding hands. I assumed you meant my uncle and my mother."

He looks at me quizzically. "It wasn't them."

Relief floods through me. Mama didn't have an affair with Uncle Jacob after all. "You saw my uncle and Peggy Foster, didn't you?"

"No, he was holding the little girl's hand. Your sister."

"You couldn't have. Anna died years before."

George looks bewildered. "Years before what?"

"Before I heard your mother talking in the cloakroom."

"When did you hear her?"

"I was ten. It must have been 1941."

"This happened a long time before that. I was a high school sophomore." George rubs his chin, leaving a spot of mud, like a miniature goatee. "I saw them the day the little girl disappeared. I didn't know she'd gone missing till they found her. That was three days later."

I hear a hum, as if I were standing under a high power line. But the wire above us only goes to the Carneys' river pump and wouldn't carry much electricity.

George is still talking. "My mother and I didn't know whether to tell the police. She told some of her friends at church, and they asked us to keep quiet. They said it would be a terrible scandal for the church. Some of the women shunned Jacob, and he must have got the message. He quit going to church."

I feel like I'm in a horror movie. I'm Anna, safe in the arms of my beloved uncle. He walks toward the riverbank, telling me how much he loves me. Then he flings me into the swift current. I scream, thrash my arms and legs, choke as water pours into my lungs, sink...

I'm brushing gooey stuff off my shirt. My hands are sticky. Throw-up clogs my throat. I bend over, and the rest comes out.

I feel a hand on my shoulder and hear George's voice. "You can wash up at the house. I'll get you a clean shirt."

We walk along the fence line. "Mom and I kept hoping it was an accident," George says. "Jacob didn't want to get blamed, so he lied. Said he hadn't seen her."

An accident? I try to put myself in Uncle Jacob's shoes. He sees Anna playing outside our house and takes her to the river without telling Mama. As they walk along the bank he gets distracted by something. He hears a splash and runs to the river. When he reaches the bank he can't see Anna, and the water is swift. He follows the shoreline downstream, calling her name. He searches along the bank. Then he runs to our house, finds Mama and Aunt Bea, and—here my reconstruction of events breaks down. I can't imagine Uncle Jacob pretending to look for her in the outbuildings, wasting precious time instead of rushing back to the river.

The alternative is even more unbelievable. Uncle Jacob grooming an innocent child, molesting her, killing her. *So she couldn't tell.*

But psychopaths don't feel remorse. Uncle Jacob had a nervous breakdown after Anna died. He lost fifty pounds and walked the hills at night. Years later in his office he told me, "I want another chance." Those were the actions of a man overwhelmed by guilt, not a psychopathic killer.

The hum gets louder.

Now I'm inside Daddy's head. He's sitting in the back pew, under that open space between the top of the cloakroom wall and the ceiling. He hears women talking in the cloakroom. He follows Mrs. Carney out of the church to question her. She tells him what George saw nine years earlier. For two days he broods—not because Mama wasted money for presents, but because his brother murdered his young daughter. The day after Christmas Uncle Jacob asks him to help get the pump out of the river. He brings along an axe...

The cuffs on the shirt George loans me cover my knuckles. When I leave their bathroom Rose takes my dirty shirt out of my hand. "I'll wash it," she says.

I thank her and head for the door, but she says, "Wait a minute," and goes into their kitchen. She comes out and hands me a paper shopping bag. "Leftovers," she says.

I put the bag in Mama's refrigerator and switch on the television set. Voices are too low for me to understand, but I don't turn up the sound. White noise is what I need.

Years passed in a blur of cards, thirty poker hands an hour, three hundred a day, ninety thousand a year. I became as interesting a conversationalist as the other gamblers: "What's the bet?"... "Get a new deck"... "I raise"... "Beats me." On good days I basked behind towering stacks of chips, marveling at my skill. On days my billfold got a workout, I shook my fist at the ceiling and cussed out God.

My income dropped the year the burly man went to prison for killing his wife, but rose the following year as neophyte gamblers learned to cash their Friday paychecks at Shep's. I celebrated Good Friday every week, as long as I avoided the eyes of the silent women who waited in the doorway.

Over time, I picked up giveaways from most of the regulars. Chi bet right away if he held trash cards but hesitated a few seconds if he had a winner. Playing no-limit, I folded if Doyle bet less than half the size of the pot and called if he bet more than half. If the Bogger's hand shook when he bet, I called. If Barney's hand shook, I folded.

But the trouble with poker was that the better I got, the less I was liked, and ultimately the less I liked myself.

I'd had one date since my divorce, with a woman who worked at the Bee Hive department store. One day as I chatted with her at the cash register, I noticed she wore no wedding ring. That night I stood for twenty minutes inside a phone booth, my hands sweating, as I tried to work up the nerve to call her. When she answered I forgot the script I'd rehearsed but managed to stammer out my name and why I was calling.

During dinner at the Steakout, she told me about her five children and her former husband, who had beaten her every time he got drunk. The last time, after she'd spent two days in the hospital, she'd filed for divorce. He was now serving a prison sentence.

"My kids and I visit him every week," she said.

I'd been drinking from my glass, and water must have gone down my windpipe. After I stopped spluttering, I wiped my chin with a napkin. "You visit the man who broke your arm? With your children?"

"He's their father." She looked at a table across the room. "See that man with the snake tattoo on his neck? He just got out of prison."

"You know him?"

She shuddered. "No, I'd never go near him. My friend said his ex-wife still walks with a limp."

A band was tuning up in the adjoining room. As I paid the

186

cashier, Ruby said she wanted to go dancing. I said okay, although I'd rather get a tooth yanked without an anesthetic.

Sitting people ringed the empty dance floor. The band started playing something so frenetic I guessed they must be strung out on amphetamines. Ruby tugged my hand.

"No," I said, horrified. Everyone else was still seated, and I hadn't danced for twenty years. "Let's wait for a slow song."

"This is a slow song." She pulled me onto the dance floor. Caring for five kids had given her the strength of a wrestler. I felt like I was having one of my typical nightmares, finding myself naked on a downtown sidewalk. I reached to put my arm across her shoulders, but she stepped away and began waving her arms and undulating.

"Come on," she said.

"What do I do?" I said, aware that everyone in the place was looking at us.

"Whatever you want."

What I wanted was to cover my head with my sweater and slink out the back door. I tried to mimic what she was doing, sticking out my arms and lifting my legs. I felt like a wound-up toy soldier.

"Loosen up," Ruby said.

Yeah, don't show fear when a grizzly attacks you.

A few people left their seats, relieved that they wouldn't be the worst dancers on the floor. When the music stopped I said, "Let's sit down," but Ruby took my hand in her superwoman grip. Unwilling to lose a tug-of-war in front of a hundred people, I stayed for the next dance, and the next. I felt as robotic as before, but now others were gyrating around me, oblivious to everyone else, including their partners. This was better than the waltzes I once endured. I could stay in one place without apologizing every few seconds for stepping on someone's toes.

On the drive from the dance hall to her trailer, we made a date for the following Saturday. I wanted to make it a weeknight because the poker games stoked up on weekends, but Ruby had to cook and clean after she got off work.

Saturday night she answered my knock and clapped her hand over her mouth. "I forgot about our date," she said. "I'm so sorry. I'm going with someone."

Behind her, sitting on a sofa, was the man with a snake tattoo on his neck.

On a breezy Sunday morning when I was forty-eight, I stood on the sidewalk outside Shep's, counting my bankroll and wishing I'd quit at midnight. Far away a church bell began ringing, two peals close together, like the supper bell Mama used to ring when I'd wander too long in the hills. Suddenly I got the urge to hear her play again. I looked at my watch. Not enough time to go back to my apartment and shave before heading north.

I drove to the farm between hills of yellowing wheat that billowed in the wind as though crop dusters were skimming the slopes ahead of me. When I turned into the lane, Daddy was hosing off his pickup's windshield, standing well back so mud wouldn't splatter his suit.

"I didn't think to wash the car before Lola left for Sunday school," he said.

After nodding to people I vaguely recognized, I settled into the back pew alongside Daddy.

Strange sounds jangled up from the basement, jerky and halting. I adjusted my hearing aids until I recognized "Amazing Grace." Was one of Mama's pupils playing the piano? For the next five minutes I watched the door behind the pulpit, where Mama would emerge on her way to the organ.

The heavy front door creaked, and the foyer doors blew open. Wind ruffled the hair of people alongside the aisle. Mama stood in the foyer doorway. She walked up the aisle, but instead of going to the organ, she lay down in the front pew. Jeannie sat on the organ's bench and began to play the prelude.

When the prelude was over, a woman with graying blond hair stepped across the aisle and helped Mama stand up. She slid onto the bench beside us and gave me a hug. Then she leaned across me and hugged Daddy, probably feeling as if she were hugging mannequins. Daddy and I looked straight ahead with poker faces.

"Why aren't you playing?" I whispered.

"My arthritis got too bad. Anyway, Jeannie's been waiting long enough."

"She could have waited a few more years. She's barely fifty."

During the sermon I analyzed a hand I'd misplayed last night. I'd hit a small diamond flush on the last card, but there was a bet and a raise ahead of me. Thinking the raiser must have a bigger flush than mine, I threw away my cards. Both men showed down straights. Instead of saving two dollars by folding, I'd lost a thirty-dollar pot. Dimly aware of the minister's drone, I shook my head, mad at myself for throwing away the best hand.

The minister raised his voice, "We reach several crossroads in life." He was looking at me. Had he seen me shake my head? Did he think I was disagreeing with him?

"At each crossroad we have a choice," he said. "We can take the high road or we can take the low road. We can help people or hurt people."

I could feel my cheeks burning. The whole congregation knew where I was sitting. He might as well have named me.

"For our closing hymn, turn to page one sixty-three," he said.

Mama handed me a hymnbook, but I pushed it away. I heard the congregation sing, "There were ninety and nine who safely lay in the shelter of the fold, but one was out on the hills away..."

When we joined the traffic jam in the aisle, Mrs. Morgan said to Mama, "Looks like our prayers have been answered."

I hurried out the door, ignoring the minister's outstretched hand, and arrived at the ranch ahead of my parents.

"What did Mrs. Morgan mean, our prayers have been answered?" I asked Mama the moment she walked in the door.

She took off her hat and scarf. "The congregation's been praying for you."

I wanted to flee and slam the door behind me, but I was hungry for fried chicken. "Why did you lie down on the pew?"

"Climbing the basement stairs gives me back spasms."

I suspected she was grateful for the crushed discs in her spine. Her osteoporosis and her worthless son gave her two excuses to play the martyr's role.

"Are you taking care of yourself?" she said. "You don't look well."

No wonder. I hadn't shaved, hadn't slept for two days, and hadn't seen the sun except when I walked to my car.

While I was setting the table, Mama got a back spasm shelling peas in the kitchen. She swallowed a dose of her pain cocktail and fried the chicken. Ignoring my protests, she deposited both halves of the breast on my plate. I chewed a bite. It didn't taste as good as her home-raised chickens did forty years ago.

"Did you say hello to Donna?" she said.

"Donna was at the church?" The last time I'd seen her, a few years after she married Archie, she was coming out of Montgomery Ward's, carrying a baby and holding the hand of a little boy. They were going to the Shady Lawn Creamery to get ice cream cones, she'd told me, her head bobbing because the boy was tugging her hand.

"She'll be leaving soon to take care of her mother," Mama said. "Hilda has cancer."

"Leaving for where?"

"Eastern Montana. Her father bought a farm there."

"Ten inches of rainfall a year," Daddy said. "Don't know how Weaver makes it pay."

Because he's a better farmer than you.

"What about Archie?" I said.

190

"That man!" Mama said. "He left Donna for another woman."

I stopped chewing.

Daddy took a small pill out of a medicine bottle and placed it under his tongue.

"Angina," Mama said. "His arrhythmia spells are coming more often, too."

He talked about his new hired man. "Best worker I've had in years."

Ten bucks says you'll fire him before harvest.

He picked up a bowl of Mama's canned apricots, put two halves on his plate, and held out the bowl to me. He'd been trying to get me to eat apricots since I was a kid.

"No, thanks," I said.

"They're mighty good."

I shook my head.

He regretfully put down the bowl. "You got any plans?" he said, always the optimist.

Yeah, tomorrow at noon I'll show up at Shep's and gamble till midnight.

They waited for me to answer, their wrinkled faces full of hope. If I said no, they would know what I already knew, that I would play poker the rest of my life.

"I'm going back to college," I heard myself say.

Instead of going home to my apartment, I drove to the Eureka Flats, a low-rainfall area northwest of Whetstone, where Archie's family owned a farm. I could have asked my parents for directions–Daddy knew where every farmer lived, and Mama kept in touch with Donna–but I didn't want them to know I was interested.

When I'd told them I was going back to college, Mama had hugged me. Daddy had asked a bunch of questions I couldn't answer. No way could I be honest: it just popped out because I'm rum-dum from playing poker for twenty hours. I imagined next Sunday's church service, Mama divulging my plans during announcements, the ladies hugging her in the aisle after the Benediction. Before Sunday I would phone Mama and tell her my plans had fallen through.

I passed a pile of rubble. According to the rumor I'd heard in high school, Archie and two other senior boys had dynamited an abandoned house. At a crossroad I took the road with the most gravel. I passed an ancient house with a gaping hole in its roof. Its windows were broken.

A vegetable garden grew behind the next house, its lush green a startling contrast to the pale field of wheat stubble that surrounded the house. A woman wearing a wide-brimmed straw hat was pulling up weeds in the garden. I parked in front by a windmill that was missing several blades.

The woman had her back to me and didn't hear me approach. She bent low, grunted, and pulled up a mass of green foliage. Lettuce, not weeds. Between us, several rows of vegetation lay strewn on the ground. I recognized radishes, spinach, and young cornstalks.

The woman pulled up another armful of lettuce and threw it away. She saw me and straightened. Her chest was heaving.

"Mark," she said in a strangled voice. She wiped the back of her hand across her forehead, leaving a smudge of dirt above her left eyebrow. Then she smiled, the creases alongside her cheeks turned into dimples, and I saw the girl who once told me to look for eggs in a tree crotch ten feet above ground.

She surveyed the wreckage around her. "This might take some explaining. Come inside."

I followed her to the back door and through the kitchen. In the living room, cardboard boxes were stacked in front of half-empty bookcases. I could see books inside a couple of open boxes.

She gestured toward an easy chair. "Give me a minute." She went into a hallway, and I heard the sound of splashing water. I examined the books that remained on the shelves. There were cookbooks, classics–Austen, Hawthorne, Stevenson, Poe–a dozen mysteries by Agatha Christie. All the books were worn, and some had taped spines.

When she came back, her face was clean. "Would you like something to drink? Tea? Water? I can't offer you beer. I poured it all down the drain."

"Nothing, thanks."

"I'm thirsty." She went into the kitchen and came back with two glasses of water. She handed me one, rearranged a doily on the arm of a sofa, and sat down. "I've got running water now, not like the last time you visited my house."

"I've never been here before."

"The house on your farm. This house wasn't much different when we moved in. It took six years for the power lines to reach us."

"How did you manage?"

"What I wanted most was a phone. I'd be stuck here for days with no car, no way to get help if my kids got hurt."

"Where was Archie?"

"His father owns property across the Oregon border." She drained her water glass.

I handed her my glass. "I'm not thirsty."

She took a drink and set the glass on a coffee table. "About the garden. Archie and his girlfriend will be moving in next week."

"My mother told me he left you."

"It's not much different than before. Most nights he went to the Tux or the Elks'. Life here gets pretty dull if you're not a reader."

The Tuxedo was Whetstone's bar, and the Elks' Club in Walla Walla had a poker game I'd coveted since I started gambling. I'd applied for membership but got blackballed, probably by a poker pro who didn't want competition.

"Luckily, Julie and Tom loved to read." She nodded toward the boxes. "I've been packing. I have to be out of the house by the first."

"I hope you'll come out okay in the settlement," I said.

"I'll get nothing."

"What about community property?"

"You're looking at it." She swept her hand around the room, at the worn furniture and the boxes. "Archie's father owns the house and the farm. That's fine with me. I just want to be rid of him."

She took the two empty water glasses into the kitchen and came back with a full glass. "I saw you in church today."

"I hear the congregation's been praying for me. I wonder who instigated that?"

"Your mother's worried about you. She's afraid if you don't come back to the church, you won't go to heaven."

"What do you think?"

She considered the question, her face serious. "I don't think whether we go to church matters, but how we live does matter."

She looked steadily into my eyes, and I got the feeling she knew something about me I didn't know.

I took a deep breath and blurted, "Is there any chance we might get together? After your divorce is final?"

She looked down at the coffee table. Seconds ticked by. The longer she waited, the worse I felt. Hesitation by an ACI prospect foretold disaster.

"I'm afraid not," she said.

Mark, no woman will ever be attracted to you.

She met my gaze again. "I was married for thirty years to one unhappy man. I don't want to spend the rest of my life with another."

"I'm not unhappy. Where did you hear that?"

"Your mother says you've been unhappy all your adult life."

I married the wrong woman. I'd be happy if I'd married you.

"It's no wonder," Donna said, "the life you've led."

"Yeah, it was pretty tough. My wife would–"

"I don't mean your marriage."

"Huh?"

194

"You make your living playing poker. Have you ever known a happy gambler?"

The winners, I wanted to say. But that wasn't true. I'd never seen Mack smile, although he'd laughed once in a while, sarcastically. Chi and Doyle acted morose at the card table. So did I, for self-protection. Looking gleeful when you win a pot inflames a sore loser. Had my glum façade carried over outside the card room? Did acting sad eventually make you sad? I remembered feeling joyful as a kid, pretending I was Frank Buck capturing wild animals in the jungle, watching westerns at the Roxy Theatre with Luke, bouncing a tennis ball against the side of our house. Everything I did was fun back then.

"Archie played poker at the Elk's." She bit her lower lip. "I know what it's like to be married to a compulsive gambler."

"I'm not a compulsive gambler."

"Sure you are."

Don't get defensive. A lot of people make that mistake. "I've always won at poker. Compulsive gamblers lose."

"Who says?"

"A compulsive gambler needs to be involved in the action. He plays too many pots, so he's bound to lose in the long run. He wins just often enough to keep him coming back."

"Why do you keep coming back? If you're not addicted, why do you keep playing poker?"

"For the money."

"Are you telling me you don't get a thrill out of winning?"

"Okay, yeah, I do get a kick out of building a big stack of chips, but–"

"I could always tell when Archie was getting ready to go to the Elk's. He'd get this glint in his eye, and the pulse in his neck would beat faster."

My shoulder hitched up and down. Donna would be a tough poker opponent. "What else did my mother say about me?"

"You've got quieter, like you're not in the same room with

195

her."

How could I explain that a pro has to rehash the hands he misplayed so he won't make the same mistake next time?

"Years ago I thought there might be a chance for us," she said.

"When?"

"That afternoon at the fair. I enjoyed your company."

"I'm still the same person."

"No you're not." She frowned and looked out the window. "That's unfair of me. I've changed, too. Maybe I've got bitter." She waved toward the garden in back. "As you saw, I'm not exactly a pinup model for joy."

"I almost asked you to go to the rodeo," I said.

"Why didn't you?"

"I couldn't work up the nerve. I knew you'd say no."

"Why did you think that?"

"My teeth. My acne."

She flipped the fingers of her right hand, as if she were brushing away a fly. "Don't be silly. I understand, though. At that age everyone's insecure." She touched my wrist, and I felt a snap of electricity. She yanked her hand back.

"My mother likes to badmouth me," I said. "Why take her word that I've been unhappy?"

"I can tell. The corners of your mouth droop down. You've got a permanently sad face, like Emmett Kelly the circus clown."

Just as well let it all spill out. "When I was selling in the Wallowas, sometimes I'd pull off the road and climb a mountain trail. I'd pretend you were with me, naming the wildflowers." I stood up. "I'd better let you get back to your gardening."

She laughed. "I'm not in the mood anymore. Let's go for a walk, for old times' sake."

We meandered among sparse wheat stalks. "The view is different from our last walk," Donna said. Except for the house behind us, all I could see were alternating hills of ripening wheat and gray stubble. The hills sloped so gently they could hardly be called hills.

Still feeling reckless, I said, "The first time we walked to the river, you said you'd enjoy living there. Remember my telling you how my parents walked to the river under a canopy of trees?"

Without turning my head I saw her nod.

"I remember thinking I'd replant the canopy, and someday we would walk under it to the river."

A gust of wind blew dust in our faces. I sneezed.

She wiped a cheek with her finger, leaving a streak of dust and moisture. "Did you ever learn how your uncle died?"

"No. I thought we were going to solve that mystery together." I recalled the set of Agatha Christie mysteries I'd seen at her house. "You'd be Miss Marple and I'd be Hercule Poirot."

She giggled, the sound I'd heard in my dreams since the day I met her. "I wish I hadn't told you I suspected your father. That got Papa fired."

"No, it didn't. I never told my father what you said."

She stopped and turned toward me, her eyes wide. "But you acted so different the next time I saw you. You hardly said a word, and you wouldn't look me in the eye."

"I was ashamed of my buck teeth."

"Oh, for goodness sake!" She resumed walking, faster than before, as if she were disgusted with me.

"He was wrong to fire your father."

"Your papa is a good man. He bought a refrigerator for the house, and he gave it to us when we moved. I think he felt guilty."

The wind picked up, howling in my right ear, making it hard for me to hear. Dust obscured her house. We walked back in silence, except for my sneezes. When we reached my car, she kissed me on the cheek.

The cheek was still tingling as I drove away. I adjusted the rearview mirror but didn't see Donna. Instead I saw the gaunt face of a gambler who hadn't slept for thirty-six hours. My hair was matted, and stubble had sprouted on my chin and jaws. I probably

197

stank of cigarette smoke. Donna would be smart to fumigate her house.

I'd told my parents I was going to college. Could I somehow pull it off? Maybe I could attend classes during the day and play poker at night, when the games were more lucrative.

Monday morning I sat across the desk from a Walla Walla College counselor. He looked at my resume. "I see you worked for sixteen years as a correspondence school representative. Salary or commission?"

"Salary. My job was to determine whether the applicant was qualified."

"What have you been doing since?"

"Working on our family farm." I hid my hands under the table.

"What are you good at?"

Manipulating people. "Talking to people," I said.

THURSDAY, JUNE 19, 1986

I stare at the murmuring figures on the television screen. It's light
outside, so I must have sat here all night. I couldn't have slept. I feel
exhausted. I go into the kitchen and see the two stacks of
stationery. The small stack only has a few pages. One more letter.

My Darling,

It's been two years since you left us. When memories
come I've got to write them down while they're fresh in
my mind. There won't be any future memories, and I
don't want to forget a single thing about you.

Sometimes I'll be working in the kitchen and I'll feel
you tug my hand, pull me toward the living room. I hear
your voice, "Come on, Mama, don't you want to have
fun?"

I remember how you kissed me when you were only a
few months old. You would open your mouth wide and
get the tip of my nose as well as my mouth. I saw you kiss
Jacob once when he was spooning applesauce into your
mouth. He looked so funny with applesauce on the tip of
his nose. He didn't understand what you were doing until I
told him.

We went to the circus last week. Two years ago I

promised you we would go to the circus in August, but you died in April. I tried to get Mark to feed peanuts to the elephant, but he would jerk back his hand. I think he was afraid the elephant would grab him and stick him into its mouth. For a second I imagined you there instead of Mark, giggling when the trunk tickled the palm of your hand. I must have said something because Mark asked who I was talking to.

I remember all the times you played on the floor with Uncle Wiggily's hollow stump bungalow. At first it was just you and Jacob until Mark got old enough. Mark bent some of the cardboard characters when he pushed them through the bungalow's door. I'm still not sure how you two managed to lose Jackie Bow-Wow. I shouldn't have let you take the bungalow outside.

Before Mark was born we would cross the highway to pick asparagus. First we would go up the canyon to your meadow. On the way you would stuff weeds down squirrel holes for their breakfast. Sometimes you would find a rock along the way and give it to me to carry. I would put it in my pocket, and you would forget all about it. I keep those five rocks in my purse. Whenever I dig into it to get my checkbook I feel the rocks and think of you. They get mighty heavy, I can tell you.

When I hear the train's whistle I instinctively think I've got to hurry and carry Anna to the front porch. Before you could walk you would hear the train toot and get excited and crawl toward the front door. I would hold you on the porch and we would wave at the engineer. He always waved at us. When you got old enough to walk, I sometimes didn't hear the whistle, but you would come into the kitchen and grab my hand.

I still go out on the porch and wave at the engineer. I ought to get word to him that you died. I don't want him to think you lost interest in his train.

I promised you we'd ride the train to Rogue River to visit my mother and sisters. You would have loved the scenery, the Columbia River Gorge, the Indians fishing for salmon at Celilo Falls. They stood on rickety wooden platforms way out over the falls, holding long poles with nets on the ends.

I remember the first time I took the train to Whetstone. I had to change trains in Portland, and I'd never seen a station that big. They had a huge blackboard with arrival and departure times written in chalk. To make sure nobody missed a train, a Negro porter walked among the benches calling, "Train time, train time." He had such a sweet tenor voice. I wished we had him in our church choir in Rogue River when Father was the minister. Some people in the congregation might have complained, but Father would have quoted a Bible verse about Jesus accepting everyone.

I know the instant you died you came alive in God's hands. I imagine you looking down at me from heaven, saying, "I'm okay," and wishing I could hear you. I remember the time you fell off the sawhorse. I ran to you, and even though your nose was bleeding you said, "I'm okay," because you didn't want me to worry. Then you started crying.

I know you're alive and happy, and yet I don't know it for sure. Jacob believes there's no life after death. He thinks that even if there was a God, He wouldn't be able to resurrect us. He says we'll always have our memories of you, but he knows that's not enough.

When we're reunited we'll pick up where we left off. We'll take the train to Portland and go to the zoo. You'll see real tigers and orangutans and giraffes, all the animals you saw in Jacob's picture book. You'll name them all correctly, even the duckbilled platypus, if they have one. We'll waddle like the penguins, and you'll laugh your head off.

We'll pick blackberries along the Rogue River with my sisters. We'll go to the beach. I can already hear you laugh as a wave splashes up to your waist. We'll play tennis together. I know you'll beat me because of my arthritis. I'll sing "Oh Promise Me" at your wedding. I'll play on the floor with your children, and I won't complain if they prefer to play with Jacob. Well, maybe I'll complain a little bit. I used to feel so jealous, watching Jacob play with you while I had to fix meals and do the washing.

Of course I don't know for sure what heaven will be like. But I know God loves us, and if He can create this beautiful world He can somehow find a way to resurrect us.

I think the reason Jacob had his nervous breakdown was because he didn't think he would ever see you again. I so wish he could get his faith back. He's finally starting to gain some weight. Bea has been worried sick about him.

Edward talks to me again at mealtimes. He can't yet talk about you, though. Jacob can't stop talking about you. It's good for both Jacob and me, I think, to talk about the good times we had with you, but it makes me sad at the same time.

The summer after I married Edward, I was supposed to help Bea in the cook shack during harvest, but I got pregnant with you and couldn't. Then the next summer you were too little to take into the hills, where the cook had to spend three weeks working in that terrible heat. You were two years old the year we switched from stationary threshers to the horse and mule team that pulls our combine. That same year we lost our lease on the Davis property. We didn't need the cook shack after that.

My goodness, I didn't realize it was so late. I've got to start supper.

Goodbye for now,
Mama

I tore up the rejection letter from the Yakima mental health agency, shredding it as efficiently as a machine. Maybe I could get a job with the Central Intelligence Agency as a shredder, since nobody wanted to hire me as a counselor. For seven months I'd been applying for jobs, sending my resume, copies of my college transcripts, letters of reference from my teachers. Fifteen interviews, no job offers.

"You'll have no trouble finding a job with a master's degree in psychology." That's what the college counselor had promised me before I enrolled.

"But I'll be fifty-three when I graduate."

"No problem. It's illegal to discriminate because of age."

And that's why every prospective employer had been so eager to interview me and so reluctant to hire me. They didn't want to get sued, but they wanted even less to hire a gray-haired rookie with a hearing problem.

Five years wasted. Five years of daytime classes, evening poker marathons, four hours sleep a night. No wonder the classroom chairs on either side of me were vacant. To twenty-year-olds I must have resembled the Ancient Mariner, skinny as a skeleton, bags under my eyes, hair wild from waking up too late to shower. Maybe they could sense the albatross around my neck, my thirty-four years as a predator.

I brushed the shreds of the Yakima letter into my wastebasket and headed out the door. At Shep's poker room my bad hearing wouldn't matter. Cards speak for themselves.

On November fourth the ringing phone woke me up. The clock on my bed stand read 6:47.

"This is Doctor Kelly," a voice said. "Your father came in by ambulance half an hour ago. You'd better come down to the hospital."

He'd spent two days in the hospital last month, after another arrhythmia spell. He'd been lying peacefully in his hospital bed, talking to Mama and me. Suddenly he sat up, whooped, and clutched his chest. Doctors and nurses rushed into the room and shooed us out while a loudspeaker bellowed, "Room three-sixteen, stat! Room three-sixteen, stat!"

We'd waited on a hallway couch until Doctor Kelly told us, "He came through this bout okay, but sooner or later one's going to get him." When we'd gone back to Daddy's room, he'd grinned and said, "You came mighty close to having a funeral."

Mama lay on a sofa in the hospital's visiting room. Back spasms, she said, from riding in the ambulance. She told me his room number. "I'll go up in a few minutes."

I rushed up the stairs. At the nurses' station Dr. Kelly put down a chart and said, "I'd guess your father has two or three hours. He may have a brief lucid spell."

Daddy was unconscious, his eyes closed. A monitor alongside his bed emitted sporadic beeps. The blood pressure needle held steady at sixty. That was a positive sign, wasn't it?

"I'm here, Dad." I patted his hand. It seemed a silly thing to do, and "Dad" sounded contrived. Luke and Timothy and I had called the folks "Mama" and "Daddy" through our twenties. One day in a restaurant we'd noticed teenagers in another booth smirking at us. We'd switched to "Mom" and "Dad" before the waitress brought our banana splits.

I laid my hand on his. I couldn't recall touching him since he'd driven me to college when I was eighteen. He'd set a suitcase beside my dormitory bunk and shook my hand. I'd felt awkward, as he must have felt.

A fiftyish woman in a blue dress came into the room and took a chair by the foot of the bed. She sat still, smiling at the wall beyond the bed. Was it her job to make sure no one died alone? I'm here, I wanted to tell her, we don't need you. And what the devil are you smiling at?

Don't get irritated. Concentrate on Daddy.

He must have gone bald gradually, but I couldn't recall a time when he had hair. I remembered the many times he'd phoned, wanting to talk, this transparent man trying to communicate with his opaque son. He could have had livelier conversations with a corpse:

We got a little rain last night.

Good.

How are things going with ICA?

Okay.

Nixon's got himself into some trouble, hasn't he?

Yeah.

Think he'll get impeached?

Maybe.

This morning I was ready to talk.

He raised himself on his elbows and looked at me, eyes focused. He said something garbled in an urgent voice. He knew what he was telling me, but his mouth wouldn't work right.

"I can't understand," I said.

He spoke again. This time I caught a few words, "... Lola... take care..."

"I'll take care of Mom," I said, guessing.

He fell back on the pillow and closed his eyes.

Mama came into the room and sat by the bed alongside the smiling woman. She stroked Daddy's forehead. "He got out of bed last night," she said. "It was after midnight. He pulled the covers up to my chin."

The beeps stopped. The blood-pressure needle began to fall,

205

fifty, forty, thirty, twenty. When the needle reached zero, without moving a muscle I opened my arms and let him in.

Mama brushed his bald brow. "That cowlick never would stay down," she said.

The woman in the blue dress left the room without looking at us.

I caught up with her in the corridor. "Excuse me," I said. "My father sat up and said something to me, but I couldn't understand it." I tapped a hearing aid. "Did you hear what he said?"

"I think he said, 'Tell Lola I'll take care of her.'"

Did he mean he would become Mama's guardian angel? More likely, he meant he'd make it through this little setback and continue to take care of her—just as she had always taken care of him.

We stopped at Safeway to get groceries. I felt intensely aware of everything around me, the rumble of the street traffic, the misty November air, the heavy gray clouds. I smelled oil that had dripped onto the asphalt of the parking space next to ours. Things I'd never before noticed seemed meaningful, like the checkered tiles of Safeway's linoleum floor. Daddy would never see those things again.

In the parking lot I set the grocery sack on the hood and groped in my pocket for the keys.

Mama peered through the passenger window. "You left them in the ignition."

Phoning the locksmith was the hardest thing I'd done all morning. While Mama watched him work on the car door, I went inside and faked an interest in lettuce, hoping nobody would connect me to the van outside with "Locksmith" printed on its side.

Neither of us talked much on the drive to the farm. I carried the sack with Daddy's wallet and clothes into their bedroom. Mama opened a bureau drawer and took out a dress shirt and a tie.

"He hated wearing a tie to church," she said. "But he has to look respectable at the funeral."

I went outside. The gray clouds were so thick I couldn't tell where the sun was. I wandered through the new orchard Daddy and Luke had planted. A few red delicious apples still clung to the top branches.

In the recently-seeded field south of the orchard, tiny green shoots had already pushed through the topsoil. I looked east. A single shaft of sunlight had pierced the clouds, illuminating the little house and the locust trees around the burnt-out homestead where Daddy grew up.

I ran to the house. Mama was in the kitchen, opening a can of tuna fish. Knowing I couldn't say a word without choking up, I beckoned her to come outside. We watched the lit-up patch spread across the highway and move toward us until we were standing in sunlight.

Mama nodded as if she wasn't a bit surprised.

At noon we ate the tuna fish and egg sandwiches she'd fixed. She took a partly-full jar of her canned apricots out of the refrigerator, forked one onto her plate, and set the jar down. I picked it up and scooped out half an apricot.

Mama cocked her head at me. "You never eat apricots."

"Thought I'd try one," I said.

By the time Daddy died, osteoporosis had shrunk Mama so small she had to peer between spokes of the steering wheel, but she still drove ten miles an hour over the speed limit. Drivers glancing in their rearview mirrors must have felt the same shock Ichabod Crane felt when he looked back and saw the headless horseman gaining on him.

I phoned Mama every day. If she didn't answer, I imagined her lying on the floor with a broken hip. One Saturday afternoon I got no answer and cashed in my chips.

She was cutting tulip stems by the porch when I drove up. "I'll run these down to the church," she said. "Be back in a few minutes."

"I'll drive you," I said.

"Don't be silly."

I watched what appeared to be a driverless car turn from the lane onto the highway, its right rear wheel dipping at the edge of the culvert. I paced for half an hour before I dug out my car keys. When I rounded a bend and saw Whetstone's houses, the ditches along the highway empty of cars, I relaxed.

I swerved onto the gravel alongside Mama's car in front of the church. Church? I stared at the building, disoriented, like a militant atheist who'd come looking for a church to bomb and got the directions wrong. "First National Bank" was etched in granite above the glass door. I had a feeling that if I pressed my nose against the glass, I'd see a couple of farmers talking crops in front of a teller's window.

Why was I seeing a bank? This building had been a church since 1940, after our old church burned down. I'd watched Daddy slip dynamite sticks into cracks in the concrete when he'd blown up a basement vault that was designed to hold money instead of the beginners' Sunday school class.

As I got out of the car I thought I heard organ music. No other cars were parked near the church, which didn't make sense because Mama's arthritis had forced her to stop playing the organ long ago.

Were my hearing aids playing tricks on me again? I opened the big glass door and stepped into the foyer. Music seemed to come from everywhere in the church. Instead of the organ's strings and reeds, I could hear bees buzzing, water rippling, birds warbling, sounds I hadn't heard for years. I pushed open the foyer's swinging doors. Red and yellow tulips splayed from two vases at the foot of the pulpit. Because the organ faced the wall, Mama hadn't seen me come in. She was hunched over the keyboard, peering up at the sheet music, glasses teetering on the tip of her nose. She sat on the edge of the bench and pumped the pedals with her toes. A painting of the last supper hung on the wall behind the choir pews. Even from this distance I could make out Judas, leaning backward at the table staring at Jesus, his cup overturned, wondering if he'd given up too much for his thirty pieces of silver.

I stepped to the right, behind the back pew, so Mama wouldn't see me and stop playing. I stood in a pool of golden light that streamed from a stained glass window. We had never sat in that light because church was always held in the mornings. The sun shone directly behind the gold center design of the nearest window. I rotated my head slightly, and crimson, turquoise, violet dazzled in turn, like a kaleidoscope. Below the design was engraved "In memory of William and Lydia Roundtree." Daddy's parents.

I gripped the back of the pew and felt the sun warm my cheek as I listened to Mama.

She turned the last page. The whistle of the flute lingered, like a mourning dove's call. She lifted her hand, and the music stopped. She sat still, head tilted, as if listening for another sound.

I walked toward her. "That's the best I've ever heard you play."

"Go on." She jabbed a finger toward a hearing aid. "Better get those things checked."

"I thought you couldn't play any more on account of your arthritis."

"It lets up once in a while." She rubbed her knuckles.

"Why don't you play tomorrow? Jeannie won't mind. I'll phone her myself."

"Don't you dare. By tomorrow I won't be able to bend my fingers."

Mama's back spasms worsened. Her orthopedist told us she might have cracked another spinal disc. He increased the codeine in her pain cocktail, which made her drowsy. On the way home from

Walla Walla one day, she dozed off and drove through a wooden railing, finally stopping in Ben Tate's wheat field. When Ben reached her, she was walking around the car, inspecting it, her left arm dangling and her nose bleeding

"Hardly scratched it," she told Ben.

He took her to the hospital, where an X-ray showed the arm was bruised but not broken.

When Timothy arrived a week later, we watched her pin gold braid to purple velvet on a Styrofoam ball, one of the Christmas balls she gave every year to her past Sunday school students, even the ones pushing fifty who couldn't have had much room left on their trees.

"Beautiful," Timothy said. "How can you make those tiny designs when you can't lift your arm?"

"Mind over matter." Mama poked a pin through a silver bead on her third try. "I'm going to play the piano again, too, soon as my arm heals. And I'm going to drive again."

Timothy straightened and looked at me over Mama's head. "How long is the car going to be in the garage?"

"A long, long time," I said.

After Mama's car came back from the garage, I confiscated her keys. I drove her to Walla Walla for groceries and doctor visits, sometimes getting to Shep's so late all the seats were filled. Then I had to suffer from the rail as other pros dragged in big pots.

She was on her knees, pulling newly-sprouted weeds in her strawberry patch, when I arrived one afternoon. As soon as she heard the car door slam, she reached for her back.

I helped her up. "Go in and lie down."

"Don't yell at me!"

"I wasn't yelling."

"You practically broke my eardrums." She hobbled into her bedroom and lay down. "Bring me some pain cocktail."

I shook the container, poured a dose into a glass measuring

cup, and helped her sit up so she could drink it.

"We've got to hire a live-in helper," I said.

"I can get along just fine by myself."

"Your arm hasn't healed."

"It's getting better." She lifted her left arm a few inches. "See?"

"You can't drive anymore. You need help with the cooking and laundry."

"Margaret already does those things."

"Your cleaning lady cooks for you?"

"Last week she made us a nice stew."

"She only comes once a week. You need help every day."

"You could move back in. I put clean sheets on your old bed." She winced. "Gave me a back spasm."

"I've got things to do."

"What? Play poker?"

I looked away. "Other things. I'll put an ad in the paper for a live-in."

"I'm not letting a stranger stay in my house." She got out of bed. One hand on her hip, she limped into the dining room, toward the phone.

She dialed. "Margaret? My dictator son says I need more help. I don't suppose you'd be available?"

Her face got animated. "Yes, bring her. See you tomorrow."

She hung up the phone and headed back to the bedroom.

"Bring who?" I said.

"What?"

"You said, 'Yes, bring her.'"

"Did I?" She collapsed onto her bed.

"You didn't mention money."

"Margaret doesn't care about money."

Next morning I parked behind the cleaning lady's car. When I opened the front door Mama was sitting on the sofa, and beside her, propped against the back of the sofa, a fat, nearly bald baby with huge eyes was waving a rag doll up and down.

"It belonged to Anna," Mama said.

"What's going on?" I said.

"Don't yell."

The baby looked at me and started bawling. "You scared her," Mama said. "Don't look so cross."

"Is it Margaret's?"

"She's a person, not an it. Her name's Callie. Isn't she the sweetest thing?"

"Would you answer my question?"

"Keep your voice down," Mama said, patting the baby's back. "You two aren't off to a very good start."

The clothes dryer had been grumbling, but now it shut off. I went into the pantry. Margaret was sorting clothes into piles. She had stringy gray hair, a caved-in cheek, and a crooked nose that had a flat surface near the tip. She smiled, revealing a gap in the front row of her teeth.

"Whose baby is that?"

"My granddaughter. I'm adopting her."

I didn't have to ask why. Mama had told me Margaret's son used to beat her up because she wouldn't give him money for drugs. The baby's mother might be a drug addict, too.

"I don't think this will work out. My mother will get a back spasm any minute."

"Margaret?" Mama called, right on cue.

Margaret took the baby, who started crying again as soon as she saw me. Mama stood up, so shaky I reached out my hand to steady her. I helped her into the bedroom.

The pitcher of pain cocktail sat on her bed stand, two-thirds full. Mama poured some into a cup.

"How many doses have you had this morning?" I said.

"I don't know." She put the empty cup on the stand and flopped backward onto her pillow.

"You'll have to leave the baby alone. Can you do that?"

212

She pressed her lips together.

"You got a back spasm just sitting on the couch. I'll tell Margaret she has to keep you away from the baby."

"Don't you dare."

"We'll have to hire someone else."

"You're not in charge here, young man. The three of us will get along just fine. Now go away and let me rest."

The baby lay in a crib by the piano, her hands weaving in the air as if she were trying to grasp something only she could see. Margaret was chopping onions in the kitchen.

"How much are you asking?" I said.

"What?"

"Your pay."

"I don't know. What do you think?"

Start low and negotiate upward. "Five hundred a month?"

"That's too much."

"Four hundred?"

"Three hundred," she said.

I was sitting at my desk in Timothy's old bedroom, trying to match doctor bills with Medicare payments, when I heard an engine rev up. I pulled back a curtain in time to see Margaret's car heading down the lane.

In the living room Mama was watching television with the sound low. The baby lay asleep in her crib.

"Where did Margaret go?"

"Shh." She pressed her forefinger against her lips. "She had a cleaning appointment."

"She's supposed to be here fulltime."

"No she's not. Most of her clients can't get by on their own. Wanda Curtis told me if it weren't for Margaret, she'd have to move into a nursing home. It's not as if I'm an invalid."

"Why didn't she take the baby with her?"

"She offered to. I said you'd help me look after Callie."

"Without asking me?"

The baby whimpered.

"I told you to keep your voice down," Mama said.

She bent over the crib. "Oh, my," she cooed, "you need changing." She picked up the baby and laid her on the sofa. "Bring me a washcloth," she said.

I brought one from the bathroom cabinet.

She sighed. "Wet it first. Didn't you ever change diapers when your children were small?"

I gave Mama the wet cloth and went back to Timothy's bedroom to finish my paperwork.

When I came out Mama was holding the baby on the sofa, singing a song. "This old man, he played three, he played knick knack on my knee." She tapped Callie's knee, making her laugh.

"That's a pedophile's song," I said.

"Fiddlesticks! I think she's getting used to you. Want to hold her?"

"No."

"She won't bite." She held out the baby toward me.

I took her, afraid Mama would drop her if I declined. Callie looked at me, and her lips curved down.

"Smile at her, for heaven's sake!" Mama said.

"I am smiling."

The baby began to wail and reached for Mama.

"You're such a sourpuss," she said, wrapping her arms around Callie. "I can't remember when I last saw you smile."

Callie cried harder. Mama jiggled her. "Heat up some water on the stove."

I turned on a burner and watched tiny bubbles form at the bottom of the pot.

Mama carried Callie into the kitchen. "Don't let it boil, for goodness sake! Hold her." She thrust the baby at me.

The baby squalled louder when I took her. She leaned back so far I was afraid her neck would break, so I cupped my hand behind her head. Her hair against my palm reminded me of a baby chick's fuzz. Mama took a bottle of milk out of the fridge and put it in the pot. Callie howled, squirming. She looked as miserable as I felt.

Mama shook a few drops from the nipple onto her wrist. She took the bottle into the living room, sat on the couch, and said, "Give her to me."

I watched the baby suck the bottle's nipple. "If I hadn't been here, you'd be lying in bed with a back spasm right now."

"You're here, aren't you?"

I looked at my watch. "When's Margaret coming back?"

"I don't know. She left our lunch in the oven."

"I can't stay all afternoon."

"It'll do you good to spend some time with us." The baby closed her eyes and kept sucking. "Take our plates out of the oven," Mama said.

I took two pie tins out of the oven and unwrapped the foil. Chicken cacciatore and oven-browned potatoes. My mouth watered. I got impatient waiting for Mama. I was used to eating alone, awash in guilt, while she lay in bed with back spasms she'd got from fixing our meal. She sat down across from me, and we started eating. I chewed slowly, enjoying each mouthful.

Mama made a face and reached for the salt shaker. "Margaret's a terrible cook. She doesn't use enough salt."

When Margaret came back I met her on the porch.

"You were gone four hours. What if my mother needed help and you weren't here?

"She said you'd stay with her."

"She never asked me. I had things to do this afternoon."

"Yes, I know."

Was she being sarcastic? "From now on you'll have to take the baby with you."

"I've been doing that, but I don't get much work done."

"Can't you hire a babysitter?"

"I can't find a reliable one. The last sitter took off and left Callie alone."

"Well, you'll have to keep my mother away from the baby."

She folded her arms. Passive aggressive.

"I've been thinking the same thing about you," she said.

"What do you mean?"

"I heard you yelling this morning."

She was upbraiding me? I should fire her on the spot.

"Callie's afraid of men. Her father spanked her when she cried."

Margaret gave me a hostile look and went inside.

There were two seats open at Shep's. Chi had a stack of purple chips in front of him. How could he win a hundred bucks from these rocks?

"You missed Omar Phelps," Chi said.

Omar Phelps! He came in once a month and dropped a bundle in a couple of hours.

I raised half the pots, expecting the rocks to fold, but they didn't. By the time the game broke up, Margaret had cost me thirty-seven dollars.

Without telling Mama, I put an ad in the paper for a live-in. Only one person replied, a big, red-faced woman who asked how much I was paying the second she entered my apartment.

"We can talk about that." I brought a chair from the kitchen, but she remained standing.

"How much are you paying?" she repeated.

She needs us. We don't need her. I had to get this interview turned around. "Have you worked as a live-in?"

"Of course." Her nostrils flared, as if I'd asked if she'd murdered any clients. "How much are you paying?"

"We were thinking of six hundred a month."

"Oh, you were, huh? I charge fifteen hundred. Sundays off."

"Maybe seven hundred."

She walked out the door.

♦ ♣ ♥ ♠

The phone rang as I was shaving. Had something happened to Mama?

"Can you come out right now?" she said.

"What's wrong?"

"Nothing. Margaret has to take Frieda to the doctor."

"She can take the baby with her."

"She has to push Frieda's wheelchair."

"This is crazy. We can't–"

"Be here by nine," Mama said.

It took me a few seconds to realize I was protesting to a dead phone. No way was Mama going to schedule my life. I fixed my usual breakfast and left the house at five after nine.

Margaret's car was gone when I pulled into the lane. From the front porch I could hear the baby crying. Mama was lying on the bed and the baby lay alongside her, howling and kicking her feet in the air. I wrinkled my nose.

"I started to change her," Mama said, "but I got a spasm." She lifted herself on one elbow, but grimaced and fell back on her pillow. "You'll have to do it."

"I don't know how."

"I might have known. First unfasten the diaper."

"I don't see any safety pins."

"The Velcro straps."

I wet a washcloth at the sink. The baby's crying intensified. How could someone so small make so much noise?

"Now lift her legs."

I did as I was told, not an easy task because the baby was kicking. "Now what?"

"Wipe her."

"I'd need a third hand."

"Oh, for heaven's sake! Take both feet in one hand." Mama closed her eyes. "You've given me a headache."

When I finished wiping the baby's bottom, I said, "What do I do with the dirty washrags?"

"There's a bucket in the bathroom. Did you say washrags?"

"I used five."

"You're hopeless. Do you think we have an endless supply?"

I took a clean diaper out of a package on the floor. Trying to recall the position of the dirty diaper, I lifted the baby's feet, placed the clean one under her, and fastened the straps—expertly, without a solitary compliment from Mama.

"It was a nightmare changing you," she said. "We didn't have disposable diapers then. Want to know how I washed them?"

"No."

"First I had to chop wood for the kitchen stove. Then I drew water from the pump and heated it. When it boiled I poured it into the washtub and stirred the diapers with a stick. All the time you'd be screaming bloody murder. You'd throw a tantrum if I didn't spend every minute with you."

The baby was still crying.

"Pick her up," Mama said.

"She'll cry louder."

"Do it anyway."

Cautiously, I lifted the baby off the bed. Her diaper shifted. Too loose. I laid her back down and tightened the straps. Callie screamed, her face red. I picked her up again. "Now what?"

"Walk with her."

I paced back and forth through the living room and dining room. The crying gradually subsided. Callie jerked her head from side to side, twisting her body so I had to hold her tightly. What was she doing, taking in everything like Donna said a cat does, seeing things from new angles?

I noticed she held her head steady for a couple of seconds every time we passed the mirror on the dining room wall. The next time we reached the mirror I stopped, and our eyes met in the mirror's reflection. I took a step back so our reflections disappeared, then a step forward. Callie smiled. I felt relieved. She wasn't afraid of me anymore. On my next trip I stopped short of the mirror, said, "Where's the baby?" and waited a couple of beats, increasing the suspense, before I stepped in front of it. Callie laughed.

I felt pleased with myself, as if I'd called a huge bet and caught my opponent bluffing.

On our third roundtrip a stranger appeared in the mirror, laughing with Callie. Five minutes later she rested her head on my cheek, and her body sagged against my chest. It was a heavy feeling, trusting, vulnerable. Something stirred inside me, the same feeling I got years ago when I held my own babies.

When I passed the mirror I noticed Callie's eyes were closed. I put her in the crib. Mama was asleep on the bed, her breathing slow and shallow. The liquid in the container of pain cocktail had dropped an inch or two. She must have taken another dose since I'd left the bedroom. Could a person die from too much codeine?

I sat in a chair by the bed, worrying about Mama, watching her blanket rise and fall almost imperceptibly.

Callie whimpered from the living room.

"She's hungry," Mama said. She crawled out of bed but teetered like a drunk, and I had to grab her elbow to keep her from falling.

"Stay in bed," I said. "I'll get her bottle."

A few minutes later I brought a warm bottle to the crib and stuck the nipple in Callie's mouth.

Mama called from the bedroom, "You can't let a baby drink while she's lying down. She'll choke."

How did she know the baby was lying down?

I sat on the sofa, cradling Callie, and let her suck the bottle again. She pushed it away and cried louder.

"Hold the bottle at a forty-five degree angle," Mama called.

Callie sucked greedily and fell asleep on my chest, the nipple still in her mouth. Unwilling to risk waking her, I held the bottle steady. My right arm began to ache.

Mama sat down by us and removed the nipple from Callie's mouth. "You can let go of the bottle," she said. A cramp shot through my hand as I straightened my fingers.

Callie stirred, her eyes still closed. "Don't wake her," I whispered.

"I declare." Mama said. "I never thought I'd see the day."

She turned on *Wheel of Fortune* with the sound too low for me to hear. The blank spaces on the board slowly filled with letters. Mama's lips moved as she tried to guess the answer before the contestants did.

"Beauty and the beast!" she cried, clapping her hands.

Callie opened her big eyes and reared back her head to look at me. Her mouth quivered. I tried to smile, but she thrust out her fat arms to Mama.

Mama took her. "You're doing better, Mark, but you've got a ways to go." On the screen, Vanna White fitted a G into a blank space. "Look, Anna," she said to the baby, "that word is egg."

When Margaret arrived at twelve-thirty, Mama was lying down in the bedroom and I was sitting on the couch, holding the baby. On the drive out here I'd prepared two lectures, one for Mama and one for Margaret, but I'd forgotten them both.

Margaret stroked Callie's hair. "She's asleep. Want me to take her?"

"No, that's okay."

"You'll stay for lunch, won't you, Mark?"

"Okay." Right now I didn't care about the poker game.

While Margaret was in the kitchen Mama came into the living room. "Let me hold her," she said.

"She'll wake up."

"Nonsense." Mama sat beside me and reached for the baby. "You can't hog her."

Margaret smiled at us from the kitchen, shaking her head.

I wandered around the farm for half an hour, enjoying the

clean air and the view of the snow-tipped mountains. I thought of Donna, the two times we'd walked to the river, the mountain hikes we'd taken in my imagination.

The dinner bell pealed, and I ambled toward the house. Mama and the baby were both asleep. Margaret watched me spoon curried shrimp onto my plate and handed me a bowl of brown rice. "You're like a different person today," she said.

"How do you mean?"

"You were rude the other day."

I wanted to protest, but that would only make her defensive. Besides, being called rude was a compliment compared to what the gamblers called me.

"You don't remember me, do you?" she said.

I looked at her closely. There was something... a woman with a swollen belly and a swollen cheek, her dark hair hanging limp as she bent over a conveyor belt at the cannery. The nightshade angel!

"Did you work at the Walla Walla Cannery?" I said.

She looked so surprised I decided I must be mistaken. "How did you know?" she said.

"Did a tub boy accidentally spray you with a hose?"

"That was you?"

"Later you came to the doorway of Shep's poker room. You had a bruise on your cheek."

She touched her hollow cheek. "A present from my husband."

"I thought Jack went to prison for killing his wife."

"His second wife."

Her eyes focused on something beyond me, and the hairs on the back of my neck rose. For an instant I was nineteen again, staring at the pile of chips I'd just won, while behind me the burly man kicked his chair into the wall.

"Jack told me the night we met that he wanted to marry me. He was so attentive at first. He would phone me several times a day, ask what I'd been doing. I was flattered." She took a bite of the curry and rice. "He changed after we got married. When he got

221

home from work, he'd make me account for every minute of my day. He found fault with everything I did. One night I cooked liver and onions, his favorite dish. He flew into a rage because I hadn't cooked stew. So the next night I cooked stew, and he wanted steak. I told him we couldn't afford steak because he lost all our money gambling. That's when he hit me the first time."

"You should have left him right then."

"That's helpful advice, forty years too late." She drank from her water glass. "Later he said he was sorry, and I forgave him. A week later he slammed my head against the kitchen door because there wasn't any beer in the house. Next time I forgot to wash his favorite fork, so I added that to my list. Don't mention poker, keep two six-packs of beer on hand, don't forget to wash his favorite fork. The list got two pages long."

Here was a chance to use my therapeutic training. "Did your father—"

She was too absorbed in her story to hear me. "Once I was late fixing supper because I was nursing my baby. Jack came home and told me to stop nursing and get supper ready. I obeyed him, but milk started spilling out of my breasts. Michael was screaming, so I picked him up. I tried to chop carrots and let him suck at the same time, but Jack took him and slapped him. I screamed and tried to get my baby back, and Jack hit me so hard I lost two teeth. When Jack was asleep I packed a suitcase with Michael's things and left. I never went back."

"Was your father abusive?" I said.

"What?"

"The daughter of an abuser often marries another abuser. She thinks that by making her own marriage work, she'll fix her parents' marriage, too."

She went rigid. "I didn't know Jack was an abuser when I married him."

"Subconsciously you knew."

"Don't try to psychoanalyze me. No man could understand the

process an abused woman goes through."

What a smug thing to say to a trained therapist. "What process?"

"Every time you placate him to keep things stable, you change a little bit. After a while, you're consumed with trying to meet his requirements. Only you can't, because he expects you to read his mind. After a few years, the old you wouldn't recognize the new you."

"You were in denial. That's because—"

"Never mind." She went to the counter and slammed a bowl of fresh strawberries on the table. "I'm wasting my breath. You'll fit whatever I say into some theory." She went into the living room.

I bit into a strawberry. The sweet flavor produced so much saliva that I couldn't have talked even if she'd stayed.

My stomach tightened as I drove to Walla Walla. Until Margaret's outburst—a defense mechanism—I'd felt a surprising contentment, feeding the baby, changing her, walking her, watching television with Mama. My anxiety increased as I neared the city limits. Usually, the closer I got to a poker game the more buoyant I felt, like I used to feel approaching a trout stream in the predawn light.

Years ago Ernie had asked me, "What's the best thing in life?"

"Playing poker," I'd replied.

"What's the second best thing?"

I'd struggled for an answer. Sex? Eating Sue's goulash? Watching football on television? Finally I'd said, "Driving to a poker game."

Not this afternoon. They say you should obey your gut instincts. What was my gut telling me?

Quit poker.

At the intersection of Third and Alder I stopped at a red light. Straight ahead was Shep's. To my right was my apartment. If I quit playing poker, what would I do with my time? I didn't even know what television shows came on at night.

The driver behind me honked, a long blast that sounded as if his horn was stuck. I pressed the gas pedal in panic, and my car lurched toward Shep's just as the light turned yellow.

Was I going to let this bully decide my future? I turned left at the next intersection. The bully followed me. I pulled over to the curb and turned to glare at him, but the driver was a teenage girl. She smiled and waved as she passed.

At Pioneer Park I bought a packet of unshelled peanuts at a vending machine. A curious squirrel approached me. I tossed a peanut but aimed too short. I was rusty. It had been almost thirty years since I'd fed squirrels with Karen and Sue, the one time I took my family to this park. I threw another peanut. The squirrel found it and darted up the tree trunk. It sat on a low limb and munched the peanut, dropping shell fragments on the ground.

Another squirrel crept toward me. I heard a squeal behind me. A tiny girl holding a milk bottle toddled past me toward the squirrel. It scampered up the trunk. At the base of the trunk the girl stood on tiptoes, holding the bottle as high as she could, its nipple pointed upward.

The mother smiled at me. She stood beside me as if we were married, sharing a moment we'd always treasure.

I gave the bag of peanuts to the woman and strolled through the park. Children flipped chunks of bread into the pond and giggled when Mallard ducks competed with white geese for each piece. Two young lovers meandered across the lawn, oblivious to everything except each other.

Wait till you get married and see what happens.

I missed being at the farm with Mama and Callie. Wandering through the park, I felt like a ghost, invisible to these happy people. Poker has a numbing effect. I could be among people, and even if they didn't like me, as most players didn't because I took their money, they couldn't ignore me, just as residents of McNealy's hotel couldn't ignore bedbugs.

I looked at my watch. Five-twenty, the time I normally ordered a tuna sandwich from Shep's counter and devoured it so fast stomach acid burned my throat. I ate a sandwich at the Book Nook's fountain, aware that I should have chosen a restaurant farther from Shep's.

Since I was only two blocks away, I might as well check out the poker game. I left cash by my plate instead of waiting for the waitress to bring my bill.

I paused in the poker room's doorway. It was an average daytime game, two sharks, a shill, a railbird who had somehow scrounged the ten-dollar buy-in, two rocks who might win a little in a game full of suckers but couldn't beat the pros. Three seats were open, but they would fill quickly once the night crew arrived. If I didn't sit down now I might have to wait for a seat. I also knew that if I sat down I would never quit poker.

The players glanced at me sourly. I went to the fountain and ordered a lime phosphate. I shuddered with ecstasy at the first sip, but I knew the high would quickly wear off, unlike poker's high.

In the mirror I saw Spittin' Joe shuffle past, heading for the poker room. It defeats a lime phosphate's purpose if you drink it fast, but I did anyway.

A seat was open to Spittin' Joe's left, the ideal location to extract my share of his Social Security check. I bought chips and sat down.

I checked my hole cards. Two queens. Joe held his cards in a shaking hand close to his face, like Daddy held a newspaper during his last years. Without turning my head I peeked at his cards. Two jacks, which couldn't beat my queens. He bet, and I raised him.

After the last card fell, he called my five-dollar bet and turned his second-best jacks face up. I studied the fringe of white hair, the tiers of wrinkles, and Joe began to look like Daddy.

I pushed him the pot. "You win, Joe." I tossed my queens into the muck, face down, and cashed in my chips. As the house man counted my chips, I looked around the card room for the last time, at the cash register that had supported me for thirty-five years, at

225

the halo of smoke that hung over the seven humped men. Then I drove to my apartment and phoned Mama. I told her I'd come out tomorrow morning, so Margaret could leave Callie if she had an appointment.

When I arrived, Margaret's car was gone. Mama was sitting on the sofa, watching a soap opera. The baby was asleep in her crib. I went outside to breathe the fresh country air. Blackbirds silently sang, and I pretended I could hear meadowlarks. A trout dimpled the water of the pond. Trout couldn't reproduce without running water, but once every few years Luke brought fingerlings from a hatchery during his spring break. Evenings, Daddy liked to throw a handful of pellets into the pond and watch the fish swarm after it. We never fished the pond, but Mama used to bring her Sunday school class out here to take turns using our fishing poles.

I stood still, feeling poker's poison ooze out of me.

Better check on Mama and the baby. As I closed the back door I heard a thump, followed by a baby's wail. I ran into the living room. Mama lay on her side near the crib, holding Callie against her chest with her right arm, her left arm scrunched beneath her at a funny angle.

"I twisted so she wouldn't hit the floor," she said.

I knelt and took the screaming baby. "Are you all right?" I asked Mama.

"I broke my arm."

At two o'clock the surgeon came into the hospital's waiting lounge and said, "She's still in the recovery room. Her bones were so thin it was like cutting paper."

226

It was late Monday evening, three days after Mama fell, when Luke unbuckled his guitar case in her hospital room. All afternoon we'd helped her try to walk, none of us wanting to believe that the weakness in her left leg and the loss of range in her speech were caused by a stroke. Now she lay with her eyes closed, sometimes responding when we asked her a question, sometimes not.

Luke strummed his guitar and started "Rounded up in Glory," singing tenor to Timothy's baritone. Mama rasped the words in a monotone. I didn't move my lips, not having sung outside my bathroom for years. Mama tightened her fingers around mine. Her hand felt small, as my hand must have felt to her fifty years before when she would make sure she didn't lose me in the Walla Walla stores.

When the song was over, I said, "Sing something funny."

They did "Old MacDonald Had a Farm." When they reached "with a cluck-cluck here and a cluck-cluck there," Mama's monotone worked fine. She knew how to do Old MacDonald's animals. She had fed them, milked them, ridden them, chased them out of her garden. Luke and Timothy did an ordinary "nay," but Mama's "neigh-h-h" tailed off in a whinny.

After the last "eeyi eeyi o," Luke leaned over and said, "What would you like now, Mom?"

Mama mumbled something I couldn't understand. Luke nodded, and they began "Precious Lord, Take my Hand."

From the corner of my eye, I glimpsed a figure in white standing in the doorway. A nurse, I thought, come to listen. But when I turned to look, she was gone.

THURSDAY, JUNE 19, 1986

The phone is ringing. It takes me a moment to realize I'm no longer in Mama's hospital room. I'm sitting at the kitchen table, her letter to Anna still clutched in my hand. I stumble into the dining room. Why isn't the phone on the wall?

It rings again, from the little table by the front door, where it's been since I grew up. I pick up the receiver.

"Mark? This is Margaret. I'm in Dayton on a cleaning job. I saw your car parked outside your mom's house. Could you do me a favor?"

"Sure," I croak, still groggy.

"Could you go to my trailer and check on Callie? When I phoned the babysitter just now there was no answer."

"Where's the trailer?"

"Space eighteen in the trailer park." She gives me the phone number of the house where she's working.

Whetstone's trailer court covers two city blocks. As I walk past trailers, doors open a few inches but no faces appear. I sense fear, the fear of bill collectors, of warrant servers, of utility workers come to shut off lights or water. I also sense the pain of broken families, of children who think they're worthless, of spouses who argue, their voices rising, following the same script Sue and I could never revise.

In one yard a little boy plays with a puppy. He smiles shyly, and my heart almost bursts.

At space eighteen I hear a baby squalling, so I go inside without knocking. Callie lies in her crib, kicking her legs into the air and bawling. She sounds hoarse. I pick her up and hold her tight, mumble, "It's okay, it's okay." She arches her back, still howling, as if she doesn't recognize me. It's been a week since she last saw me.

A package of diapers is on the table, so I lay her on a sofa and change her. A lukewarm, almost-full bottle of milk is also on the table. She grabs it out of my hand and sucks ferociously.

When she's through drinking I put the bottle in the refrigerator and pick her up. She snivels as if she's about to start crying again. I try to walk her in the small room—one step, detour around the table, another step, turn around. I pat her back and whisper to her. She's still whimpering. I locate the bathroom and turn her so she's facing the mirror. She goes quiet for a few seconds before she resumes fussing. I turn away from the mirror, say, "Where's the baby?" then pivot back. She gives the other baby a tentative smile.

Anna's rag doll lies on the table. While we waited for the ambulance, Mama asked me to give the doll to Margaret. We sit on the sofa, and Callie grabs the three strands of red yarn and whaps the doll against my leg.

Callie's asleep in the crib when Margaret arrives an hour later. She hovers over the crib.

"No excuse is good enough. I can't let her babysit again."

"What about your cleaning appointments?"

"I'll take Callie with me. I can't get much work done, but I can't really afford to pay a babysitter, either."

"What will you do?"

"I know someone who might volunteer."

Too tired to think, I start toward the door.

"Don't go," Margaret says. "There's something I want to tell you."

We sit at the table. "My name used to be Peggy Foster," she says.

Air hits my teeth. My mouth must be hanging open. Peggy

Foster. Burke Foster's daughter. The girl Uncle Jacob hugged just before she went away.

"When I moved back to Whetstone I didn't tell anyone. I was afraid I'd have trouble getting clients. The worst thing an unmarried girl could do was get pregnant. That's why my mother sent me away, so nobody would find out. They found out anyway."

"I never knew why you left," I said.

"I went to live with my aunt. I was only sixteen years old. I didn't know what to do."

"Did you keep the baby?"

"I gave her up for adoption. It was the hardest thing I've ever done, but I didn't see how I could raise a child by myself."

And Uncle Jacob, the coward who pretended to search for Anna in the outbuildings, knowing she'd drowned, showed his cowardice again by failing to take responsibility for his baby. Handing Peggy a few bucks at the depot doesn't count.

"It's getting warm in here," Margaret says. She takes a small fan from behind the couch and plugs it into an extension cord. She sets the fan on the table. The fan purrs, and a welcome breeze cools my face. My T-shirt is stuck to my chest. I pull it free. Margaret turns the fan so it's pointed toward the crib.

"The adoption agency wouldn't tell me anything. I don't know her name or where she is. All these years I've longed for her. I used to imagine she was with me, doing things together. I'd be in a thrift store and she'd see some little thing, a jewelry box maybe, and I'd hear her voice, 'Mommy, come and look.'"

Margaret plants her elbows on the table and cups her chin in her hands. Her fingers cover the deformed cheek–maybe an instinctive reflex. "I'm blessed, really, getting a second chance with my granddaughter."

"I've been trying to figure out how my uncle died."

"Jacob? Mom wrote that he drowned."

"Did she mention his hand was severed?"

"No." Margaret's eyes get as big as Callie's.

"Your father might have killed him."

She straightens up. "My father? Who says?"

"He had a motive. Did you know about the school wagon incident?"

"What school wagon incident?"

I tell her, but when I get to the part about Uncle Jacob pinning Burke to the wagon's floor, she interrupts me. "So my dad killed him because of the school wagon thing? That's ridiculous."

"He had a stronger motive."

"What?"

Could she really be this naïve? "Maybe he found out my uncle was the father of your baby."

"Jacob? Where on earth did you get that idea?"

"You spent so much time with him. Once I saw you crying, and he hugged you."

"I told him I was pregnant."

"He drove you to the depot and gave you money."

"My mom didn't have money for the ticket. A boy from school was my baby's father. He got me alone behind the gym one night. Nobody called it rape back then. It was always the girl's fault if she got pregnant."

She strokes the plateau of her crooked nose with an index finger. "I was terrified my dad would find out. He would have come after me with his razor strop."

There goes Burke's motive for killing Uncle Jacob. Or does it? Mama said Uncle Jacob acted like a father to Peggy. Maybe there was another reason he drove her to the depot and gave her money.

"Maybe Burke had a different motive."

"You're serious, aren't you? Why are you so fixated on proving my dad killed your uncle?"

Because if he didn't, my father is the only suspect. "What if Uncle Jacob was your father?"

She stares at me, her mouth open, revealing the gap between her teeth.

231

"We used to hear Burke yelling at night." I'm talking fast because her face is darkening. "What if your mother went to Uncle Jacob for comfort and they had an affair? Burke found out about it and killed Uncle Jacob. Then–"

"Stop right there!" She holds up both hands, as if she wants to shove me backward onto the floor. She closes her eyes and takes deep breaths until her shoulders go limp. When she looks up, the lines in her face have smoothed out. "I don't know why I waste my energy getting mad at you. You know what your trouble is?"

My trouble?

"You live in an imaginary world. You spend all your time playing poker. You have no experience in the real world."

I don't, huh? I've always lived in the real world. I had to size up a poker player and decide whether he was bluffing. I had to figure the odds of hitting a flush on the last card. I had to make an ACI prospect think I was doing him a favor by enrolling him.

"Jack lived in a fantasy world, too. He thought he deserved whatever he wanted." She pats my wrist. "I'm not finding fault with you."

What the heck are you doing, then? Sue, my mother, Donna, now you. Every woman I know seems eager to point out my flaws.

The baby starts fussing, and Margaret leans over the crib. She picks up Callie, who lolls against her shoulder, still asleep.

It's time for me to leave. I stand up, but Margaret says, "Sit down."

So you can dredge up more of my flaws? I sit down.

Margaret strokes the baby's hair. "When I moved back to Whetstone I was bitter. People recoiled when they saw my face. I couldn't afford surgery on my cheek. I couldn't afford a dentist, either. I got so ashamed I couldn't look people in the eye. The only jobs I could get were cannery work and cleaning houses."

Callie murmurs in her sleep, and Margaret jiggles her. "Then I met a white-haired angel, someone I knew years before. Your mother." She lays the baby in her crib and sits at the table again.

"She recognized me at the Post Office. The first morning I went out to clean her house, she knew something was wrong. She asked me to sit beside her on the couch, and before I knew it I was pouring out my life story. I talked for an hour."

Margaret laughs. "I got up to start cleaning, but she said, 'Let's forget about the cleaning today.' Then she told me her story. She said for two years after her daughter died, she was lost. She had all this love for Anna left over, and she didn't know what to do with it. Then Jacob said something that made her think. He said, 'It seems wrong that someone so happy should leave a legacy of sadness.' Your mother realized she couldn't let all that love sit in her heart unused. She had to give it to others. That way Anna's love would go on rippling outward.

"While your mother talked I'd been looking away. Then she went quiet for so long I looked at her, and she gave me such a radiant smile. I felt my heart fill up. I don't know what we talked about after that. When it came time for my next appointment, she paid me for four hours' work, even though I hadn't lifted a finger."

Margaret gets up from the table. "I've got to eat something. You hungry?"

"No."

She opens the refrigerator door and takes out a package of cheese slices. She puts it on a plate along with some soda crackers and sits down. "Up till then I'd felt bitter about cleaning houses. Like I deserved something better after the hell I'd gone through with Jack."

She tears off part of a cheese slice, slips it between two crackers, and munches. "I resented my customers. Most were old women, living alone because their husbands had died. After I left your mother's house I started thinking about them. Some were one sprained ankle away from a nursing home. They'd taken care of their husbands right up till the end, and now there was no one left to take care of them. I decided to help them stay in their homes. I wound up doing a lot more work without charging for my time.

233

And you know what? I've been happier ever since."

All at once I'm so tired I can't keep my eyes open. "I've got to get home before I fall asleep."

"That was the second time your mother rescued me. You were right. Dad did yell when he got drunk. He'd take off his belt and threaten to give me a whipping. I was terrified of him, and Mom never protected me. That's why I kept running to your mother."

Margaret stands up when I do. "For years your mother's been telling me how unhappy you were. But the first time I saw you holding Callie, your face was lit up like a Christmas tree."

Back at the house I collapse on my bed. I fall asleep within seconds.

THURSDAY, JUNE 19, 1986

When I wake, the bedroom is darker. I go into the kitchen. It's still sunlight outside, but the clock reads six fifty-one. I've slept for seven hours and feel refreshed for the first time in a week. My stomach growls. Mama doesn't have a microwave, so I warm up Rose Carney's leftovers in the oven. I devour the meatloaf and baked beans.

I put Mama's letters back in the cardboard box, along with the two envelopes—one containing Mrs. Wilson's letter and the empty one in Daddy's handwriting. I lay my ugly crayon drawing of Uncle Wiggily on top, but then I wonder why Mama didn't write my name and age at the bottom, like she did on my later drawings. I turn the sheet over. On the back in the top right corner, Mama did write something. *Anna Roundtree, age three.*

"Good job, Anna," I whisper.

I return the box to Mama's bureau drawer. Her purse lies on the bed where I tossed it the night she died. I open the clasp. Underneath a compact, a folded letter, a hairbrush and her coin purse, I feel rocks at the bottom. I line them up on the blanket. These must be the five rocks Anna found on their walks and handed to Mama. She carried them in her purse for fifty-three years, waiting for Anna to ask for them again. No wonder the discs in her spine got disjointed.

I put the rocks in my left pants pocket. Their combined weight makes the pocket sag, so I transfer the three smallest to my right pocket.

The letter is so frayed it's separated at the seams. Mama fastened the parts together with Scotch tape. The letter is in Daddy's handwriting, undated, but I know when it was mailed because I've seen the empty envelope. A week before they got married. I read the final paragraph twice.

> You wrote that you will keep me so busy after I arrive in Rogue River for the wedding that I won't have time to tease you. We'll see about that. One more week and we'll be together for good. I know you will hate to leave your family, but you have family waiting for you up here, too.
>
> Sincerely,
Edward

I remember chasing the woman in blue down the hospital corridor, hearing her repeat Daddy's last words, "Tell Lola I'll take care of her." He didn't mean he'd take care of Mama. He meant he'd take care of Anna until Mama joined them.

I put the letter in the bureau drawer with the others. I wash and dry the Carneys' plastic containers. The kitchen clock shows it's after eight, and farmers go to bed early. I'll return them tomorrow.

How many days has it been since Mama died? Two? Three? Let's see, the surgery was Friday. Sunday night she died... no, it was Monday.

Monday, not Sunday!

I run to my car. As I start the engine I see the front door is ajar. Who cares?

When George comes to the door his face shows concern, not irritation. Old ranchers know that a knock late in the evening often means someone's in trouble, and he can see that I'm agitated. He closes the door behind him. Farmers feel more comfortable talking on a porch than inside a house.

"You all right?" he says.

"Yeah, I'm fine." I hand him the paper bag with the plastic containers.

He takes the bag, goes inside, and comes back with my shirt. It's been ironed and folded.

"I forgot to bring your shirt," I say.

"Don't worry about it."

"Tell Rose the food was delicious."

"We've got more if you'd like."

"No thanks, but I appreciate the offer." I'm getting better at farm folks' talk. "I've got a question. When you were in high school, what time did school let out?"

"Four o'clock."

"What time did you get home?"

"I don't know. The bus had to take that loop up Smith Springs Road. I'd guess I got home about five, maybe a quarter till." George reaches for his shirt pocket and grins. "I'll probably do that when I'm lying in the coffin. Scare people half to death." He squints at me. "Odd questions."

"So the afternoon you saw Uncle Jacob and Anna at the river—it couldn't have been a school day, right?"

George thinks for a minute. "You're right. It was Sunday. My mother fixed dinner after we got home from church, and I didn't wait for desert. I grabbed my fishing rod and headed for the river. A friend of mine told me he'd caught a sixteen-inch rainbow under the Bolles Junction bridge."

"Did you go to school the next day?"

"No, Monday morning Pa drove me up to Uncle Fred's place. North of Huntsville. I helped him seed barley every spring."

"When did you get back home?"

"Let's see… Seeding took three days, so I must have got home Wednesday night." The sun drops below a locust branch, and George puts up his left hand to shade his eyes. He looks as if he's saluting with the wrong hand. "Mom told me they'd found the little girl's body. I didn't even know she'd gone missing. That's when I told Mom I saw them at the river."

"My aunt says Anna disappeared the day after Palm Sunday. Monday, not Sunday."

Farmers don't make good poker players. Watching George's face change, I would have guessed he'd taken a second look at his cards and realized he'd hit a flush.

He whistles. "So I saw them the day *before* she drowned. All these years Mom and I wondered whether we should have told the police. She thought nobody would believe us. And it could have been an accident." He shakes his head slowly. "I'm glad we didn't tell the police. At least we didn't do any harm."

No, not much harm. You only got an innocent man murdered.

The setting sun blinds me as I drive back toward the ranch. Afraid I'll cause a head-on collision, I pull onto the highway's shoulder and shut off the ignition. In five minutes the sun will set. Up the hill to my right I see the guardian angel, the tombstone Donna thought was a woman. It leans inward, toward the place where Anna and Uncle Jacob lie, at peace now. Daddy lies there, too, maybe not so peacefully.

To my left, the sun's last rays illuminate our old combine, pulled first by horses and mules, then by the tractor that sits beside it.

I have a few minutes to kill, so I cross the railroad tracks and walk past the shop and the pile of scrap iron to the machines.

The combine's header is missing, but the header wheel that gave me blisters is still next to the grain tank. The combine's wheels and the tractor's linked treads are half-buried. The tractor and combine look like toys, miniatures of the giant machines I recall from long-ago harvests.

A rusty chain hangs from the tractor's hitch. I lift the chain and feel it slide through my fingers. The hook at the end catches on my thumb.

238

And now I know what happened to Uncle Jacob.

The sky is pink when I start my car, purple when I approach Whetstone. Ahead, I see Aunt Bea cross Smith Springs Road, which intersects with the highway. I pull onto the shoulder. She starts climbing the first of the wheat hills that continue past our ranch all the way to Waitsburg. I get out of the car and watch until she disappears over the crest. Almost ninety and she's climbing a steep hill at dusk?

Yes, and three nights ago she stood at the top of a hill, watching me set fire to Mama's letters.

I'm too wired to go back to the ranch, and I won't be able to sleep because of my long nap. I drive half a block past her house and park facing it. I can sit here as long as she can walk. Didn't I once sit through a forty-eight-hour poker game?

It's after midnight when I see Aunt Bea appear under a street light, striding toward her house.

What's this? She's passing her house, heading toward me. Has she recognized my car? I crouch low on the passenger seat and count to sixty. When I straighten up she's nowhere in sight. I turn the car around and drive slowly down the hill. I take a left at the bottom, just as I did Tuesday morning. I park by the railroad tracks and get out. Pinpoints of light appear in the field across the tracks. Deer's eyes.

The depot is boarded up, unused for so long the planks covering the bottom of the door have come loose from their nails. Unable to resist the challenge, I kneel, lift the loose boards, and push the bottom of the door. It gives way. I wriggle under the planks and stand up. I can't see anything.

If I were ten years old I could be Sherlock Holmes, waiting in the dark for a swamp adder to slither down a bell rope. But I'm fifty-four, and I fear spiders. I take a cautious step and collide with something solid. A wooden bench. The oil stove and the ticket window must be to my left.

Something rustles, and I stop breathing. My eyes adjust to the dark, and I make out the dim outline of benches. There's something in the middle of the back bench that doesn't belong there.

"Jacob?" a voice says.

"It's Mark, Aunt Bea."

"His train was due at seven forty-eight. What time is it?"

"I can't see my watch."

I feel my way along the row of benches and sit beside Aunt Bea. The bench is hard, like a church pew.

"His train came a long time ago," I say. "I met him on the road as he was walking home."

"Reverend Taylor and I were having Bible study."

"I know."

"That's all we were doing. You can't believe what people say."

"No, you can't. Someone said Uncle Jacob and my mother had an affair, but they didn't, did they?"

"No. Lola would never do a thing like that. Neither would Jacob. He loved me."

"You said his shirt was buttoned wrong the afternoon Anna disappeared."

Her laugh is musical, unlike the magpie's squawk I recall from my last visit. "His shirt was buttoned wrong all morning, too."

I shift my position, but it doesn't help. How did I sit through hour-long church services?

"I know how Uncle Jacob died," I say.

Her face turns toward me.

"He did find my father that morning. They took the tractor across the snow to the river. Uncle Jacob backed it close to the bank and unraveled a chain from the tractor's hitch. Then my father got on the tractor. That puzzles me. Uncle Jacob did the seeding and harrowing that fall. The one time my father got on the tractor, he drove it through the side of the barn. So why did Uncle Jacob get in the river?"

"Jacob was a good swimmer," Aunt Bea says.

"So was my father. I heard he jumped into Wallowa Lake and

240

rescued one of his nephews."

"Ethyl's boy. I was there. Edward didn't really know how to swim. All he could do was dogpaddle. He had all his clothes on, even his shoes. It's a miracle they both made it back to shore."

"Uncle Jacob reminded him how to work the tractor's gears. Then he took hold of the pipe and lowered himself into the river so he could wrap the chain around the pump."

Aunt Bea listens intently.

"The cold water must have numbed his hands. He had trouble getting the chain right. He needed more slack. He yelled at my father to back up, toward the river. My father might have heard him wrong, but I think it's more likely he got the gears mixed up. He put the tractor in forward instead of reverse. Uncle Jacob had the chain wrapped around his wrist. The chain pulled his arm one way, and the pump pulled it the opposite direction. Something had to give."

I hear a car approach. A sliver of light appears on the floor under the planks.

"It was an accident," I say.

"You sure?"

"Yes!" Why did I say it so loud, and why am I sweating all of a sudden? I swipe the back of my hand across my forehead. It's as wet as if I'd just stepped out of the shower. I try to pick up my train of thought. "The next morning I saw him erase the tractor's tracks with a shovel. You can't blame him." My voice sounds defensive. "If the police had found those tracks, they'd have thought it was murder."

We sit silently for a few minutes. Then Aunt Bea says, "You almost got it right."

"Almost?"

"Edward told me what happened."

Why would Daddy confess to Aunt Bea? He'd told me once how to deal with a neighbor's dog that kills chickens. "Shoot the dog and bury it, and don't tell anyone."

Maybe he wanted to convince Aunt Bea it was in her interest as well as his to keep quiet. Without the insurance payment, the bank would foreclose, evicting Aunt Bea along with us.

I jerk to attention. Aunt Bea has said something.

"I didn't catch that. You were saying my father confessed what he did."

"No, he told me what I did."

"What?"

"Jacob couldn't find Edward, so he asked me to help him get the pump out. I told him I'd never been on a tractor. He showed me how to shift the gears."

I hear myself wheeze. The depot is full of dust.

"Jacob yelled 'Back up!' I thought I shifted into reverse. I'd never—"

I wait silently.

"I felt so guilty. I stopped going to church. I couldn't look anyone in the eye."

"You didn't do it on purpose."

"That's what I keep telling myself. But sometimes I wonder. That's what's haunted me all these years."

I elbow my way under the loose boards that guard the depot's door, grunting with the effort. Aunt Bea scoots through like a teenager. She's had lots of practice.

SATURDAY, JUNE 21, 1986

Today the church is packed. I'm sitting in the left front pew, trying to persuade a drop of water to evaporate before it leaks out of my eyelid. One after another they stand to tell their stories, women in their twenties, thirties, forties, fifties, even a couple of awkward men. At a time when they felt alone and unloved, Mama's radar had blipped.

"Page thirty-seven," the minister says. Somebody from the pew behind hands me a hymnal. I take it to be polite, although I do not intend to sing.

"Amazing Grace" starts as a whisper, not because the singers plan to build to a crescendo for dramatic effect, but because they don't want to sing "that saved a wretch like me" with such fervor that they draw appraising glances. But when they reach, "I once was lost but now am found," their voices swell, and the hairs on my arm tingle. Suddenly I want to sing, too. I hunt for a bass voice I can hitch onto. A bass rumbles from my right, half a note flat. By the time I get my mouth open all I can hear is the melody, led by Luke's tenor. I clamp my mouth shut, unwilling to mimic my own brother an octave too low.

"Was blind but now I see," soars through the church, almost lifting me off the floor, and I can't hold back any longer, I've got to sing. I try for low G but wobble between A sharp and B flat. I grope lower, knowing G must be down there somewhere, and my

243

voice warps downward like a phonograph turned off with its needle still in the groove. Luke's voice falters, and I'm afraid I will throw off the whole congregation. Then I hear the piano's hard thunk, and I aim for its lowest note and hit G dead center. Following the plink of the piano, I sing, "And grace will lead me home," every note true, dipping to C sharp as if I'd been singing on key all my life.

It hits me that the church must have switched from the organ back to the piano since I was last here. I force myself to look front right, past the table I'd been avoiding. But the organ is still there, and Jeannie is swaying and pumping into the last verse.

I hear the other bass again, on key now that he can follow the piano. And now I hear a quavering tenor and more new voices, way too many for this little church, and I realize we would be in trouble if a fire marshal walked in—if he could count all the singers.

I cock my head toward the back of the church and fiddle with my hearing aids until I hear the other sound. It's coming from way in back, not the sad whistle of the organ's flute but the song of the meadowlark.

We go up to your meadow sometimes, Callie and I. Ever since Mama's funeral I've babysat her weekdays while her grandma cleans houses. She's two and a half, almost your age when you left us.

It takes us a long time to reach your meadow. Every few feet Callie stops to check out a weed or dig in a mound of loose dirt above a gopher hole. The ground squirrels are long gone, so she can't push weeds down their holes for their breakfast, like you did. When she hands me a rock to carry, I put it in my pants pocket so I won't get it mixed up with the five rocks you gave Mama, the ones I found in her purse. I carry your rocks in my right coat pocket, which I keep buttoned so I won't lose them.

Halfway to the meadow Callie gets tired and holds out her arms. I like to carry her, to feel her weight against my chest. I understand now what I missed all those years, rarely holding my own kids, standing stiff as a fence post when Mama hugged me and pecked my cheek.

As I carry her, I tell her some of the things we'll do when she gets a little older. We'll ride the train to Portland and go to the zoo. When the circus comes to Walla Walla, we'll feed peanuts to the elephants. Maybe Donna will go with us. Both of her parents have died, and she's selling their Montana farm. I phoned her the other day, the first time we've talked since she left Whetstone. She wants to go for a walk with Callie and me.

Fifty years of winter cloudbursts have washed out most of your meadow, Anna. Like some people, the rain never seems to get

245

things right. It wastes itself when the ground is frozen and withholds its nourishment when the wheat is growing.

From the bottom of the gully I lift Callie onto a dirt ledge, all that's left of your meadow. I climb up beside her and we look around. Across the gully, Russian thistle covers the hillside up to the fence. The only flowers we see are tiny violets in April and the prickly blossoms of yellow star thistle in August. Tumbleweeds still clog the fence. Some things don't change.

One September afternoon, while Callie sat on the ledge watching a beetle maneuver past a dirt clod, I closed my eyes and tried to picture you three up there. All I saw was the snapshot, Daddy hoisting you high over his head, your face indistinct. That's the only photo of you in existence. Maybe they couldn't afford a camera and Mama borrowed one that day to take your picture.

As I carried Callie back from the meadow, mid-afternoon, way past her naptime, she laid her head in the crook of my neck and dozed. When we reached the canyon's mouth—asparagus grew there during your time—she raised her head and smiled at me, then plopped her face against my neck and patted my back. Love overwhelmed me, the same love Mama must have felt when she carried you.

I go to the other place alone, the wild place on the hilltop where you four lie, at least the part of you that changes and disappears. Virginia creeper smothers the fallen locust trees and curls over the headstones, which I'm sure is okay with you and Daddy and Uncle Jacob, though it must bug Mama.

It's been two years since we carried Mama up that hill, your three brothers and three of her old Sunday school students. We set the casket down by the freshly-dug hole between your tiny stone and Daddy's. Sweat trickled into my mouth. It was the hottest day of the year, and I had no hat. Because we'd come straight from the church to the cemetery, I still wore my suit with its red flower, one of the roses Aunt Bea picked from Mama's garden and pinned to the pallbearers' lapels. After the minister said a prayer, we dropped the blossoms on the casket. Aunt Bea laid the extra roses on the graves of Uncle Jacob, Daddy and you.

Luke asked if I wanted a ride back to the house. I said I'd walk.

I walked along the fencerow where the hills and flatland converge, under the two black walnut trees Daddy planted before we were born. By the time I reached the patch of wheat stubble south of the canyon, where you and Mama picked asparagus on your way home from the meadow, the adrenalin I'd been running on all week had drained away. My forehead felt dry and hot, as if I had a fever. I wished I'd worn a hat.

I paused under a tree, the first tree in the line of ancient locusts that ran from the canyon's mouth to the highway.

Up the canyon to my right was your meadow, the place Mama liked to go when her three sons wore her out, where she would lie among the wildflowers and gaze at the clouds, remembering.

Straight ahead was the house where my brothers and I grew up, where they would be waiting to say goodbye before they left for Seattle. A ten-minute stroll and I could relax in Mama's recliner with the air conditioner humming, sip a glass of cool water, my first drink since breakfast. No wonder I was thirsty.

Twenty yards up the canyon, a scraggly apple tree clung to the steep hillside. Two magpies sat on a leafless branch near a nest. A raven landed on a lower branch. The magpies fluttered around the raven, shrieking. A third magpie flew over my head, then another. They lit as close to the raven as they dared, flapping their wings and squawking. The raven hopped onto the branch that held the nest.

I started toward the tree, planning to scare the raven away, but then I remembered why I'd shot magpies as a twelve-year-old. Like the raven, they were predators who ate the eggs of robins and meadowlarks. I looked south and saw more magpies flying toward the tree, some so far away they must have come from the river forest. How did they know their fellow magpies were in trouble? And why were they trying to help other magpies? Didn't predators live by the law of the jungle, every beast for itself? Or were the magpies driven by an altruism gene, an unconscious desire to protect the young of their species?

Ignoring the screeching magpies, the raven lifted an egg out of the nest with its beak and flew across the canyon. All the magpies followed. The raven landed on a hillside, and the magpies lit a few feet away, surrounding it. The raven pecked at the egg and broke its shell apart. The magpies stopped chattering.

The raven flew away, but the magpies stood in a quiet circle around the eggshell. Then they left the hillside. Some disappeared into the line of locust trees; others flew across the highway, toward the river. I watched them till they got too small to see. That's when I realized I was following them, taking the path alongside the locusts that you and Mama took on your way home from the meadow.

I passed the worn-out seeders Daddy had pulled under the trees. Just beyond, partly sunk under two feet of topsoil from winter run-offs, were the steam engine and stationary thresher that had harvested wheat before I was born. A falling locust limb had crushed the roof of the cook shack where Aunt Bea fixed three harvest meals a day for twenty men, rising at four in the morning to bake bread, finally lying down under the shack at midnight, after she'd washed the supper dishes.

I should have turned back when I reached the Osage orange trees near the highway. The ground was littered with their poisonous green fruit, the thick hides knobby like basketballs. Looking at them made my stomach queasy. Got to go home, I remember thinking.

I crossed the highway and pushed through dead kochia weeds, not caring anymore whether cheat grass stuck to my socks. Ahead was the little house where I lived till I was four, where you lived all your short life, three long years that changed so many lives.

A wild rose bush, straggly and gaunt, had survived near the north wall. Its few blossoms had gaps between their remaining petals, like the missing teeth of young children.

Shingles on the north side of the roof were yellow with moss, but on the south side only wooden slats remained, the shingles blown away. The windows had no glass, and the front door was gone. Below the doorway was a jumble of boards and moss-covered shingles, what was left of the collapsed porch.

I heard a train's whistle but couldn't see a train. This porch was where Mama held you while you waved at the engineer. I'm glad he waved back.

Along the fence that led to the river forest, a few scattered elderberry bushes were all that remained of the canopied lane. I touched my forehead. Burning hot, not a drop of sweat. I needed shade. Under those cottonwoods, the temperature would drop ten degrees.

I walked south along the fence, knowing it was a mistake. A ring-necked pheasant exploded from the wheat stubble, and I flinched. Vines choked the elderberry bushes, twining around their branches like the pythons I once captured there. Forty-five years ago, if I crawled deep enough into the canopy, it became the jungle of Ceylon, teeming with rhesus monkeys and leopards.

I thought of you, Anna, your last walk under the canopy, the one time you walked to the river alone. *The path the wee people take.*

Were you the little tiger, prowling through the jungle looking for parakeets and tapirs? Not to eat, of course, to play with. They were your friends, as were all the birds and animals, all the people in your life, every weed, every beetle, every cloud. You loved everything, and everything loved you.

Except the river. You loved the river, but the river betrayed you.

My head throbbed, the beats synchronized like the drums of jungle villagers. The river cottonwoods grew taller. Not far to shade. Straight ahead, two ravens circled above the trees.

I stumbled out of the wheat stubble into a meadow blanketed with daisies. Dragonflies hovered an inch above the flowers. Cottonwoods flanked the meadow, their fluffy white balls floating above me in the still air. It felt cooler already, though I hadn't yet reached shade.

I could hear the murmur of rapids, but a huge bush hid the river. I smelled water and the lush scent of wild roses. The bush was loaded with blossoms, pink petals on the outside that shaded to white inside, yellow tendrils of pollen in the center, like a child's drawing of the sun. Small black bees buzzed among the blossoms. I warily touched a branch, remembering the hostile thorns of tame roses, but these thorns were gentle.

On the other side of the bush I waded through more daisies. Now I could see water. A great blue heron rose from a pool and flapped upstream, its wingspan almost as wide as the river. Across the water, dark-green trees blended into lime-green bunch grass on the steep slope beyond. A black and gold butterfly flitted past my nose. I staggered across a pebbled beach, aiming for the shade of a willow at the river's edge. The water was greenish nearby, blue toward the middle, so shallow I could see pebbles all the way to the far bank.

My chest fluttered. I must have fallen, but I felt myself rising, floating.

If I hadn't reached shade I would have died, a doctor told me that night in the hospital. That's where Timothy and Luke found me an hour later. They had driven slowly along the highway, looking for me, past the graveyard. They guessed I might have walked to the old house. When they didn't find me there, Luke thought of the river. He doesn't know why.

During my night in the hospital, I wrote down every detail I could recall, trying to reason it out. If what I saw when I opened my eyes was a memory, I must have been lying where I collapsed fifty-three years later, for the river looked the same. But winter floods change the river's channel. And how could I remember something that happened when I was a few months old? Was I hallucinating from heat stroke? Or was something else happening?

Although I'd seen only one blurred snapshot of you, I recognized you right away. You had big eyes and long brown hair that flattened wetly against your neck. You were standing knee-deep in a riffle, laughing non-stop as you splashed water at Daddy and Uncle Jacob, who splashed you back. Their overalls were rolled up, but it didn't matter. You were all three soaked. Daddy's black hair was plastered against his scalp except for the thatch in front that stuck up in your snapshot.

When you aimed at Uncle Jacob's face, high above yours, he ducked behind his elbow, laughing. When you splashed Daddy, he grinned, the equivalent of a laugh from anyone else.

A bird screeched to my left. I looked back across the daisies. Through a gap in the cottonwoods I could see the little house, but the fence I'd followed was no longer visible. A narrow grove of trees stretched all the way from the house to the river forest. I saw a flash of silver in the grove, metal glinting in the sunlight.

When I looked back at the river, you and Daddy were watching Uncle Jacob. He reached into the riffles and brought up a small flat stone. With a sidearm motion he threw it upstream. It skipped across a pool, brushing the water three times before it disappeared among the cattails on the far bank, leaving dimples that rippled outward, as if trout were feeding on a caddisfly hatch.

Daddy found another flat stone on the river bottom and tossed it upstream. As I expected, it clunked into the pool and disappeared. Luke and I had tried to teach him how to make rocks skip, but he never could. Skipping pebbles is an art. You have to picture the rock skipping before you let it go.

You picked up a chunky rock and threw it overhanded. It landed two feet away, drenching you. Uncle Jacob laughed, but Daddy stared past me toward the river bank. I turned to see what he was looking at.

Mama stood among the daisies, holding a tin pail. She wore a blue and white checkered dress and a wide-brimmed straw hat. A wisp of auburn hair straggled across one cheek. She watched you, smiling.

You and Uncle Jacob were bent over, hands on your knees, peering into the clear water. He handed you a flat stone and pantomimed how to throw sidearm. You threw the rock underhanded. It looped in a high arc, landing at the tail of the pool where the rapids began. Uncle Jacob clapped. You looked at Daddy to check his reaction. Something about his face made you turn toward the shore.

At first you didn't seem to recognize her. She was ten yards away, and your eyes may have been bleary from the water. Then you squealed, "Mama!"

You didn't wade to shore, you tried to sprint, and you fell headfirst with such a big splash I felt drops hit my face. You got up and ran barefoot across the pebbled beach. Mama dropped the pail and braced herself, arms outstretched, as you launched yourself at her. You wound up with your arms around her neck, legs around her waist, face pressed against her cheek. She squeezed you tight.

You stayed that way a long time, dripping water all over Mama. She stroked your hair.

She gave Daddy a stern look. "Her hair's filthy."

"We played outside in the dirt all morning," he said.

"I don't suppose it occurred to you to wash it."

"Uncle Jacob found Jackie Bow-Wow," you said.

Mama rubbed your back, rumpling your wet shirt. "Where was he?"

"By the chicken house. He was buried under some weeds. We were digging a cave for the Bushy Bear."

"With my good spoons, I'll bet."

"We washed them," Daddy said.

"I know how you wash things. You never heard of soap."

Daddy waded toward the bank. "What's the bucket for?"

"I thought we could hunt for wild strawberries."

"Yay!" you shouted. I wish I could have seen your face.

Daddy slogged through the water onto the shore. When he reached you and Mama, he stopped. He looked at her and she looked at him. You put one arm around each of their necks and pulled them close until your foreheads bumped together. Mama's hat fell upside down among the daisies.

I glanced at Uncle Jacob. He stood in the riffles, beaming at the three of you.

Daddy nuzzled Mama's cheek with his nose. Then he kissed her on the lips, something I'd never seen him do.

You cupped your hands under their chins and pushed, tilting their heads back.

"No kissing," you said.

Then you all three laughed. I can still hear you.

ACKNOWLEDGEMENTS

My heartfelt thanks to my wife, Libby, my first reader and confidant always; to Robin Stratton, a writer's dream editor, whose advice I fought ferociously until I realized she was right—every time; to Sue Matley and Myra King, my writing partners; to Tiffany Cain, Vivian Fetty, Pat Henry, Bruce Matley, and Karen MacIvor, who read early drafts of this novel and gave me valuable feedback; to Don Davis for his help in photography; to all the friends, family members, and professional people who gave me helpful information and encouragement.

Made in the USA
Middletown, DE
06 May 2017